Praise for David Haynes and *Live at Five*

"One of the liveliest novels I've read in a long time. David Haynes is blessed with a wonderful sense of humor and a perfect ear for dialogue. As soon as his characters open their mouths, you're hooked."
—Jill McCorkle

"Haynes' comedy about the gap between image and reality is charming, intelligent, and significant.... [His] earlier novels, including *Somebody Else's Mama,* portray African American, middle-class family life. Here he moves into a larger social arena, but without sacrificing his intimacy with his characters, or his gently ironic humor."
—*Booklist* (boxed review)

Live at Five's "dialogue and the strength of the women [are] qualities that sent *Waiting to Exhale* into the stratosphere."
—*Washington Post Book World*

"Touching and wickedly funny.... With this novel, Haynes should establish himself as a sharp-eyed observer of race and class issues."
—*Publishers Weekly* (starred review)

"Fortunate [is] the reader who enters the ever-expanding world of David Haynes, a writer blessed with an ear for the truth and the talent to bring it to light in ever-delightful ways. *Live at Five* is a look at the gap between image and reality that combines the satire and humor of the film *Network* with the superbly realized voices of African-American men and women that have become Haynes' trademark."
—*Dallas Morning News*

"Insightful.... *Live at Five* succeeds as a warm and funny tale."
—*Cleveland Plain Dealer*

HARVEST AMERICAN
Writing

Live
at
Five

. . . .

LIVE
at
FIVE

DAVID
HAYNES

A Harvest Book

Harcourt Brace & Company

San Diego   New York   London

Requests for permission to make copies of any part of the work should be mailed to:
Permissions Department,
Milkweed Editions,
430 First Avenue North, Suite 400
Minneapolis, Minnesota 55401-1743

Published 1996 by Milkweed Editions

The characters and events in this book are fictitious. Any similarity to real persons, living or dead, is coincidental and not intended by the author.

Library of Congress Cataloging-in-Publication Data
Haynes, David. 1955–
Live at five/David Haynes. —1st Harvest ed.
p. cm.
ISBN 0-15-600503-4
1. Television news anchors—United States—Fiction. 2. Single mothers—United States—Fiction. 3. Afro-Americans—Ficton.
I. Title.
[PS3558.A8488L58 1997]
813'.54—dc21
97-22027

Printed in the United States of America
First Harvest edition 1997
E D C B A

In loving memory of my father,
Paul Haynes,
1905–1995.
Thanks for the tools, Dad.

ACKNOWLEDGMENTS

Thanks to the Ragdale Foundation and the Virginia Center for the Creative Arts for the time and quiet space to create this work.

Also, to Christy Cave and Kate Havelin for checking the television stuff. Any discrepancies between this story and "real" television life are strictly the result of my imagination and not of their careful reading.

Live
at
Five

. . . .

Live
at
Five

. . . .

Mousse
and
Styling Gels
Don't Help

. . . .

Along with everything else, I also wanted to tell
you how nice your hair has been looking lately.
You are a credit to the race.

Mrs. Delores Smotherson
St. Paul

Brandon Wilson fussed with his hair, picked it with his right
hand and pressed down with his left to make sure there weren't
any little hairs sticking up. The light in the men's room wasn't as
good as the light at the make-up table, and it was hard to tell
whether or not everything evened up okay. There was nothing
worse than going around with a lot of little wiry hairs sticking
out of your head—especially when you were on camera in front
of thousands of people. Every time it happened—and no matter
what he did it seemed like it always happened—he got sacks of
letters from these old sisters asking him didn't his daddy teach
him to comb his hair right. He found it discouraging. Where he
thought it might have been white people out there laying for
him, it was instead our folks, particularly these little old black
ladies, just waiting for him, waiting on a slipup: a *dat* instead of
a *that*, a grease stain on his tie, one hair sticking out on his head.
Didn't those broads have anything better to do than hound a
brother who was just trying to make something of himself? He

3

was supposed to be worrying about what the top story should be and whether or not they should broadcast the graphic footage of the car wreck on I-94. Instead he was spending time worrying about his hair.

Black people and their hair. Maybe he should do a story about that, about why we were all so fixated on hair. On who had the good hair and who had the nappy hair, and whose head was full of lint and whose didn't get combed this morning. The thing was, each of those ornery old heifers out there who were always so worried about his short afro, they all knew the truth, which was that you got what you got, and on most days what you woke up with was what it was gonna be like the rest of the day, and it didn't matter how much afro-do you sprayed into it or how long you picked at it. Black folks' hair had a life all its own.

After a thorough inspection Brandon decided his hair looked okay, and really he should have been on his way back to the newsroom but he was hiding from Dexter Rayburn, the new station manager, and until he could think of a better place to hide he intended to stay right where he was. He figured the bathroom was a pretty good hiding place, seeing as how Dexter looked like the sort of person who didn't use one.

Dexter had been sent in from corporate to "clean things up." Brandon knew "clean things up" meant, among other things, doing something about the ratings of the five-o'clock news, the program that he co-anchored with Mindy St. Michaels. As a matter of fact, yes, the ratings were in the toilet, particularly since Channel 7 hired that new punk—the little bastard—and yes, they were dead last, fifth out of five, and yes, in fact, more people did watch reruns of "The Facts of Life" than Newscenter 13, but in no way did Brandon feel that it was his fault. In the first place, St. Paul wasn't exactly the news capital of the United States. Their editorial meetings in the morning were more like prayer meetings: everyone praying that some poor loser out there would shoot his wife, or that a building—any building—

would burn down, and that it would happen within a couple of miles of downtown St. Paul so they could get a camera crew out there before the overly efficient fire department put it out. There were also prayers that none of the other stations scooped them on whatever measly story came along, anything that remotely resembled news. They could scoop the 5:30 national headlines but people would only put up with so much of that Bosnia shit, so what they ran was an endless series of soft news—human interest crap that he was sick to death of. How many dog washes and charity bowling tournaments could a man report on before he started blathering in front of the camera like an idiot? A lot of days whether or not "Natalie" and "Tootie" got dates really was more compelling than their news broadcast. Furthermore, KCKK was the cheapest news operation in town. They didn't have satellite trucks or Doppler radar, or anything flashy for that matter. He and Mindy sat behind brown plywood desks with the call letters tacked on them, right in front of the actual newsroom. Behind them, the rest of the news staff, crazed with boredom, spent the broadcast crawling around on the floor, off-camera, whispering rude remarks, flying paper airplanes and looking for other ways to start Mindy giggling. Mindy was a giggler—almost everything struck her as funny: sock puppets, stupid face tricks, elephant jokes. She was from the school of professional women who believed that as long as you smiled and had a sunny disposition, the business community would welcome you with open arms. She'd spent four years in a college sorority where the standard response to almost anything was to open one's eyes and mouth real wide and to gasp the word, "FUN!" When she started anchoring she read every story with a determined cheeriness—whether it was about a basket of puppies delivered to Children's Hospital or a plane crash in which hundreds of people had been killed. Brandon had had to teach her to go through her scripts and highlight the serious-face stories in one color and the happy-face stories in another.

He had spent the better part of several years praying that she would remember her code.

Brandon knew that this was just the sort of information Dexter had files full of. He also knew that "clean things up" meant cleaning up the talent—himself and Mindy for starters, and that as far as the network was concerned the reason the ratings were in the toilet was pretty clear. One needn't look any further than Channel 7. After hiring pretty-boy Dane Stephens, they had skyrocketed from fourth to second place; or KMN where good old Arne Peterson had been reading the news since the invention of electricity and whom all the old Swedes and Norwegians just loved. Brandon knew some of those old geezers had their sets permanently tuned to Channel 6, and he figured the news director over there must have to keep Arne propped up with a stiff two-by-four to keep him from toppling over in his chair. Arne must be 107. Sure, he'd die one of these days, but not soon enough for Brandon. Channel 6 was still number one at five, Dexter was here now, and the only ones watching Brandon were a scattering of vindictive black crones, and not too many of them at that.

He leaned into the mirror, stretched his mouth out, and pulled the skin at the corner of his eyes. Not bad for thirty-eight (thirty-two on his official bio). One of the good things about being black—you aged pretty well. Not like poor Mindy. She had been looking pretty skanky here lately. Mindy was as worried about Dexter as he was. In this business your fate revolved around guys like Dexter. These guys lived by one credo, and according to that credo KCKK was failing because they were dead last. He'd been around a month, this Dexter, watching them read, taking notes in his red folio, whispering to various consultants. He'd made them sit for hours in front of the camera while one of his hired guns slathered them with different shades of makeup and draped them with colored swatches of cloth, baking them under the lights while the crew switched from the amber gel to the rose to the blue and then back through the cycle again. Poor Mindy. The incessant handling made her so nervous, her giggle had turned into more of a shrill rattle. She'd already had a couple of "procedures," as she liked to refer to her face lifts, and the makeup girl had to work overtime as it was to keep Mindy from looking as if she were in a state of constant surprise.

The ruthless part of Brandon regretted that he hadn't exploited his advantage, that he hadn't done something such as have a meeting with Mindy and Dexter in a brightly lit restaurant so Dexter could see up close how far over the hill she really was. Because one never knew, sometimes it was one or the other, and it never hurt to jimmy the odds a bit in one's favor. As sleazy as that sounded, he knew she would do it too, do whatever it took to get a leg up. It was too late for any of that now, he knew. He also knew that as much as it might come down to him or her, it could just as well be that both of them would be getting the ax. Today was D day. Dexter had finished his month of "getting the lay of the land," and today he would announce his reorganization of the newsroom.

Ron Anderson from the sports team sauntered into the lavatory, popping gum, his six-foot-four frame gliding as if he were still out there on the court.

"Hiding in the men's room, I see."

"Fuck you," said Brandon.

Anderson peed into the urinal what Brandon thought was an awfully large amount of liquid. He whistled his way to the sink, washed his hands carefully, and groomed himself in the neat but casual way all ex-jocks do, wet comb raked across the scalp, a hand behind it, adjusting things ever so carefully.

"You're a pretty cool customer," Brandon said.

"You know it. Sports is safer than a nun's pussy at a gay bar. You guys, though. Ha!" he scoffed and made another pass through his strawberry blond hair.

As if, Brandon thought, there were all these people out there who were tuning in just for the sports part of the show. "Heard anything?" he asked.

"Nah. Why? You worried?"

Brandon shrugged.

"Come on. They never fire *you* guys. They got quotas and shit."

Asshole, Brandon thought, and then said, "Dexter Rayburn is ruthless. All he sees is the book."

Anderson dried his comb on a paper towel, turned to Brandon and said, "I'm out of here. Got me a lunch date with that hot new babe down in sales. Wish me luck. Oh, and one more thing, your hair looks good today. Almost like you combed it."

"Thanks a lot," Brandon said. "Tomorrow I'll save myself the trouble and just glue the shit on like you do."

"Check you later, buddy," Anderson said, and winked and pointed at him.

Motherfucker, Brandon thought. The station was full of creeps like him. Winking, pointing creeps.

Ron was probably right, though. There probably was a quota. Every station had to have at least one, and KCKK had two, him and Kimberly Darnell. Of the two of them, he was probably a lot safer. For one thing, Kimberly was still just a reporter—on the pothole and shopping-mall beat, no less—and no one had really paid her much attention. The other thing about her was she was too dark. Shades darker than Brandon, and he didn't know how she got hired in the first place, paper-bag color being the usual cutoff in the industry as far as he can see. She was way past that, way down somewhere past copper-penny color, closer to tree bark, in the beef-gravy area. These station owners didn't want to take any chances with their audience, especially not in a market like this one, where there were so few African Americans in the first place. Not that Kimberly wasn't good at her job, because she was. She was still young, and given time and a few good stories— maybe a blizzard or a big scandal at the state house—she might go places. But not here, not in the great white north.

Brandon was in the safe range—just this side of the paper bag, sort of a chocolate-milk color with a little extra milk thrown in.

And he had a contract, too. For an anchor chair. Which said—and his agent reassured him it would hold—that he'd be working *in an anchor chair only* at KCKK through the fall of next year. So what's the worst they could do? Put him on "Dawn Report?"

Thinking about that made him more anxious, because as far as he could tell from the ratings, no one watched "Dawn Report." No one. Brandon didn't even know the guy who did the show. All he knew was he was some guy who had been around the station forever, and who used to be Crinkles the Clown, and who had an iron-clad life-long contract from the days when local kiddie shows were hot, and that the only reason they had "Dawn Report" was to give this guy something to do until he died. Rumor had it he was retiring. And wouldn't that be the perfect slot for Brandon?

In his anxiety, Brandon ran his hands through his hair, and out popped a row of rogue wires, back by the cowlick on the crown of his head. He had to pull out his pick and start all over again.

No one would ever discover him on the "Dawn Report."

To be discovered: that was the only reason he had moved to the Twin Cities in the first place. This place was legend: it was where the networks scouted for talent. Though Newscenter 13 might not beat Action 6, when the bigs were in town they scanned through every local newscast at least once. But no one watched "Dawn Report." No one.

He finally got the hairs tucked back in. There went his dream, down the dumper. Ever since he was five, when his father brought home their first TV back in St. Louis, Brandon knew that someday that would be him in there. Which was how he had thought it worked at first; he thought that people were actually in the television set, singing and dancing, having dinner, and telling stories. And when he got older and he knew better, he still wanted to be on. He was going to be Bob Gibson, on TV in the World Series, at bat for the Cardinals. Then he decided he would be the Jackson Five—all five combined—or Bill Cosby or Ali, any of those folks. And what they had in common that he wanted was that they got to be in that box, and he loved them and so did everyone else. He was going to be in there, too, and he'd worked hard on his dream—through college and J school, and through Podunk stations all over America. In Racine and several Springfields and Evansville and Texarkana, and he'd finally made it here, to a major market, just this side of the big time. And now here was Dexter Rayburn to drop that dream in the dust.

Maybe it wasn't hopeless. He was still young—looked younger still. He had credentials; he had a great tape. There was that affirmative-action thing. Anderson was right. Stations all over the country had a quota to fill. So he'd take a step back, move down a market. So what. A lot of smaller markets had a lot more going on than here. It was all about luck, anyway. Luck and timing—being on the air when the big story broke, asking the right question to the right person at the right time. Breaking into the big time was all about catching a break, and you could catch one anywhere. He'd been in the Cities five years and the only thing he'd caught so far were a couple of bad colds and a sunfish at Lake Calhoun. And Sandra.

His sweet Sandra.

Sandra would come if he moved on. He'd bet she would. She'd always talked about how dead it was here, anyway, and how she wanted to be closer to Tennessee where her folks were. Indianapolis. Louisville. Nashville. He'd have his agent get on it today. Maybe Dexter was doing him a favor after all.

"My man!" Dexter said, popping his head in the bathroom door. "Just who I'm looking for. My office. Five minutes. Be there." He said this with a flat smile. He made a gun of his hand, aimed it, shot, and left.

Shit, Brandon thought.

Maybe he should do a star number. Walk out on him . . . or better: he should go in there with his lawyer and his agent and let them do the talking. That was it! He wished he'd thought of it earlier, and he headed toward his phone in case they happened to be sitting around their offices just waiting for his call.

Mindy was sitting at her desk. Just sitting there. Straight and tall. Hands folded on the desk.

"You okay, Min?"

She nodded.

"You meet with Dexter?"

She nodded. She was smiling like the runners-up who were forced to stand around after they'd lost and be happy for the new Miss America.

"And?" he prompted.

She sniffled almost inaudibly. Trembled. "He's making me a redhead," she said. A trooper, Mindy choked back her tears.

Brandon nodded in sympathy, patted her on the back as he walked past on his way to see Dexter. The Minster had caught a tough break. But not that tough. He, and according to her only a few other guys (only four, really, she had told him), knew that she was naturally red anyway.

Dexter's office door gaped open like the mouth of a hungry crocodile. Brandon heard him in there whistling as nonchalantly as a mama's boy with a happy note from the teacher. Brandon tapped the door frame.

"My man!" Dexter smiled. "Have yourself a sitdown."

A
Kind
of
Love

. . . .

When Nita saw Skjoreski she was gonna kick him in his white ass.
The muthafucker had promised her he was sending somebody
over yesterday to fix the damn hot water heater. Hadn't nobody
come yet, and she had all these trifling niggers on her behind because there hadn't been no hot water since the weekend. What
she ought to do was quit on his ass. Let him find some other fool
to caretake this rattrap. If she could afford to quit, she would,
but as it was she could barely afford the one fifty-five a month,
forget about the three hundred he usually charged for the two-
bedroom units. Where would she find an apartment half this size
that would take her and the three kids for that kind of money?

Caretaker . . . huh! Fools up in here thought that meant she
owned the damn building. All it meant was she was the one got
the complaints when something went wrong. Like from this
witch here. Nita tried to head the nosy wench back toward the
door. She'd barged right in and made herself comfortable. If the
old thing weren't the one watched her kids after school, she'd
eighty-six her ass.

"What else you want me to do, Mrs. Carter?" she asked her.
"I been calling him since Sunday morning. Says he'll get to it as
soon as he can."

"How folks supposed to live without hot water? It's unsanitary."

"I'd've fixed it myself if I could, and believe me I tried. I'll call him again if it makes . . . Better yet, you go on back to your place and you call him yourself."

"Who I'm calling is the health department. If I don't get me some hot water. Today." Mrs. Carter left, slamming the door behind her.

Bitch.

Nita dialed Skjoreski's number again and got the answering machine again: same drone, same silly request to "leave a message at the beep tone."

She slammed down the phone. She knew better. His other number had a machine on it, too. Lazy bastard never picked up the phone. Never. And the damn machine was already full of messages from her. Both machines were. It was ridiculous. Not only that, but here she was, like all these other folks, washing herself with a cold rag, and then trying to get the kids to do it, too, and worried about whether she'd get a note from the school nurse about how dirty their hair was getting, and not being able to wash the grease off the supper dishes or rinse out a few clothes in the sink. What was more ridiculous was that fools like this one—fools who couldn't run a damn one-car funeral— ended up owning buildings that people like her had to live in. It was a good building, too—had sound, solid floors and walls and good copper pipes and decent wiring. Had one of those good old oil heaters in the basement that ran like a dream and kept these radiators humming all winter. She knew this building top to bottom, cause most of the time it was her crawling around its belly fixing things. And if she couldn't fix them, she was more often than not down there scuttling around with the workman to find out how to, so that the next time something broke she and these other folks wouldn't be sitting around waiting on Skjoreski to get to it. She had soldered pipes and changed the fuses and patched and repatched the hoses to the washing machine so many times that they looked more like tubes of duct tape than anything else. This was a damn good building. All it

needed was some paint in the halls and some tuck-pointing outside where them bricks had come loose, and if Skjoreski weren't
so cheap he'd have an investment would last somebody a lifetime. But he nickled-and-dimed them to death. If he'd changed
the damn junction box two years ago, he'd have been ahead now
with the money he'd spent on fuses. Every time Mrs. Carter
ironed and ran her microwave at the same time she blew a circuit. But, no, he didn't put one penny in the building that he
didn't have to. And why should he? To him the building was a
tax deduction, and when he'd run down the depreciation on his
taxes, he'd sell it to the next fool, and so on, until they depreci-
ated it to death. She knew about that shit from her business accounting class at Metro State. She knew about how they
distinguished between investment-grade and tax-benefit real estate, and how if this building were in Highland Park or Crocus
Hill, it might be worth something, but as it was, stuck here on
Marshall Avenue, in this neighborhood, it was only worth renting to poor folks and running into the ground. And why not.
After all, up and down the block there wasn't nothing but other
run-down houses—a couple of them crack houses these days—
and the city didn't put much money into enforcing the housing
codes or sending police here or making the street look nice. A
couple blocks over, things were picking up. Rich young white
folks buying in and putting in gardens and fancy wrought-iron
fences. They were as far over as Laurel Avenue now, and someday
they'd get over here. But not for a long time, not until this block
was rubble. They'd just bulldoze it and build condos.

Not if it was her building. She'd paint the halls a dazzling
white and hang some decent curtains out there instead of those
faded rags Skjoreski had. She'd put some new grass out front
and pave the lot in back and put stripes on it so the folks with
cars would park straight and not every which way. She'd change
that junction box, and more than anything, she'd run the trash
out of here, like them ornery lazy-ass niggers upstairs, and she'd

15

screen folks before she rented to them in the first place, not like Skjoreski who'd rent to anybody brought him a money order for the deposit.

Some days she thought she just might have herself a building like this one. Or a house, a nice little house like those over there in the Midway, with a little yard she could garden in, a room for the girls, and a separate room for Marco. Marco was eight and was already carrying on about how he didn't want to be around those girls all the time, his sisters Rae Anne, six, and Didi, five. He'd have his room, and there would be a room for them, and one just for her. A place for all of Nita's things, too, where there wouldn't be this one's or that one's hands, fingering them, accidentally or on purpose. A place to read quietly or to watch her stories. A place just to go and be by herself. Alone.

All her life she'd never had such a place. She had shared with her two sisters when she was coming up, moved out of there and in with André and his mama when Marco come along, and then her girls. And now they were here. Some days she got sad and down, and she couldn't imagine how she was ever gonna get that house. Or any house. She'd be here with her kids and their kids too, maybe. Here or some place just like here. Like Cece across the hall. The girl slept in the front room, had her two youngest in the middle room, and her older girls and their two babies in the back. Been here eight years, and ain't going nowhere.

And thinking of Cece always gave her resolve, reminded her she could do better. She *could* move up and move on. She would finish her accounting degree at Metro one of these days ... quit cashiering, get her a job downtown somewhere paid something, and make a decent life for these children. And so what if it took her three or four more years. Between Wards and the kids she could only manage a course or two at a time, but so what. She was on her way.

And who knew, maybe somebody'd come along and help her. André, his lazy butt, he didn't do a blessed thing for her or these kids, not now and not ever as far as that went. Oh, sure on birthdays or at Christmas, he might drop around with a cheap stuffed toy or a bag of groceries. *Might . . . if* he was working, and *if* he hadn't partied up all his money, and *if* he remembered what day it was. Not marrying that nigger was the smartest thing she ever did. Those four years living at his mama's, all she'd heard was everyone she knew talking like "Marry the boy. Them kids need a daddy." She figured André had already done his daddy thing, or at least the only part of it he was interested in. He was done with it. If he was still around all she'd have was that much less room and one more mouth to feed.

What she hoped was there was another man out there: a real man. Not a boy, like André. A man with a steady job, a man who knew what he wanted in life and had some idea of how to get it. A man who could come in and be a real father to these children. Help them get dressed in the morning and help them with their homework. Take them to the park on Sundays and to the fair, and sit up with them when they were sick or just scared. A man who'd let her work on *her* dreams, too, and not expect her to be here all hours of the day and night, whenever he wanted to come home and have some fun. A man in her bed, who was gentle and kind, a man there for her and her only, and not for every other bitch who walked up and down the street in a tight dress. She didn't know any men like that. Her mama had had one, then he died, and now she'd got herself another one (even if he was kind of a lazy one). Martina, a girl she worked with, had one (or so she said), and there was Mr. Miles who had the house behind them, who helped her start her raggedy old car sometimes in the winter when it was below zero, and who chased the hoodlums out of the alley and then helped her sweep up the busted glass and litter they left behind. He already had him a wife and some kids of his own.

She didn't understand it. She kept herself up. She was only twenty-four and she only weighed ten pounds more than in high school. Lots of these Negroes claimed to like a little flesh on a woman. She dressed as well as she could afford, as well as her Wards' discount allowed. And she wasn't common—switching her behind up and down the street, talking loud and laying down with anything—like a lot of these wenches out here did. Maybe *that* was it: maybe she was supposed to get down in the gutter with them. But she knew what kind of men you met down there. The street corners and the jails were full of those men, and they wouldn't be taking her any place she'd dreamed of going. She wanted those other men, but where the hell were they? Every once in a while she got talked to, down at the college or at the store, but she knew that that wasn't nothing, cause a lot of these men would talk to anything in a skirt to see if they can get some play. Once in a while they turned out to be halfway decent, and once in a while one of the decent ones even asked her out. She went when she could, when she had the energy and the time and her mama could look after the kids for a few hours. Things went okay until they find out about the kids. The serious ones, well, there's not many of them wanted to hook up with a woman with kids. Not many of them had figured some other man's children as part of his plans. She can't say she blamed them.

Sometimes she wished she had waited. Wished she didn't have the damn kids—it would be easier without them. Easier to finish up school and move up a little. But as far as a man was concerned, she knew that kids being a problem was a lie. Lots of sisters out there with no kids in the same boat she was. Most of the men in jail or on probation. The others married or gay, and the few that were left, well there was a lot of women out there scratching around for them, like chickens in a worn-out yard. And when a woman scratched up something she liked, she'd better be prepared to put up a fight, better be prepared to use every trick her mama taught her and a lot she hadn't, cause the good men had plenty to choose from, always had two or three on the line at a time, and if it was something you didn't give him, there were plenty other girls out there ready to take your place. Give all she can, give till it hurts, give till she ain't got no more to give, and in the end she'd be lucky if she came out with anything more than a broken heart and maybe another baby to take care of.

Things could be worse. She had her kids, and she loved them and they loved her back. At least *they* loved her — didn't matter what she looked like, or how she dressed, or how much money she got. At least she had that.

And she had her mama and her sisters. And old simple André; even he loved her, too, she guessed, in his own juvenile way. He'd come by with his measly gifts and his million-dollar smile. He'd fuss over his kids and they'd wallow in all that affection like piglets in a slop pit. She would make popcorn and they'd sit around the living room watching TV together, just like a real family. And she'd let him stay the night a lot of times, and he would, and it would be nice. If she tried real hard she could believe it was real, and sometimes he would stay a few days, but often in the morning he would be gone. It was a kind of love, she guessed.

She wasn't banking on it, though. Wasn't banking on André or any of those other imaginary men out there. In the end you could only count on yourself. She had her own program in place, and while it might be nice to have a warm body along for the ride — especially on those cold-ass Minnesota nights, she wasn't rerouting her trip to pick up anyone.

"Nita!" Her name was shouted from down the hallway. It was that damn Skjoreski. Finally. She opened the door, and there he was down by the back steps.

"Where the hell you been?" she asked him. "Been calling you all weekend."

"Come see what I got," he said.

"Better be what I think it is or you and me finta fight." She followed him out back. On the truck he had two water heaters wrapped in blankets, lying on top of some old mattresses.

"Got a good deal on em," he said.

The cheap ass muthafucker, she thought. Bought some damn used water heaters. And they were too small, besides. "How's one of those supposed to do for all us? We got fifteen people living in here. More on the weekends, sometimes."

"I'm putting them both in."

"This don't make no kind of sense. Why don't you fix what you got, stead of all this."

"This is cheaper," he said, smiling at her with his sleazy skin-flint teeth. "Coil's shot to hell on the one we got. Can't get the parts, and if I could, they'd cost me as much as these two. Dennis! Let's get to work." He called to a boy in the cab of the truck.

"Got my boy with me today. Playing a little hooky, so I'm putting him to work." The boy turned off the radio and climbed out to help his father. He was a chip, Nita saw—same sandy hair, same pug nose. He'd be a big man, too, in a few years, like his father, probably with the same beer gut.

"This is Nita, my caretaker," Skjoreski said, introducing them.

Nita said, "How do you do," and the boy smiled shyly through his scowl.

"He's thirteen," his father said and rolled his eyes in a way that Nita figured was supposed to indicate something. She had no idea what.

"Prop the doors open for us, honey," Skjoreski ordered, and then said, "Hop up there, son, and get the other end."

Nita set a cinder block by the back door. Skjoreski stood behind the truck, bullying the boy into carrying the other end.

"It's heavy," Dennis whined.

"Take your time. Easy," Skjoreski encouraged.

"It's too heavy!"

"Careful! Don't drop it. You'll break the goddamn glass inside."

Nita was disgusted. Too cheap even to hire a mover, he took his own son out of school for this. "Hang on a second," she said.

She sent the boy to the basement to hold open another door and took over.

"You go on up there," she told Skjoreski, "and lower down first. I'll steady this end." He agreed, and she figured the bastard probably planned for this to happen. That's why he waited till her day off to bring the things over here in the first place. She stood the first one gently, then the second. Skjoreski jumped down off the truck, already puffing and sweating from the effort. Served him right.

"Now," she said, "you get the top end and back down. I'll follow you." Skjoreski gave her a look and she knew it was because he wanted to be on the back end, but there was no way she was having all that weight lowered down on her, and she sure wasn't letting him do it to that boy. And, anyway, she hoped maybe he'd lose control of the whole mess and it would crush his fat ass.

She had the first load, anyway. She bent down to pick up the bottom. There was an unfinished lip of metal there just waiting to cut into her hands. "Wait a minute," she said. She ran downstairs and grabbed a pair of gardening gloves and went back for another try. "Let's go," she ordered. The heater didn't seem that heavy, though it was just heavy enough and Skjoreski that much taller than she that she had to carry it in an awkward stooped position. They maneuvered through the door, and as Skjoreski started down she could feel the weight shift to his end.

"Jesus, shit," he said.

"You got it?"

"Yeah. Come on."

The bottom step came sooner than she expected and she almost dropped her end. "Hang on." She followed him back into the corner by the furnace room, back where the old tank stood, idle.

"I know you're not expecting me to help you get *that* out of here," she said, indicating the old heater, which was bigger by half than the other two combined. She wanted him to talk for a minute or two because she was too tired to go out there and wrestle with the other one.

"Nah," he said. "One of these days I'll come over and bust it up with a sledgehammer and take it out piece by piece."

"Tell me what day so I can be someplace else."

He laughed, and Nita knew "one of these days" would be the same day he came over and rebuilt the front steps and put a new lock on the back door and bought a new fixture for the light outside Mrs. Carter's place in the upstairs hallway.

"How you gonna hook up two water heaters anyway?" she asked him.

"See right back here," he said and then indicated a place where the pipe from the old heater branched in a T. "Here is where the water for your side of the building separates from the water that goes on the other side. That," he pointed to the first heater, "is your water, and that," he pointed out to the truck, "is theirs. Now that's what you call thinking."

A tight-fisted dog was more what she thought. But then she was relieved that she wouldn't be fighting for water with Cece and that mob of hers across the hall or Mrs. Carter, who spent all day washing everything in her house in hot soapy water, including all her clothes. Between those two apartments some days they used up all the water in the hundred-gallon tank that had just died. That's probably why it died in the first place. On her side, the downstairs front was still empty and that left just her and Mrs. Stephens, who was real quiet and lived alone. Upstairs was Mr. Reese—an old white man, the only one on the block—and then those heathens up above her who'd moved in last week. Lord knows they didn't bathe much. Two or three of them up there—she couldn't keep track of who went in and out, weren't more than teenagers and kept all kinds of hours and didn't care when they turned that stereo up. She'd warned them and even called the police on them once or twice, but there was something about them made her afraid. Skjoreski should never have let them in the building in the first place. She wanted him to take care of it. The sooner the better.

"You gonna do something about them boys upstairs?" she asked. He was reconnecting the water pipe from the old heater and attaching it to the new one. To his credit he had planned it all out . . . had purchased (or found, probably) plenty of piping and had even drawn himself a little diagram. She had to remind him, however, where the main utility valves were, though she hesitated for a moment, not completely trusting that the fool wouldn't flood them or blow up the whole damn building. Too damn cheap even to call the gas company.

"I went up there," he said. "Nothing's broken. They paid the rent on time. What do you want me to do?"

"Mr. Skjoreski, I'm trying to raise my children here. They need their rest so they can get up in the morning and go to school. How they gonna sleep with that mess going on up there? And I know they got something going on, and you know they do too, and there are laws in this city. As the landlord, you're responsible."

"Look, Nita, I did my job. If you got evidence, take it to the police. There's no law against having parties. They're your neighbors and you're gonna have to find a way to get along with them."

"Why'd you rent to something like that in the first place?"

He laughed. "How am I supposed to tell the good ones from the bad ones? You tell me."

She laid the wrench down on the floor, the one she'd been holding for him, and started for the steps. If she kept holding the wrench there was a good chance she would knock his brains out.

He just didn't get it. None of them did, not the police, not anyone. They didn't understand how people like those boys intimidated decent people like her right out of the neighborhood. Everyone left, like most of the good people around here had already done. Left it to those vultures who tore everything down. So all that remained was empty land for the developers.

She'd leave too. If she could. But for now she was trapped, and she hated it. Hated how helpless this felt. Damn. There had to be something she could do. The apartment downstairs was vacant; and soon she'd be surrounded by them, sandwiched in.

That wasn't going to happen. Not while she was alive.

"Mr. Skjoreski, you rented that place downstairs yet?"

"Why? You want it?"

"No. But I do want to know who's going in there. Seeing as how these are my neighbors and I got to get along with them."

Skjoreski came down off the ladder. "So?"

"So, how bout you let me take care of it. Earn some of that big rent discount you give me."

"Think you can handle it?"

She crossed her arms and stared him down.

"Well, you know my rules. Deposit up front, hundred bucks. Cash. No Section Eight and no dogs."

She nodded yes to his rules and ran upstairs to her apartment so she could start composing a newspaper ad.

Adios, Good-Bye, and Good Luck

. . . .

*Why you always on there acting white? Why
you can't talk like regular folks?*

Mary Lovelace
Brooklyn Park

Dexter had his feet up on the desk. The top half of his body rocked back and forth to a beat that Brandon heard only as a sibilant pump. "What up, What up, What up," he chanted in time to the bass. He snapped the off button of the Walkman. "The Beasties play some funky shit, man. You down with it?"

"They're all right," Brandon said, figuring the politic thing to do on a day like this was to go along with the program. Actually he hated rap music. He hated it a lot and he always had. Yeah, he understood the anger and the poetry and the rhythm, but he wasn't particularly crazy about watching some street toughs making megabucks and bitching about "the man." Who did they think "the man" was, anyway? And, anyway, after a while it all sounded the same to him. Give him an Anita Baker CD any day.

"I saw these boys at the Garden a while back. They turned it out." Dexter opened a desk drawer and dropped the Walkman in.

The other thing Brandon hated was white people who tried to act like black people. Like certain rappers. And this guy. Or at least around him they acted that way. He bet Dexter Rayburn didn't play this when he was sitting in the corporate offices in New York. He was a fool, but he wasn't stupid. You didn't get to be director of the Broadcast Media Division of Carl K. Karuthers Industries at his age unless you played the game and you played it straight. What was he? Twenty-nine? That's what the rumor said.

Dexter stared at him with a self-satisfied smile. He nodded his head up and down slowly as if he'd been examining and was pleased with the merchandise.

"Brandon Wilson," he said, and kept nodding and examining and smiling.

"That's me," Brandon said, shrugging. This scene had not been in his life plan. He hadn't planned to be sitting across the desk from a barely pubescent brat like this one who controlled his fate. A guy who was ten years younger than he. By this point, he was supposed to be in New York, with an aisle full of secretaries and producers of his own. Guys like Dexter were supposed to be coming to him for favors.

"You ambitious, Wilson? Don't answer that. . . . Hell, you wouldn't be here if you weren't. It's a tough scramble up and out of the hood. Fighting that street. Fighting the man. You did it, though. Clocked them dues, got your shit together."

Brandon's parents were teachers and they lived comfortably in suburban St. Louis. Brandon didn't tell Dexter that. He just nodded and listened.

"I come in here cold, I mean, I don't know anything. I look around this two-bit piece-of-shit operation out here in the middle of the goddamn frozen tundra, and I'm thinking to myself, Dexter, you've, like, died and gone to hell. I'm seriously bummed. You know what I'm saying?"

Brandon nodded.

"I'm thinking, hey, why bother, can't make a silk purse out of . . . I mean, hell it's not even the ear. It's a goddamn cow's ass-hole, is what it is."

Sow, Brandon thought.

"You got no equipment, no budget, that fucking weather girl's still pasting numbers on a goddamn weather map. First broadcast I go to—shut the door, will ya—here's Wilma . . . what's the weather broad's name?"

"Siverson. Wilma Siverson."

"Yeah, that broad. She's on the air and I'm thinking, what the fuck. I mean how old is this broad, a hundred and fifty? And she's still on the air? She's got guys out there making cue cards the size of billboards."

Brandon began mentally to make a list of possible gifts for Wilma's retirement party.

"So the Dex man is a pretty depressed little puppy. The Dex man don't like being depressed, and I'm thinking about throwing in the towel, walking out on this shit. And then you know what happens?"

"What?" Brandon asked. He really can't imagine.

"I see this guy, is what happens. I'm looking through a stack of old tape and I see this guy. You know who that guy is, Wilson? Know who he is?"

Brandon shook his head.

With a lot of drama, Dexter unfurled a finger in his direction.

"Me?"

"My man!"

Brandon pointed to himself just to be sure.

"My main man! I see this brother, and I feel like . . . like . . . I have been digging around in this pile of shit and here is this, like . . . pearl. This beautiful black pearl."

So, he thought. I'm a pearl now. Could be worse. Brandon had been sitting in his best "dignified" posture, back straight and tall, his arms laid in a relaxed manner along the arms of the chair, fingers idle. It had taken twenty years in the business to perfect this manner. Brandon felt a stiffness setting in, but sensed it was still too early let his guard down.

Dexter rose from his chair and began pacing around his

desk. "My problem is, then . . . what?" He fired the question at Brandon.

"You, uh . . . you. . . ."

"Exactly. You got this pearl and it's worth a fortune and it's surrounded by *shit*. Disgusting."

"Absolutely," Brandon said, nodding, though he was completely lost.

Dexter grabbed at his chin and took on a pensive air. "When you got a pearl covered with shit, someone's got to get his hands dirty digging the mother out of there. That's a man's job, Brad—can I call you Brad?"

"Brandon."

"Brad. I say to myself 'it's the big leagues now. They sent you out here to Saint Plaid to see if you had the balls to do a man's job.' And you know what, Brad? The Dex has got him some balls. Since he was this big." He indicated about an inch between his thumb and forefinger. "They sent me out here to kick butt, Brad, and you know what day it is?"

"Brandon. Brannnndon. Like Brando, with Ns in it."

"It's butt-kicking day, Brad. You ready to see some butt kicked?" Brandon nodded eagerly. A good butt kicking was always enjoyable, especially when it wasn't yours.

"Great! But first, a man needs two more things besides balls for my job. You know what they are?"

"Uh, let me see, uh . . . ?" Damn, he thought, this was just like those damn pop quizzes in fifth grade social studies. The right answer was Lake Ontario. He couldn't come up with it then, either. "Uh, brains?"

"Vision," Dexter said. "You got to have vision, and I ask myself, 'Does Dexter Rayburn have vision?'"

"Yes?" Brandon ventured. He thought that this was the correct response but was a bit confused about the flow of the conversation.

"So far I'm batting a thousand," Dexter said. He stood looking out the window, staring as if out there were all of Manhattan or Camelot or Oz, instead of the backside of the St. Paul City Hall. He reached around and stroked his dark brown ponytail. The ponytail was short and evenly trimmed and it was fastened at the nape of his neck with a silver binder. Brandon thought there was a good chance that it was a fake ponytail.

"Imagine," he said. He turned and framed Brandon's face, making a square with his two hands. Dexter had framed himself for Brandon as well, the thin face, intent eyes behind round black-framed glasses. "Move way out." He backed up with his hands. "A media . . . empire. Television. Radio. Newspaper. Publishing houses." He numbered those with his right hand. "And the crown jewel of that empire. KCKK. Move in closer. Major market. Good demographics. Who's number one at five, six, and ten?"

"KCKK?" Brandon ventured.

Dexter bent over Brandon's shoulder. "Move even closer. A television news set. State of the art. The world at your fingertips. Monitors that rise like mist to show . . . whatever the fuck you want them to show. Computer-animated graphics that put the work of a thousand Disney illustrators to shame. Writers who understand what you're up against out there, night after night, slugging it out with the boys down the street. Them big boys who want nothing more than to leave your ass face down in the dust. Anchors with an image as solid and sound as those guys carved on . . . that mountain out there, you know the place—it doesn't matter, that's my vision. And who do I see in that chair?"

Now, Brandon felt the way he did when he was in second grade and his teacher, Miss Dahl, asked for volunteers to stand behind John Glenn when he came to their school to make a speech. He had raised his hand sheepishly, because he couldn't believe it was possible that someone like him—among all these other deserving well-scrubbed hard-working faces—might be picked.

"Me?" he said, almost coyly.

"My man!"

And Brandon relaxed in the chair, or at least he relaxed a little. It wasn't the big adios, good-bye and good luck. It could still be a lot of things, but at least it wasn't that.

Dexter rubbed his hands together and stared at Brandon. Brandon held his stare, though the inside of his stomach spun. Sure, he was on television every night in front of thousands of people, and yes, he'd been doing it for years. But it was one thing to look into that red light, and it was quite another to be staring at one of them—one of those thousands of anonymous faces. Staring him right in the eye.

"Do I make you nervous, Brad?"

"Not at all," he lied.

"Good, because you know what the third thing is?"

Not to be nervous? he wondered. Nah! Too easy.

"Trust. Whom do you trust, Brad?"

"A number of people, I guess."

"Give me the list. Come on." He beckoned him as if he wanted him to follow him.

"My parents, for starters. They've always done right by me."

"Mommy and Daddy, good. Good. My father is Mr. Invisible and my mother—the Nazi bitch from hell, but hey, parents. I can dig it. Go on. This is interesting."

"My girlfriend, Sandra." She was fairly trustworthy, Brandon thought, always carrying on about things such as honesty and monogamy and being open with each other.

"Never," Dexter stopped him, "and I want to emphasize this, *never* trust a woman."

Brandon suppressed a cringe. Apparently that had been a wrong answer. He wanted to ask Dexter who that was in the picture on his desk? Girlfriend? Wife? No, the guy didn't wear a ring. Of course, he was the type who wouldn't wear one. On the rumor mill he'd been reported to be sniffing around the same hot new babe that Ron Anderson was after.

Dexter caught him eyeing the photo. He picked it up, slurped a big sloppy kiss on it, and then mouthed the words "ball breaker." He placed the picture face down over his crotch and said, "Go on. We don't have all day."

"Let's see," Brandon said, and thought, who else was there to trust? The business was anathema to friendship. Moving every three years—or less. Everybody crawling over everybody to get to the top.

"I'll cut to the chase," Dexter said. "Do you trust *me*, Brad?" It wasn't a millisecond before Brandon recognized his predicament: answer too fast and be thought a suck-up, answer too slow and be thought indecisive and disloyal.

He could not answer at all and be out of a job.

He waited what he thought was just the right amount of time—timing was everything in this business—about three long seconds, and then he began.

"Yes," he said, slowly, nodding as he said it, ending with his most reserved smile. Timing *and* delivery.

Dexter removed his glasses and put them on his desk, amid a jumble of papers and do-nothings. "A little lukewarm, wouldn't you say?" and before Brandon could respond, he added, "Personally, I wouldn't trust my ass as far as I can piss, and while I do all right in that department myself," he ever-so-slowly lifted the picture from his crotch, "I ain't one of y'all.

"What's important is *I* trust me. Me. I get sent out here to this goddamn godforsaken wilderness. You know why? Because this is the kind of place they send the pricks they want to get rid of. They figure if you fuck up out here, who gives a shit. Karuthers would unload this dump if he could find some sucker who'd pay him half what he leveraged up his ass to buy it for. A goddamn load of shit," he said, and with his arm he swept most of the crap from his desk.

"Who'd *you* fuck with?" Brandon asked, laughing.

"I *fucked* Karuthers's daughter."

Brandon bit his lip, his tongue, anything else he could bite to stop himself, but he couldn't stop. He started laughing again. Dexter laughed with him.

Then Dexter's laugh sputtered out like a car running out of gas. He retrieved his glasses from the floor. "I was on my way to vice president—youngest ever. They were all pulling for me, all them big fuckers. Then this little . . . *piece* . . . snags me at the Christmas party."

"Was it worth it?"

"Is it ever? No, tell you what. Ask me that when we're done here, you and me." He jumped up as if he was going to come across the desk at Brandon. "It goes back to trust, Brad."

"The name is B.R.A.N.D. . . ."

"Fuck Brandon. What kind of a goddamn pissant name is that anyway for a black guy. You think people want to watch some nigger on television named Brandon?"

Brandon jumped up.

"Fuck no. And sit your ass down. From now on your name is Brad. Got it? Brad. Short and simple, the way *they* like it." He pointed out the window behind him.

Brandon sat down, slowly, not sure whether he should sit, kick this guy's ass, or head for the door.

"What are you gonna do? Take a swing at me. Go on! Do it!" He opened his arms to receive the punch. "That's like fuckin suicide for your career. Such as it is."

"I've got a contract and I don't take. . . ."

"Fuck your contract and fuck what you will or won't take. Karuthers has so many lawyers that if you and your contract ever saw a dime it would be from your casket. You want to talk replacements? We got so many lined up, if you and me started screwing the broads in that line our dicks would fall off before we got to the end of it. Good-looking broads, and white guys and black guys, and any one of em'd be happy to come in here for half what we pay you. So, the next time you get any big ideas, you remember that."

32

Dexter sat down and straightened his tie, wrapped today into a perfect Windsor knot.

"You know the one thing you got going for you, Brad—you don't mind if I call you Brad?" Dexter sneered at his own sarcasm.

Brandon didn't move a muscle.

"What you got going for you is . . . me—I like your ass. Why? Cause you're *my* ticket out of this graveyard."

"And how's that?" Brandon couldn't tell whether his voice was shaking as much as he was inside.

"Like I said. I saw you on that little monitor, right there, behind you on that credenza, and I said to myself that nigger . . ."

"Do. Not. Use. That. Word. Around. Me."

"Christ, all right, so goddamn sensitive all the sudden. But I'm telling you, *you* got it. Here, in the middle of this chintzy two-bit operation, somewhere behind all the crappy packaging, *you* got what people tune in for."

"There's a lot of smart, good-looking people around here."

"Fuck smart. Fuck good-looking." Dexter rolled his head back in exasperation. "You don't even know, do you?" He came around in Brandon's face. A dangerous place, perhaps, because Brandon wasn't too sure he wanted the job anymore.

"It. I.T. They don't even have a name for what you got. And I don't even know how to describe the shit to you. But I know it when I see it, and you got it, buddy. Ronald Reagan had it. Brokaw, Rather, all the big boys got it. Shit, Diane Sawyer's got so much of it, she's got it dripping off her backside. Guys like that, they tell you to buy, you buy; they say jump off the fucking cliff, people jump by the thousands. If I could bottle what they got, I'd be a billionaire tomorrow." Dexter scoffed. "Hell, yes, you got it. And you don't even fuckin know it."

"I'm on in an hour," Brandon said, standing.

"You're a lazy son of a bitch, aren't you Brad?"

"I didn't get here being lazy."

"You're sitting on a fuckin gold mine, but you sit out there at that cardboard desk next to that blond cunt and read that sob-sister shit they give you. Tell me I'm wrong."

Brandon opened the door to leave.

Dexter fished a yellow legal pad off his desk. "Back here, to-morrow morning, you and me," he said. "Nine-thirty . . . no, make that ten. Hang on. You got homework."

Brandon turned to hear what it was.

"See this pad. I got five pages of ideas—killer ideas—to send your ass over the top."

"Such as?"

Dexter smiled coyly. "You show me yours and I'll show you mine. Maybe I'm wrong about you Brad. Maybe you like reading all that soft shit about some kid whose cat got stuck in a tree. Tomorrow morning. Ten."

Brandon stared at the man's back for a minute. He sure talked big for a little guy. Little wiry guy—the kind who looked like he spent all his spare time jogging. "Why should I?" Brandon asked, and then regretted it, instantly and deeply.

Dexter turned, sneered. "Suit yourself. And, uh, Brad, you have a good show out there tonight."

Brandon closed the door. He picked his way across the news-room to their desks—his and Mindy's. They had real desks, too, thank goodness, just behind the plywood boxes that were the set. Mindy was sitting at hers, staring at her image in a little compact. He figured she was probably trying to remember what she looked like as a redhead. She handed him a stack of paper. Tonight's script. The lead story: sixth-graders collect pennies for peace.

"How'd it go, Brandon?" she asked.

"Brad. Just call me Brad."

3 Rooms,
No Vu

. . . .

Nita bundled her register receipts, taking extra care to make sure she'd marked all her voids on the master tape. It had been one of those days with everybody changing their minds at the last minute, long after she'd rung them up. She'd rung up eighty-nine dollars for this Asian woman before the poor thing discovered she'd left her checkbook at home. It took her an extra half hour to organize the mess, and she feared she'd missed the deadline for tomorrow's want ads. Skjoreski had given her a week to rent the basement apartment, said he could have somebody in there "before she could say Jackie Daniels, ha ha," and that she better not blow her big chance. Even if she got the ad in tomorrow that left only five days to do this right. Letting Skjoreski fill the apartment was not an option, not after he rented to those trifling boys upstairs. And not that Skjoreski had had any luck anyway. Miss Jenkins had moved out to her daughter's place over a month ago, and didn't nobody want the dingy place so far. Who'd want to live down there? All the windows above your head so anybody could look down on you. And you could smell the damp when you opened the door; on a humid day you could see the moisture dripping down the walls. Poor old Miss Jenkins, down in that dungeon. She couldn't even keep her violets alive down there. The only good thing about the apartment was it stayed cool in the summer. But in the winter, even right there next to the boiler, it never seemed to heat up down there. That kind of damp cold could kill a person, too.

She'd composed the ad in her head, and then scribbled the words on a piece of Marco's notebook paper. There wasn't a whole lot to say about the place. Three rooms. Garden level. No pets. Two hundred dollars a month. She couldn't believe Skjoreski had the nerve to charge that kind of money. He must not even want to rent it. It was probably his secret love nest, and she thought she had heard him down there sometimes, opening the door with his key. One time there was a light left on in the back room — last month, it was, when there hadn't been anybody by to look at it for a week. He was the only one could get in besides her, and she hadn't left any lights on.

She wished she had time to post an ad up at some of the colleges. Those students were always looking for rooms, and maybe some white kids would be adventurous enough to come here. Of course, with her luck they would bring one of those giant stereo systems and blast everybody out the building. And she despaired that at this price she wouldn't find anybody halfway decent who would even consider the place. She hoped that it *was* Skjoreski's love nest, and that he would stay in love and keep it for just his honey and him, a quiet private place that nobody knew but them.

The want-ad line was busy so she quick dialed home.

"Mrs. Carter, the kids get in okay?"

"I'm not stayin late today. I got me a meeting."

Answer the question, bitch, she thought. "Mrs. Carter, I'm running fifteen minutes behind is all. I swear. I'll be in the door at five-fifteen. Five-thirty latest."

"We contracted five o'clock, as I recall."

Stingy bitch, too. Nita tried to sweet talk her. "Now, I take care of you real good, don't I, Mrs. Carter? You know Miss Nita always puts a little something extra in your pay." And a fifth of bourbon along with it every other week.

"Your boy got him a black eye or something. All shiny looking."

"What happened to him? Put him on the phone."

"You'll see when you get here," she said, and hung up.

Shriveled up old wench. She ought to spend another quarter just to tell her where she could get off. But then she'd hurt her feelings, and then she'd be left high and dry with no one to watch the kids till she got home from work. She wasn't gonna have her kids run up and down the street like a lot them out there did. And she wasn't gonna have them in that apartment by themselves, where who knows what they could get into. There were all kinds of crazy folks out there, too. Some crazy enough to come right in your house and snatch your child. A person couldn't be too careful these days. The bus dropped her kids off at the corner at ten after four. Mrs. Carter met them at the door and gave them a little snack. Then they could watch cartoons or read books. Nita was usually in the door by five. She gave Mrs. Carter five dollars each day she sat with them. Nita knew that was cheap child care; she knew women who paid a hundred dollars a week, but, even so, twenty dollars a week! More than that, if she traded Friday to have Sunday off. Nita barely cleared two hundred a week after all the shit they took out. No wonder these other women sat on their behinds all day and watched the stories. Women couldn't afford to work cause they couldn't afford child care. Her mama helped out when she could, but Mama worked the day shift herself. Mama would look after the kids on the nights that Nita had school and sometime on the weekend, if she was up to it. In her own ornery way Mrs. Carter was a blessing. She was patient with the children, and she worked so cheap, Nita knew, because she liked them and watching them gave her something to do. She liked to fuss, but Nita wasn't in the mood for her silliness today.

She got through to the want-ad people on the next try. She read them the copy she wanted and then the woman asked for her credit card number. The flush of shame she felt whenever they asked for this information always surprised her — after all, she hadn't done anything wrong. They just don't give those credit cards to people like her.

"Will you take Ward's?" she asked.

"Visa? Master?" the woman prompted.

"Is there any other way I can pay for it?"

"You can mail us your order with a check, or pay with cash or check here at the office."

"I really need to get this in today. Can you help me?" It was worth a try. Sometimes you caught someone with a sympathetic ear.

"We're open till five if you want to come on down. You know where we are, on Minnesota Street?"

Nita replaced the phone in the cradle. She forgot about thank yous or good-byes. Time! There was never enough time to get everything done. Everything that needed doing: the kids and the caretaking and school and work, and, and, and. And forget about having any other kind of life. Any fun. Or love.

She could make it if she hurried. What's the worst Mrs. Carter could do—kill the damn kids? Not even she was that evil.

Mrs. Carter stood in the hallway outside Nita's door, arms folded across her boxy little chest. The pulsing rhythm of a bass guitar reverberated up and down the hallways. Shit, Nita mumbled. They're up there at it again.

"I know," Nita said to her, heading her off.

"It's getting on six o'clock," Mrs. Carter said.

"Something came up and I had to go handle it. I'm sorry."

"You said five fifteen, five thirty at the latest, remember?"

Nita eased past her into the door. "I did my best. Hey, you all!" she yelled to the kids. "Everything go okay here?" The TV was on but it couldn't be heard. Didi ran out and wrapped her arms around her mother's legs.

"How you doing, precious?"

"You know, just cause a person's old don't mean she ain't got a life. Back in my time they had a thing what was known as consideration. I guess those . . ."

At the same time she was getting this lecture from Mrs. Carter, Didi was telling her about a trip her all-day kindergarten class took to the zoo, and the ceiling upstairs thud-thud-thudded like God's own marching band.

"All right, shit, Mrs. Carter. I said I was sorry. What is it with that damn noise up there? How long has that been going on?"

"Since just after the kids came in."

"That loud? Didn't you say anything?"

"I'm an old woman. I don't need the aggravation."

"Mommy, there was a bear."

"Baby, I'll listen all about the bear in a few minutes."

"This is gonna stop," she said to Mrs. Carter. She headed out the door and up the steps. She made a fist and pounded the door four times as hard as she could to be sure they heard her over the music. She smelled the green sweet ripeness of marijuana, sickening sweet almost, like the smell of geraniums on fire.

"Whasup!" the one that opened the door said. He was the one they called Sipp. She could hear in his voice the reason: hadn't been too long he'd been up here from Tupelo or one of those places. "Come on in, sister. Gentlemen, we got us a visitor."

"Yeah!" one of the other two cheered.

She wanted to tell him that in the first place she was not his sister, and in the second place this wasn't the sort of place she wanted to visit. Not ever.

"No. Thank you," she said.

"You looking fine tonight, Nita. Ain't she looking fine, Cecil?"

"Look good enough to eat," Cecil said. Sipp laughed—a nasty

exhalation, really. She was whelmed by the smoke and the noise. She wanted to snatch that stocking off this nigger's head. He was shirtless, built as if sculpted, every muscle defined. A faint pink strip outlined his full lips, red lips that stood out regally against his rich black skin. He disgusted her and attracted her at the same time.

"I'm fixing to sit down to dinner with my kids. I need for you all to turn this music down."

"Hey! Claudell. Turn that down, man."

The sudden absence of noise left a vacuum.

"How's that," he asked her.

"Thank you," she said, and turned and walked down the steps.

"Any time, any time. Wooooooo weeeee! Look at that."

She sat down to dinner with her kids. Macaroni and cheese and canned peaches. It mostly stayed quiet, but every now and then there was a short but loud blast of the beat. They were taunting her with it, she knew. Come on back up, sugar. Put on your tough act for us. Walk for us, sugar. Come on, do the wild thing. They made her feel so dirty, like she was something made to please their nasty imaginations.

They tempted her too. Not with their music or their dope or their nasty talk. They made her want to play with her own power. She made them turn that stereo down; what else could she make them do? Jump through a hoop? Dance? Make love all night, like they claimed they could?

A blast of stereo, then another. COME ON UP. COME ON UP.

She picked around in the macaroni for the crunchy parts, for some texture. She tried to concentrate on Didi's story about the zoo. There was snake. A monkey. A tiger with stripes.

"The big blue fish lives there," Didi told her.

Rae Anne was in her kittenish mood. Flirtatious and quiet and independent and helpless. She looked at Nita and then averted her eyes and then giggled. Nita reached over and rubbed her head.

"What happened to your eye?" she asked Marco.

She was gonna focus on what was down here. On what was real.

"Nothing," he said, a mouth full of food slurring his words.

"You're gonna choke if you do that. Nothing, huh? It just got like that on its own."

"Yeah." He smiled as if he was proud of his answer and proud of his eye. Purplish swelling arced below his eyelid on the left like a shadow on his coffee-brown skin.

"You wasn't in a fight or nothing?"

"Maybe a little." He looked down at his plate.

"A little, huh. I know one thing. I know I better not be getting no behavior notes. You understand me, boy?"

"Yes."

"Yes what?"

"Yes, ma'am, yes."

"Finish your peaches," she said. She never knew whether she handled things right. She tried to, but then nobody taught you this shit. She tried to work with her kids the same way her mama did with hers. Maybe a bit more patient. She tried to throw in a little Bill Cosby, too, and she had done pretty well. But she wasn't a dad like Bill, and she always wondered whether dads handled things some other way. Things like this fight her son had had.

COME ON UP. COME ON UP.

"Why are they doing that, Mama?" Rae Anne asked.

"They're ignorant, baby. Forget about them."

"Tell them to stop."

"Don't worry, baby. I'll take care of it."

Her mother arrived at seven to watch the kids. Nita hadn't even changed from her work clothes yet, and there wasn't time now. If she hurried she'd run into class just before the professor. It was accounting again tonight. She didn't know what the big deal was. Any fool could see the money you spent went in one box and what came in went in the other one, and once you learned

41

the different forms, that was pretty much that. She'd already finished the textbook, and the workbook, too—she couldn't stop. She liked this kind of stuff. It was fun to play around with money, to pretend that it was you who was compounding all that interest. And she was good at numbers and fast on the keypad and had already memorized all the fancy names that only meant things like "you don't own it yet, the bank do" and "it's wore out and worth less this year than last," like her car was—amortized into the ditch. But they made you sit through the whole thing. There were still five weeks left, so she kissed the kids good night and got her things for school. Bless her heart, Mama had agreed to take care of the dishes.

The music stayed low, but the beat could still be heard at the front door. COME ON UP.

She sat at her desk on the side of the classroom, two rows back from the door. Her pulse beat to the rhythm: COME ON UP. COME ON UP.

Be easy to go up there, too. Fill your lungs with smoke, lay back and surrender to the beat. There weren't any tax tables up there. No deficits or debits or obligations. They didn't have nothing: kids, worries—nothing she could see but a good time. No furniture, no nothing but that stereo and its beat, and so what if they had nothing? What did she have? A job where she was on her feet all day, three mouths to feed, a building to look after that wasn't even her own, this class and that class, and, and, and . . .

And she put her head down on the desk and felt her eyes fill up with tears. She felt herself drifting away, to sleep, and knew she had better not. If she was gonna make it. . . . She swallowed back the tears, sat up straight and tried to focus on whatever the hell tonight's lesson was about.

A
Thousand
Words

. . . .

Just what I don't need when I come in from
work in the afternoon: an uppity Negro like
you. Give me some Dane Stephens any time.
                      Shirley Anne Simms
                      Minneapolis

Off in the distance from Sandra's bedroom, downtown
Minneapolis glistened like a jewel-encrusted ring. Her apartment
sat on a hill, in Bloomington, and her unit was on the top floor.
From here the city seemed safe, remote, a picture on a postcard
on a rotating rack in the drugstore.

She turned on the bed, mumbled something. He hoped he
hadn't awakened her. He was restless. Good wine and good sex
hadn't helped.

Dexter. The image of the man's leer was tattooed inside his
eyelids. His slight, yet somehow substantial body leaned back in
that swivel chair, his feet on that desk. Somehow it didn't fit, this
image of Dexter—it was too vulnerable, too open. Dexter should
be standing, legs apart and planted like pillars, arms crossed at the
chest. Or coiled on his desk, set to strike. No warning. No mercy.

Guys like Dexter, they were the ones you saw speeding down
the freeway, ninety miles an hour, weaving lanes, cutting people
off. If they hit somebody—what the hell. That's what insurance

was for. His type had high-risk hobbies. They free-fell from planes. They spelunked. They scuba dived in shark-infested waters. They ran their work lives the same way: risks, thrills — damn the consequences.

Where did they come from? What ingredients created such monsters? Was it genetic, or perhaps it was childhood trauma that made them the way they were? Who knew? All Brandon knew was that it was a mystery, the same kind of mystery as how Kirby Puckett could hit with perfection and regularity a small round object hurtling toward him at ninety miles an hour, or how the morning sky could still be so beautiful when the temperature hit twenty below.

He perched on the arm of a leather-upholstered wing-back chair. I *am* aggressive. I *am* ambitious, he thought. But nothing like Dexter. And he couldn't help believing that there had been a test of some kind back there, that his feet had been placed in the fire and his response measured. And what had he done? He had sat there passively and taken it. Were he like Dexter, he'd have backed the motherfucker up against the window and busted his lip. He would have laid down the rules as to what the program was going to be. He'd have had him shaking in his fifteen-hundred-dollar boots and shitting in his Armani suit.

Outside the window the streets were dead. Night sounds were the wind and the distant complaint of a yard dog. He liked the quiet out here, the anonymity. No one in Bloomington watched Newscenter 13, or so it seemed. At the market, at the tennis court, at the health club, no one recognized him. Everyone in downtown St. Paul — where his penthouse was — seemed to. Especially all the old ladies. Brandon had developed a force field around him that he turned on. It told them to keep their distance. At those times he put on his dark glasses, glowered, and just generally radiated a bad feeling. It usually worked. People pointed and stared and the old ladies followed him with their eyes. But they never approached him for autographs or small talk.

It was nicer out here, at Sandra's. He liked her taste, the simple patterns she favored, floral and feminine, soft pinks and beiges. He liked imagining that this was *their* home, but Sandra said she wasn't ready for that. For that matter, neither was he.

"Come back to bed," she said. She lay on her side patting his pillow.

"I didn't mean to wake you."

"You can't sleep?"

"It'll pass." He hoped.

"No job's worth losing sleep over."

He sat at the edge of the bed. "That job is my whole life," he said. "It's everything I've worked for."

"You're a prime fellow, Brandon Wilson."

"What is this?" he laughed. "A high-school graduation speech? I'm the one who usually gives those."

"Well, it's my turn tonight." She curled around behind him, draping herself across his shoulder.

"This is the nineties," she said. "No one stays in one career his whole life. Use your imagination. There's lots of things you can do."

"When did you ever hear me say I wanted to do anything else? I like the news. Writing it. The deadlines and the pressure. I like that it might actually make a difference sometimes what I say. I like the power, too, I guess."

"Produce a show, then. Or go on the radio. Or write for one of the papers."

"I like *television*. I like being *on* television. When that camera turns on, I turn on. You've never been out there, so you can't understand." He slid down till he was prone, Sandra still curled behind him. She liked her sleep. She slept like a puppy and was already fading away.

"You don't deserve to be talked to that way," she said, and yawned.

"Because I'm Brandon Wilson, right?"

"Because you're a person. Like anybody else. You have to ask yourself: Do you really want to work where such is the standard of behavior?"

He didn't answer. There were a lot of Dexters out there. Maybe not as blatant, but journalism attracted jerks the way a dead squirrel attracted flies.

"Maybe you should move on," she suggested. "What are there — five, six stations in this town? A thousand around the country?"

"There are only two ways you move in this business. Up or down."

"You'll be fine. I believe it, honey. You know I do."

"But?"

"But nothing," she said, but he knew her disclaimers. But be yourself; but don't compromise; but look out for the Dexter Rayburns of the world. Behind him she surrendered to sleep, her breath coming even and calm. He covered her with the comforter.

"Night, love," he said.

He knew the only way he could stay in the game was to go along with Dexter's game. Play better, play smarter, but he had to play, or his career was over. He went down the hall to Sandra's study, found a legal pad and began making notes.

In the morning two workmen in the newsroom were attaching a new front panel to the anchor desk. The pale blue covering looked like marble and had two chrome strips running across it. The station's call letters had been neatly stenciled between the chrome strips in such a way that they appeared to be raised.

Brandon was impressed, though less so when from the back he could see it was just another piece of plywood, gussied up a bit for the camera.

He saw that someone else had been gussied up, too.

"You like it?" Mindy asked. Already this morning her hair was several shades down from its platinum high—today an odd beige color. "Dex says we have to take in stages. You know, give the people a chance to get used to it."

"Dex?"

"That's what he wants me to call him," she shrugged. "Want to hear something funny? Yesterday, during our meeting, I think he tried to hit on me."

"The guy's young enough to be your son."

"*Step*son. And only if I had married his *very* rich father who was *very* old. Or better yet, my son-in-*law*. He's got plenty of money, don't you think? He'd be a good catch for one of the sponge sisters."

Mindy's daughters had been giving her a fit lately, having some sort of long-distance competition with each other to see who could get the most goodies out of mom.

Brandon couldn't help himself. He had always harbored a deep and solid, lust-filled attraction to white gals like Mindy. Even if, like Mindy, they were sort of frivolous. And he had to admit that underneath all the paint and frills there was something rather decent about her. She wasn't one of those lock-yourself-away-in-an-ivory-tower types. Some agent along the way had convinced her that "good works," as she called them—without the least bit of sarcasm—were the key to her continued success in broadcasting. One could find her every night of the week at this charity auction or that recognition banquet, performing her heart out, singing her renditions of "My Way" and "America the Beautiful." She passed out candy hearts and her own crimson-lipped kisses in nursing homes all over the state. Sure, all on-air staff did these things. It was written into their contracts: get out there and keep the public happy! Brandon did as little as he could get by with, always signing up for things like parades and judging beauty pageants—the stuff where there was some crowd control and people were kept at a distance. Mindy liked getting dirty. She enjoyed "rubbing elbows with America," as she called it—again, no irony. That was part of what attracted him—the contrasts between them. Mindy's extrovert against his private person, her effervescence versus his circumspection, even his black skin next to her white. They'd briefly been lovers, right after he first joined the station. She had called it off because her daughters were fourteen and sixteen at the time, rebellious enough as it was, and she felt her only chance to get them through adolescence was to assume the role of chaste mother, even if it was the late eighties and she was divorced, financially independent, and therefore free to do whatever she wished. Still, anyone could see that there was some sort of chemistry between them, even Jack Pruitt, the now-fired station manager, and it wasn't long before they were teamed to do the news at five. And even though Mindy wasn't exactly what he would call a serious journalist—he even doubted that she knew what most of the stories she read were about— they were basically a good team, he thought. The best he'd been part of. She had that quality Dexter kept going on about, and to- gether they had timing, like the lovers they had been. Each knew the other's rhythms, knew when to yield, knew when her partner was not quite on the mark. He often wondered whether in a more high-profile operation, one with some production values and some decent support, they just might be on top. Not that that was even her goal. She, of course, couldn't care less about the news. She liked the money, the notoriety, the glamour. Her news sense told her that it was a good idea to work PR into the show for any charity that asked and she would spend the entire half hour doing that if he let her, headlines be damned. It could be worse. She read the hell out of the TelePrompTer, had finally learned to alter her tones to match the mood of the story, and, most importantly, she pronounced all the words correctly, even the tongue-twisting names of Middle-Eastern despots.

He reached out and fingered a lock of her hair.

"Glamorous, huh?" she asked.

"You're gonna let him do it to you?"

She shrugged, "Got to keep the sponge sisters in college. You know, college, where you need all that resort wear and plane tickets to Daytona." She picked up her daughters' picture and simpered at it. Posed together, they were blond and pretty like their mother. "This little princess," she said pointing to the one on the left. "Dear sweet Jennifer Anne. She called me up last night. She says, 'I saw the cutest outfit today. It was just to die for. On Michigan Avenue. I must have it. There's a spring mixer coming up. I don't have one nice thing to wear. I just must have it. I'll die. Oh, mother, please.'"

"You sent her the money, of course."

"Fed-Ex'd it, honey. Of course. Here's the choices: send the little witch the money or have her on the phone for three days whining to me about how she's the only one who doesn't have new boots and she can't remember the last time I bought her anything and how much I spent on Jessica that I didn't spend on her. Or worse, they call daddy—Mr. Moneybags—and then that wife of his calls me up about how my daughters are spending her children's lunch money. This dress I'm buying her costs like maybe half of what Big Daddy charges for using his proctoscope once, and he's up to at least fifty butts every day . . ."

"Fed-Ex'd it, huh."

"Overnight delivery. And you know what? They really do get it there on time."

"And the hair thing?"

"Blonde, purple, green, pink—my hair's been colors in this business that don't even exist anymore. But you know what, Brandon? I make them send me to some place nice, like to Horst's spa. I get a manicure and a pedicure and a facial. And I just have to have a new wardrobe to go with my new hair color, don't you think?" she batted her eyes and pouted.

"You're shameless," he said.

"I'm a forty-something-year-old woman in a teenager's business. I've got the sponge sisters in the most expensive colleges on earth and ten years on a mortgage out at the lake. I call it practical."

"He come in yet?" Brandon nodded toward Dexter's office.

"Speak of the devil," she whispered, and picked up the phone so as to look busy.

Dexter sauntered across the newsroom. His leather gym bag gaped open with clothes and a shoe and a racket handle. He stomped through the office, not acknowledging a soul.

"Bad day on the courts, I guess," Mindy said.

"Just in time for our ten A.M."

"Good luck, and friend, could you get a clarification for me?"

"Sure."

"Is *all* my hair supposed to be red?" She puckered her lips in a smooch.

Brandon tapped the door frame.

"Goddamn, motherfucking, pissing, shitass, fucking hell."

"Good game?"

"Don't fuck with me, Brad."

"Just asking." He raised his hands in protest. He couldn't tell if Dexter was sweating or wet from the shower. His shirt was rumpled, and he looked like he had dressed in hurry. "Racquetball?" Brandon asked.

"I bet this wimp from promotions a hundred bucks I could take him. Cocksucker turns out to be a goddamn shill. I even let him get up on me, too. I handicapped the bastard. Let him try me again. I'll wipe the floor with his ass." He bent over the rug and squeezed a stream of water from his ponytail.

"You wanted to meet?" Brandon asked.

"Yeah, yeah, yeah, so talk to me. What do you got?"

Brandon opened his daybook to review his notes, but before he could answer . . .

"See, here's the thing, Brad. What is television about?"

Another damn quiz. He opened his mouth to answer.

"Nah, fuck that. Pictures. Period. The whole goddamn thing is pictures. There's nothing else to it. Each one of those pictures is a story. You take your president. You put him in front of a bunch of flags on the deck of a battleship. What's the story there?"

"President's making a military speech?" Brandon guessed.

"No. Fuck no!" Dexter came around the desk. "Forget the speech, forget the reason he's there. Forget the news, for chrissakes." Dexter made the frame with his hands again. "Look at the picture, Brad."

Brandon looked through the frame. He saw Dexter, still flushed from the game. Or else excited about his performance.

"What you see is," and Dexter enumerated with his fingers, "the battleship, which is power—enough power to blow most of those monkey-suck countries off the map. The flag, which is we all love this country to death and all that shit; and the man, in the center of the picture, standing tall. You know the rest. The bastard doesn't have to say shit.

"Another picture: a little girl stuck down in a well. Clock's ticking. She hasn't had any water in a long time, Brad. There's the frantic mother. All the sisters and aunts are gathered round, weeping and shit. There's the dad—they won't let him go down there, but he's right there holding those ropes and hauling that dirt. There's the rescuers and the paramedics. You got the story?

"Forget all that J-school crap about unlicensed day care and failing infrastructure and emergency response teams. This is about that poor schmuck sitting out there in television land. He works in the widget factory all day, attaching A to B. He sees some rug rat pulled out of a well down in Dogpatch somewhere and he's thinking, 'That's me down there. I saved her ass.' And he even goes to his checkbook and sends Daisy May twenty-five bucks in a get-well card. Pictures, Brad.

"Now, let's get down to it. It's five o'clock. Let's say we're over there in Minneapolis. The TV's on Channel 13. We're in some gimp's house, some old dame with a bum leg—after all, who else watches the crap you put on? Couple folks with busted remotes who can't get up to change the goddamn channel after the soaps. On comes the news. You got two people up there. Black guy. Nice looking man, thirty-something, sharp dresser, articulate. Personally you might not like your colored, but it's obvious he's not one of the ones would snatch your purse. There's a white chick. She's been around the track, you can tell, but she's keeping herself up pretty good. They start reading the news—it goes back and forth. What's the story, Brad?"

"Come on, Dexter. It's the news. The news is about the news."

Dexter laughed. "You believe that shit?" he asked, and laughed some more. He was perched on the lip of his desk now, shaking his head derisively.

"You and Mindy. That's the story. Remember, Brad," he said, holding up alternating hands. "Picture. Story. Picture. Story. That's all this shit is."

Brandon can't believe this guy. "My business is to report the news," he said. "You know, when I was at Columbia . . ."

"You know what people want to know when they tune in, Brad? They see this handsome black guy, and they see this white chick. What they want to know is, are you fucking her. Are you fucking her Brad? She's still a good-looking broad."

"My personal life is . . ."

"Beside the point, actually. The point is: Picture. Story. You know, it's funny," Dexter said. He walked around and sat at his desk. "You spend all that time and money at some big university. They tell you about"—he deepened his voice—"Objectivity and Ethics and Integrity and Documentation. All that antique shit went out with Walter Cronkite. Picture. Story. You think I'm making this shit up? They got whole companies, hundred-million-dollar computers, all they do is study who watches what and why. You're in this penny-ante station still living in the goddamn 1960s. Example. If this was the sixties you know very well you wouldn't even be sitting at that desk with a white woman. Research says it's cool now—as long as—guess what? As long as she ain't blond."

"So you change the woman's hair? Just like that?"

"Problem. Solution. Just like that. And by now I'm sure you know what our other problem is."

"Wild guess. We don't have a story?"

"Quick learner, Brad. So," Dexter said and he leaned back in the swivel chair, feet up on the desk, hands behind his head—the position that confused Brandon and that he despised. "Homework time. What you got?"

Brandon fumbled open his daybook again. "I took a few notes here," he said. "Oh . . . uh . . . one thing I thought was, it would be nice if we started a consumer series. Have it as a regular feature. Investigate rip-offs and tell people about discounts and ways to save money."

Dexter waved his hand for Brandon to continue.

"We could use a new open, too. We've been on this same one since I got here. It's really old."

Dexter turned his lips up disdainfully.

"Oh, and what would be great would be if we could do movie reviews. Get a kid from one of the alternative papers. After the reviews, Mindy and . . ."

Dexter cut him off. "You been listening, Brad?"

"I thought I was."

Dexter removed his glasses and squinted into the distance. "Well. I guess I should shake your hand. Great ideas, man. What you got? Fifteen? Twenty of em there? Just as strong, right? Really fine—and hey, you know what, go with them. You got my blessing. Here." He scribbled a memo on a pad and ripped it in

Brandon's direction. "Memo to finance. Carte blanche. Open account. You do all that shit. I don't give a rat's ass about it. Take it."

Brandon reached for the paper and Dexter pulled it away.

"Hang on," Dexter said. "What do I get?"

"Best news operation in town," Brandon said.

Dexter waved that away. "Look, man, I'm giving you a lot here. I'm telling you to get what you need. Do what you got to do. You want graphics, get some graphics. Some hot shit reporter out there? Hire him. You need money? Spend . . . let's say . . . a half-million bucks, even there I'm putting my ass on the line. You think Karuthers wants to drop another nickel in this cesspool? Fuck no. I'm going out on the limb for you, bud. And, the only thing I want to know is, what do I get?"

"What do you want?" Brandon asked, sick of the game.

"Just one tiny little thing. I want a story."

"A story?"

"Channel 7. Their *Action News* report, or whatever the hell they call it. You know that show?"

Brandon nodded.

Dexter made the frame again. "You're a young woman. You've just got in from a hard day in the typing pool. You're single. You pop one of those diet dinners in the microwave, and get ready for another evening in front of the tube. On comes this guy, this Don? Dean?" Dexter snaps his fingers.

"Dane Stephens."

"Yeah, that cocksucker. Little prick looks like he's thirteen. That guy, he reads the news and every once in a while he kinda closes his eyelids together just so, and then he turns and talks to that cunt next to him and rubs a finger across his lips, laughs at her little jokes. I don't need to tell you the story. Broads out there eat that shit up."

"I hate to disappoint you, Dexter, but that's not me. I don't do that shtick."

Dexter spits like a cat. "Give me some credit." He pulled

something from his sports bag. "Think man. Try to keep up with me here." He held a hand mirror in Brandon's face. "Here is the person whose story we've got to tell."

Brandon saw himself in the mirror. His eyes were wide, and he appeared calm, if a bit perplexed.

"Who is Brad Wilson? Tell me, cause that's what we've gotta tell the people out there."

Brandon dropped his eyes and considered the query. He reimagined the life he had always wanted to have. He conjured a life of adventure and courage, raised in foreign capitals, the offspring of spies. Someone who had fought wars, who had spent years in the trenches, covering carnage for UPI. That life—the one that was so different than the one he actually had. Though he had never set out consciously to seek the high life, he had somehow always expected it to find him. And where friends also approaching forty had begun the ritual of lamenting lives not lived, Brandon had years earlier come to terms with an existence that in some hard-to-explain way actually often thrilled him with its predictability and lack of stimulation.

"I'm an ordinary person," he said. "I went to school and played sports. I went on to college and started working in TV."

"They're tuning out in droves, Brad. Click—another share. Click."

Brandon thought hard. He wanted that piece of paper. He could turn this operation around in no time with that kind of cash. "I . . . uh, enjoy all kinds of music, I enjoy the theater. I, uh . . ."

"Click—another share. Click."

"Look, Dexter, I'm an ordinary, boring, average . . ."

"Click! Click! Click! I don't give a shit about all that crap. Hell, I didn't ask for your fucking bio. No one else wants it either. Look in this mirror. This face here. Look at it. What is it?"

"It's me."

"Forget you. Look at the face. What is the face?"

"It's a guy. A face."

"WHAT KIND OF FACE!"

"An oblong face, a handsome face, a man's face, a . . ."

"Say it! Goddamn it!"

"A black face!" Brandon shouted and knocked the mirror away. It shattered on the floor. "There! Satisfied?"

Dexter returned to the swivel chair. "Picture. Story. What's the story?"

"I'm sick of this shit. You tell me."

"Well, he's got a spine after all," Dexter smirked. "Story: Here's a guy who started at the bottom. Lived in a rundown neighborhood. Had to fight his way to school everyday and back. Barely literate mama, but hard-working salt-of-the-earth type, God bless her. She was gonna see to it that at least one of her kids made it. Hell, the kid even gang-banged for a while. Got strung out on smack—but this kid and this mama were determined. He gets it together. Gets a scholarship. Plays a little college ball—yeah! Took years of hard work and struggle, but he made it to the top. But he never forgot about the folks back in the hood or about mama. He knows how hard the struggle is. But this is America, goddamnit, and he's made it. And, if he can make it, anyone can."

Brandon applauded. "That's a beautiful story, Dex. Can I call you Dex? And it ain't got shit to do with my life."

"Who the hell is talking about your *life*? I'm talking about stories here. The story that goes with the picture."

Brandon shook his head. "That story's a damn fantasy. The odds of a kid like that getting off the streets are next to nothing. People believe that shit cause it makes them feel better."

"BINGO. Brains and looks, too. I am the luckiest guy on earth."

"I'm not making up some bogus life story to support your racist myth."

"Who asked you to? Now you're pissing me off. Just when I think you're coming along, you say some stupid shit like that." He stood in the position Brandon always imagined him in—legs apart, but firmly planted. "Last time, Brad. Picture. Story. You been in this business your whole fucking life. Get a clue. We don't make this shit up. You know the pictures. You know the stories. Sexy broad with a beer can. If I drink it, I'll get laid. Picture. Story. The goddamn stories are just out there, man. You said it yourself. You tell the stories that make people feel good. You tell em what confirms what they believe. No, wait. You even got me confused. *You* don't tell them shit. The picture does. You're the picture Brannndon," he said, emphasizing the Ns. "And unless folks out there see what they believe and believe what they see, they'll keep clicking until they find it somewhere else. Got it?"

"Yeah," he said. "I got it. I don't like it, but I got it."

"You with me?" Dexter said, waving the paper with the carte blanche on it.

Brandon felt the saliva run in his mouth. He swallowed to keep from drooling. "Depends on where we're going," he said.

"You're either with me or you're not."

"I said it depends."

"Integrity. More of that J-school shit. That and a quarter will get you a call home to that Mommy and Daddy you love so much."

"Tell me exactly what you want me to do, Dexter. Let's get real specific and get this over with so we can get on with it or not."

Dexter sat, pulled up to his desk and rubbed his hands as if to warm them. "It's simple," he said. "We got our story. Boy from the ghetto makes good. But somehow, people can't quite buy it. Why? Because they haven't experienced it—not with *this* boy. And there's something about him that doesn't let the story be automatically true like it is, say, with your Richard Pryor types. Face it. Brad, you're a pretty white guy when it comes right down to it."

"I been black all my damn life."

"Hell, you speak better than me, better than most everybody out there. And your name isn't Roscoe or Washington or Rufus. It's Brandon, for chrissakes. Don't get offended. It ain't me, hey I grew up with guys just like you all my life. Smart, rich little black pricks. You guys never fit the story. Born with that silver spoon. The trouble is people didn't see you earn it. They see you sitting there, and it's like you just showed up. Like you don't deserve it. Take the white chick again—what's her name—Mandy?"

"Mindy."

"Now, while people don't like the idea of you and this white gal getting together, they can live with it if they think maybe you earned it." He anticipated Brandon's protest and waved it away with his hands. "So we relive the experience for them. Right there on the five o'clock news every night. The good people of St. Paul and Minneapolis watch their very own Brad Wilson as he starts out in the slums and rises to the anchor chair. The question is how? That's your damn homework."

Brandon closed his eyes. Who knew? "What do we do, make some docu-drama?" The whole thing was so preposterous, he couldn't take it seriously. Somebody must have dropped this guy on his head.

"That could work. A graphic thing, right? At the beginning of the news every night. Come on. Work with me here. What else you got?"

"You're the answer guy."

"Come on. Fuck that. Think. How do we get people to experience your rise into good old American middle class? You could follow some poor kid around. Do a sob piece or investigate some welfare queen. Shit, come on Brad. What the hell goes on down in that damn ghetto."

"Dexter, I have absolutely no idea. I have never lived in the ghetto one day in my whole life."

Dexter stood up, clapped his hands, clenched his fists and shook them. "Brilliant. Fucking brilliant. Check this out. We put you in the ghetto. We get you a rundown apartment somewhere—in the projects or something. And we do the news from there.

No! You do the news from there. Back and forth to Mindy in the studio. Yes! Damn, damn, we're good."

"That is the most bizarre, asinine . . ."

"I grew up in Chicago. This broad who was mayor, what's her name—Byrne. Campaign stunt. She moved into the projects. Right in there with the garbage and the rats. The chick's numbers went through the roof."

Brandon remembered that story, remembered reading it on the air. He remembered a part of him thinking it was a good idea. A mayor should have to get out there and live like her constituency did, get out of her limousines and designer apartment and see how the government treated the real people. The other part of him was horrified.

Dexter came around the desk again and squatted in front of Brandon's chair. "You're a journalist, man. We both know that, and I already told you I don't give a fuck about the news. That's not my job. I'm handing you the opportunity of a lifetime. All the money you need. The staff. I'm giving you the story of your life. You go down to the community. With *your* people. Tell their stories. Tell what it's like to have to live in that shit down there— with the drugs and the gangs and the hookers. Top story. Every night. Good journalism."

"I have to live there?"

"It has to look like you do. Hey, five weeks. We start just before May sweeps. You're down there full time at the start, then slowly we pull you back in."

Brandon sat, quiet, thinking. He looked at Dexter, who was still squatting and staring at him.

"This is easier than a two-dollar whore, man. Just get yourself a quiet place in an okay building. A little run-down, but livable. Anonymous, with a back door, so you can come and go without a lot of attention. We keep this real quiet. Just you and me. This gets out and we're dog meat, both of us."

Brandon looked back and forth, from the window to Dexter. Back and forth. He somehow couldn't keep his eyes on him.

"I'm putting my whole career on this, Brandon. I'd bet my first-born child. Come on. You in?" He stood up and placed the paper on Brandon's lap. "Come on, man."

Brandon folded the paper into his pocket and shook Dexter's hand. He went out to find the place where he could make the stupid plan work.

Adventures in American Literature

. . . .

No one wanted the damn apartment. The last old man had taken one look in the door.

"Two hundred dollars? Shit."

He hadn't even gone in.

Nita had arranged a few sticks of furniture abandoned by former tenants to give the dump a more lived-in look. She found some old shelves and placed a few whatnots on them—little china dogs and dolls, a sea shell, a chipped vase. It hadn't helped.

One man—one who came and looked the first day the ad was in the paper—said he would be back, but that was three days ago. He'd probably rented a much nicer place. The paper was full of choices, and a person would have to be pretty desperate to settle for this. Nita didn't want him, anyway. He was too young, and it would just be more of the same thing she had upstairs.

She locked the door. The old man who had rejected the apartment had already pulled his car away from the curb.

On her way upstairs she ran into that Sipp from upstairs.

"Hey, bitch," he said, grinning from ear to ear, opening his arms as if he expected her to jump right into them.

"I'm not your bitch. You better watch who you . . ."

"Scuse me, baby. You just look so gooooood standing there in that door."

"I ain't your baby, or none of your nothing else, for that matter. Now, if you'll let me pass, I got work to do."

"Crannnnkeeee today. Won't give a brother even a little play." He stood to one side of the stairwell, leaving just enough room for Nita to scoot by.

Black dog, she thought. She crossed her arms and gave him time to go on about whatever it was he was doing. That damn grin. What did he have to smile about anyway? She'd bring him down a few pegs.

"As long as you standing here, let's take care of some business," she said.

"Ooh, I love me a woman take care of business." He squeezed his face together in delight. She couldn't keep from snickering.

"First, you need to get some names on this mailbox. Postman won't leave no mail unless you got it marked, clear, and with everybody stay up there's name on it."

"We don't get no mail, sugar. Not unless you playing post office."

"You get a damn light bill."

"Not if they don't know where you live." He cackled like that was real funny, a country-boy kind of laugh that touched something somewhere inside her. Despite herself, she found herself acting coy and cute. She put her hands on her hips and cocked her head to one side.

"Let me find an electric bill in here for you. See don't I come up there and throw it in your face."

"Ahhhhh. You put the hurt on me now. That's cold blooded."

"Be colder when they shut off your power."

"Looka here, I'm gonna run upstairs and get me some tape and put some names on that mailbox right now. I'm a changed man. You done converted me." He turned around to go.

"Hang on. I got something else."

"Lay it on me, sister." He opened his arms again. He looked good again today, she thought. He wore a skin-tight black T-shirt and some fairly new jeans with a crease pressed down the front. She couldn't imagine how them jeans got looking so nice. Not wanting to seem like some kind of tramp, she set her face hard.

"What I got for you is a request. That you please don't make me have to come up there about that damn music tonight. Please."

"Anything for you, baby."

"Well, good." She smiled. She knew she was acting cheap. But he *was* kind of cute, and if it worked. . . .

"I'll be back directly with some names," he said. He sprinted up three steps at a time. A nice butt on him, too. Real nice.

"Mrs. Carter! How long you been standing there?" She was up in the hallway by Nita's door.

"This my home. I figure I stand where I want to."

Nita opened her apartment and tried to block the way, but the old wench just pushed her way on in.

"You don't need to be skulking around the hallway snooping on folks."

Mrs. Carter waved her hand. "Wasn't studying ya'll. Came down to get me some air."

"I'm starting my supper now," Nita said, hoping to get rid of her.

"No, thank you. I got some lima beans soaking. And I *was* standing there long enough to hear you flirting with that trash from upstairs."

"Flirting! You better hush with that mess." Nita was indignant. The old woman made her so mad sometimes she could strangle her. Look at her. Set herself right down and made herself comfortable. Moved all her school books from where she wanted them. Nita would never find her place.

"I heard what I heard," Mrs. Carter said. "I may be old but I still know flirting when I see it."

Nita dropped the package of hamburger on the counter. "For what would I want to mess with something like that?"

"That's my question for you. They ain't nothing but trash. I don't even speak to em myself."

"For your information, and not that it's any of your concern, I was doing caretaking business."

"More like taking care of your *own* business. I'm just trying to warn you. Woman can't be too careful these days."

Nita scoffed. She never knew what it was with these little old black ladies all over the city thought it was their job to look after folks—folks they didn't even know. Just yesterday another old sister had come into Wards, talking about how if she was Nita she wouldn't be wearing that color red cause a brownskin women just look ashy when she wears it. Who asked you, bitch? was what she wanted to say, but that was the sort of thing they fired you for on the spot, and for all Nita knew she had been the secret shopper, one of the ones they sent around to make sure you were being courteous.

Flirting. Ha! "As if you'd know," she mumbled.

"I heard that. I been around. You don't know what I know."

Nita broke up the ground meat and dropped it in the skillet where it sizzled. She wiped her hand on the dish towel, then fished around a drawer for a spatula. "Tell me then," she said, giving a stir to the meat.

"No, no, no, see, I'm not the kind goes around bothering folks who already know everything. No, ma'am. Not me."

"Well, then," Nita said, then chuckled. Guess I shut her up, she thought.

"Folks think they can use you. Take advantage of you all kinds of ways. Mrs. Carter knows when to keep *her* mouth closed."

"Tell it, honey." Nita salted and peppered the meat. The pieces on the bottom of the skillet had already browned, so she turned the flame lower.

"That's right. I do. I know me something else, too. I know some trash like that upstairs'll give a gal nothing but grief."

"You know that, huh?"

"They the kind knock an old lady down for her last quarter. Ain't never worked a day in they lives. You keep messing with him, see what happens."

"Nita!" Sipp yelled. Mrs. Carter smirked.

He sauntered in with a roll of masking tape.

"Ain't one thing to write with in that whole place up there."

"I got something," Nita said. She dug through the piles of papers on the dinette, fishing up a blue highlighter. Mrs. Carter kept smirking.

"How you this afternoon, ma'am?" Sipp asked.

"Just fine. Thank you for asking." She didn't look at him—kept smirking at Nita.

Nita scowled at her. "Here it is," she said, handing Sipp the marker

"Right back with it." He bounded down the steps.

"Least he can write his name," Mrs. Carter said.

"Shush." Nita closed the door gently. "That's rude."

"I'd check my purse before I talk about rude."

Nita ignored her. She added the sauce and the seasoning packets to the hamburger, covered it, and set it on the back of the stove. When it was time to eat she'd add the noodles and heat it up a few minutes.

Sipp opened the door and tossed Nita the marker. "Thanks a lot," he said.

"Any time."

"Any time, indeed," Mrs. Carter whispered.

"Later," Sipp said, starting to leave, and then opened the door again. "Say, Nita. We having a little party Friday night. Why don't you come on up?"

"Seems to me they got a party every night," Mrs. Carter said.

Nita cut her eyes at her. "I don't know," she said. "It's a long week, and I got the kids and . . ."

"You'll watch the kids for her, won't you?"

"You mean I ain't invited to the party?"

Nita rolled her eyes and Sipp put his hand to his heart in fake shame.

"I'll let you all know, okay?" Nita said.

"I'll see you Friday," he said. He winked at Mrs. Carter and left.

"Don't say nothing to me, Mrs. Carter."

"Mmmph, mmph, mmmmmph."

"And what does that suppose to mean?"

"No, no. You didn't want me to say nothing."

"Time for my nap," Nita said. She held open the door.

"Yeah, you better get you some beauty sleep, girl." She strutted and switched her way over to the door.

"Now, if you make fun of me, I'm gonna have to hurt you."

"Yeah. Borrowing pens. Inviting folks to parties. You know what else I noticed?"

"Have a nice evening, Mrs. Carter."

"He opened the door and walked right in. Just like home."

"Bye," Nita eased her on out the door with the slightest of pushes.

Silly old thing.

Nita scanned her apartment to see what needed doing. Pleased that things seemed fairly neat for a change, she settled in to get her homework done.

She pulled from her stack the text for her short-story class. She'd taken it because she needed a humanities elective, but it turned out to be not so bad. Some of the stories were fun to read. She hoped tonight's reading would be one of the dull ones, though. Hoped it would send her right to sleep. She could nap for about a half hour, till just before the kids came in the door. She settled on the couch, then got up and locked the door. A woman really couldn't be too careful.

She wrapped herself in the afghan and turned to page 157. Oh, yeah, this story, she thought. She wasn't getting anywhere with this. So far, it was two or three professors talking about all the sweet young college girls they had got to come home with them.

She'd been trying to get through it for two days now, but a lot of times there didn't seem to be anything to get hold of. A lot of times there were just meaningless words on the page. Some pages she read three times to wring a clue from, and what she really couldn't figure out was what the big deal was. Her own professor said these were the best writers America had to offer the world, and Nita thought if that was true, than the world shouldn't be wasting too much time on them.

I arrived at Cornell, a young man, free, with no responsibility save planting the seeds of wisdom in the minds of a thousand nubile coed beauties, all eager for the lessons I had to teach.

What was this shit? Everybody in this story was full of it, full of himself, full of words didn't nobody use.

"I'd like to have a conference," she said. Her breasts rose from pink angora as large and inviting as summer moons rising in the east.

Oh, yes, we'd confer.

"Name please?" I asked, a ploy, a professional stance, concealing my most unprofessional aims.

Oh, it's one of those kinds of stories, she thought. The books were full of them, stories where men ran everything and the women either ended up on the bad end of the deal or were just there as toys. Where were the stories where the women came out on top? Had someone gone through the books with scissors and cut those out?

Maybe I'm spoiled, Nita thought. Maybe cause I do so much for myself I forgot that a lot of women out there must like to have someone else in charge. But did it have to be either/or? Wasn't there some world where a person could make the choices she wanted—have the family she wanted, make her own way in the world—and still have a partner? Apparently not. Even back in high school, back when she first decided she wanted to have the child that came up to be Marco, Nita knew that rather than multiple choice, life would turn out to more of a true/false kind of thing. You chose, and if you picked wrong, it wasn't so much you got marked down as it was you had to spend the rest of your life explaining your answer. Nita had no explanations that satisfied all them out there asking the questions. She'd chosen single motherhood for no other reason than she knew she would be a good mother and it was what she wanted to do. She'd chosen no man yet because there hadn't been a man worth choosing. As if it were anyone's business, and yet the television lately had been full of men—white men and black men, and some women too— who had decided it was her fault that there was no more money and that the streets were full of hoodlums and that . . . well, that apparently everything else. Choices? In case you hadn't heard, girls, the government had run out of those, too.

"Mama!"

"Open the door, mama."

"You home, mama?"

Nita tumbled off the couch in a daze. Damn, she'd fallen asleep in the middle of the reading. Which was what she wanted, but she'd show up for class unprepared.

She dragged the afghan with her to unlock the door. "You kids caught me sleep." She yawned and then bent to receive three juicy kisses.

Skjoreski called just as she was spooning fruit cocktail into bowls for their supper. She told him, no, she hadn't rented the basement yet, but she was working on it. He reminded her she had till tomorrow, and that he had some other folks "just ready to sign a lease." Fine, Nita thought. If he can rent it himself, better for him. She'd done the best she could. All she was out was some time showing the apartment and the five ninety-five for the ad. She'd petty-cash that back to Skjoreski one way or the other. Who knew? He might even get someone halfway decent. They'd even settled down upstairs. She'd seen to that. The pounding through the roof was faint: you could hardly hear it over "The Facts of Life." If she got them to set those speakers on some phone books it would be even better. She could get them to do that, easy. They didn't run nothing around here anyway. She did.

She called the kids into supper. Marco came right away. The girls whined—they didn't want to miss the end of the show.

"This food'll be cold by then. All's happens is Tootie and her dad hug and make up. You seen this one." She snapped off the set. They pouted but went to their places at the table where she dished them each some of the casserole. They said grace, and Nita was getting Rae Anne some juice when there was a pounding at the door.

"Looking for Sipp," he said. He was large and menacing and wearing a leather jacket.

"Wrong place," Nita said, closing the door, but he pushed it open. She tried to block his way.

"He got something I'm looking for."

"What are you doing?" She raised her hand to hold him back, but he shoved her aside and pushed his way into the apartment. "You can't come in here."

"Where he at?" the man said. He was looking around.

"Get out of my house! Now! Right now! I mean it. Get out of my house! He don't live here. Get out of here!" She was screaming. She saw that the kids were gone. They had gotten away.

"Tony!" someone yelled from the door. It was Sipp. "Wrong place, man. Upstairs. Sorry about that, Nita."

"Yeah," the man said. He gave her a look like he owned her.

She closed the door. Bolted it. She saw that she had been clutching her fork so hard that she had pressed its image into her hand.

My kids!

She looked and they scurried from beneath the table and ran to wrap themselves around her.

They ate, or tried to eat, but no one was very hungry. Everyone was quiet, too.

She sat with them in front of the television. She couldn't even see what was on.

"No, Mama," she said, when she called her to tell her. "I'm not going to school tonight."

I may not leave here ever again, she thought.

They sat and they watched, huddled together as if in front of a fire for warmth. There was another knock.

"Don't answer it, Mama," Marco said. Her man. Her little man—but he was no man. There was no man here.

There was another knock.

"I'm scared, Mommy," Didi said.

"It's okay, sweetie. Everything's fine," she said, and she tried to sound calm and unafraid. She would not have her children live this way—afraid in their own home. She had to show them it was okay.

"Nothing to worry about at all."

She walked to the door and swallowed her own fear. "Always check the peephole first," she said, and she almost laughed because there wasn't one of them over there who would reach the peephole for years without a chair, and maybe a box or two on top of that. There was a man out there, and it was eight o'clock and it was no one she knew. She cracked open the door, leaving the chain on. She wished she had a knife or a skillet. Without the distortion of the lens, he looked sort of familiar.

"What you want?" she asked.

"The apartment," he said. "I came about the apartment."

Just a Little Place to Get Away from It All

. . . .

*You don't look like regular folks. It's something
about you different. I don't know if it's your hair
or what. It's been my experience, though, that
light skin folks think they better than others.*

Mattie Lewis
Roseville

She acted as if she were afraid of him, so Brandon smiled pleasantly and tried to put her at ease.

"The name's Wilson. Brandon Wilson. I'd like to take a look at the place you're renting."

Her face appeared thin, or perhaps it was seeing her through the cracked door made it seem so.

"Awful late," she said.

Behind her he could see a bunch of kids. He wondered how many she had in there.

"I've been at work," he said. "Got here as soon as I could. Is this a bad time?"

"Just a minute." She closed the door and he heard some scuffling around. Sounded like she was shushing kids and throwing things around. He strolled down the hall. The dim light obscured the condition of the walls. Every other fixture seemed to be missing a bulb. Where there was light he could see the need for a coat of paint. At some point the plaster had been a pale industrial yellow—God, there was a lot of that color in these places. Here, it was faded and cracking off the walls onto an ancient orange rug. He didn't hear much noise in the hall, save a faint bass beat of a speaker amp. Nothing to lose sleep over. The walls had absorbed the smell of various fried foods and boiled vegetables—smells of home, he thought, and felt oddly comforted. At the end of the hallway at the bottom of the stairs was the requisite back door.

"Where you going?" she asked.

"Just looking around."

"It's in front."

She led him down the short flight to the main entrance. They turned and walked down another set of stairs to a door set at an angle to the hallway.

"In here," she said, fiercely.

She was hard-looking, intense, and she wouldn't look at him at all. She flipped a switch, flooding the room with muddy gold light.

"This is it," she said.

"May I?" he asked.

She raised one hand to indicate she didn't really care what he did as long as he didn't bother her.

He entered a fair-sized room. Head-level windows divided the walls on two sides, and a homely chandelier—a beige speckled globe on a silver chain—indicated what must be intended to be a dining room. Ugly green shag carpeting clashed with the brown paneled walls. The whole place smelled of wet cement.

Everything about the apartment was hideous. The tiny half-size refrigerator was fairly clean, just as the stove next to it almost was. Someone had left a shelf behind and a rotten old upholstered chair.

"This stuff come with the place?" he asked.

"Belongs to the building. Bring your own furniture."

He nodded, relieved. He tried the water—decent pressure. He peered behind the appliances. Nothing suspicious.

"Bathroom?" he asked.

"Through there," she said.

Not many words, this one, he thought. She flipped another switch for him, illuminating a room half the size of the first. Off to the side there was a tiny closet, and next to that a bathroom. Though all the porcelain was a little rusty, it was also almost clean, and the pressure was good here, too.

"Bugs?" he asked.

"Where?"

"Any bugs down here? You know. Roaches? Spiders?"

"You see any bugs?"

"Just asking." He wandered back to the front room, shaking his head. People had to live in these places. It was hardly the worst he'd seen. He'd been in one last night where the caretaker had had all the food in the house suspended off the floor in baskets to keep the mice out. Another one had looked as if it had been trashed by a heavy metal band. This basement apartment was far from the worst. In fact in many ways, it was about the best. It was solid-looking and clean and . . .

"Your place is upstairs, right?"

"Yeah?" she sneered.

"You keep your kids quiet?"

She looked at him as if he'd asked her if they were human babies.

"Hey, a person has to check on everything," he said. "I like a quiet place, and I can't be having a lot of noise upstairs when we're working."

"We?"

"I. I mean me."

"You won't hear nothing from my kids," she said and went and stood in the door.

"Two hundred, right?"

She nodded.

He opened his wallet and started pulling through bills, pulling up the edges of all the twenties. "I'll take it," he said.

"Wait a minute," she said, shaking her head as if he'd said something shocking. "Not so fast."

"It's still for rent, isn't it?" Damn. That was the other problem. A couple of these buildings—the ones that were almost decent—they wouldn't rent to him. If there was an ad in the paper and the place was empty and you had good cash money, there was no reason on earth to say no. When he got his investigative team going, that would be the first thing they'd be looking into.

"Yeah, it's available. But people . . . a person don't . . . no one has. . . ," the woman sighed. "Come on up and look at the lease."

He followed her upstairs and this time she let him into the apartment. He smelled fried meat—burgers, he bet—and the soft plastic, powdery smell of children.

"Sit down," she offered. She rifled through a file box in the corner.

He was amazed at the clutter. Every surface held a book or a toy or a cheap souvenir of some kind. Beside him a cube table had a smearing of dust on it—a rather cute table like the ones his parents had bought in the sixties—a polka dot pattern on this one. A closer look told him it was a milk crate wrapped in contact paper.

Little faces peeked around the corner. They gasped.

"Hello, there," he said. An awfully cute picture, he thought, like possums peeping over a tree branch.

The woman stood up with the folder she found and ordered the kids back to bed.

"Way past time," she scolded.

"Guess who that is, Mommy?"

"It's a man wants to rent an apartment and a man who don't want to be bothered with y'all," she said, and then to him, "Excuse me." She handed him a copy of the lease and shooed the kids down the hall.

"He's on TV," one of the little faces said.

"You'll be on the TV, too. Story of how I killed your behind. Now, go on in there before I have to tear you up."

"Sorry bout that," she said. She pointed to the paper in his hand. "That would be your lease."

"Boilerplate," he said. It was copied from a do-it-yourself legal book—solid as steel or more holes than a colander, depending on who your lawyers were. He wrote a note in the margins and initialed it.

"I wrote here," he showed her, "Month to month, thirty days notice, three month minimum."

"I don't know if you can just . . ."

"Look." He stood up, brushed his seat. Crumbs of some kind fell off, and he thought, damn, another suit to the cleaners. He'd put it on Dexter's tab. "Is there someone else in charge I need to talk to? You don't seem to be too sure about anything."

"I'm the caretaker," she said. "I decide about this apartment."

"Fine," he said. He handed her the lease and reached for his wallet. "What do you need? First and last? Cleaning deposit?"

"You carry that kind of money? What do you do?"

This little bit of money? he thought. A couple of odd twenties? He really had come down in the world. He figured an explanation of some kind must be in order.

"It's what your kid said. I'm on television."

"Really?"

"I do the news at five. For a couple years now."

"No kidding?" she said, sort of smiling. "I guess I don't get home by five too often. And the kids watch "The Facts of Life.""

"They and everybody else," he said. He made a note to himself to get on the people at promotions. Some of those bus cards would be nice. Some advertising where this sort of person might see you.

"So, how much?" he asked.

The woman shook her head and went and sat down in the

chair. "I got to be honest with you. You look like a decent man and all, but I got these kids to think about. I'm trying hard to do the right things. I have to be careful who I rent to. Up there . . . ," she pointed and shook her head some more.

He heard the faint pumping of a bass.

"A problem up there?" he asked.

"Naw. They just noisy sometimes. They have a lot of people in and out."

"What kind of people?"

"See, I can deal with them. I can. But if I got one downstairs, too? You know what I'm saying?"

"I give you my word," Brandon told her. "You won't have one bit of noise from me. Okay? I cause any problems for you or your kids, I'm out of here."

"Well . . . ," she reached for the lease. "Still. If you're some big TV person, what you want with a place like this? Don't make sense."

"You're pretty smart. Things must run pretty well around here. How many tenants?"

"Fourteen. Legal. And you didn't answer my question."

He laughed. "Persistent, too. You and me'll do all right."

"Won't *be* a you unless I get an answer satisfies me."

"Can't say it'll satisfy you, but here goes. It's not easy being in the public eye. People stop you all the time. Want your autograph. Want you to get them or their kids or their dog on TV. There's no privacy. I have to get away from it sometimes. Go some place nobody knows who I am."

"And you figure this is the place?"

"Last place anybody would look for me."

"And you figure nobody will know you're here?"

"Not unless you tell em."

"And that's your story?"

"Only one I got." He smiled his TV smile.

She held out her hand. "Two hundred up front, plus a hundred dollars cleaning deposit."

He peeled the bills off into her hand, rather enjoying the "Let's Make a Deal" feeling of the transaction.

Later, on the bed behind Sandra, caressing her back, he felt her once more drifting off to sleep.

"I may be away for a while. Some nights at least."

She aspirated some words and they sounded like a sigh.

"A couple of weeks. A month, maybe."

She rolled to face him. "A month? Going where?"

He felt bad that he had alarmed her, felt cheap and mean that he had chosen such a time to tell her, after a wonderful evening, after love.

"It's an assignment for Dexter. I'm not supposed to talk about it."

"Not even to me?" She sat up, pulling a sheet up with her.

"It's complicated," he said. He'd rehearsed this conversation in his head. It wasn't going the way he'd planned.

"Too complicated for an uneducated chick like me, I guess."

"I knew you wouldn't understand."

"What's to understand? Nah, see, don't run this transparent shit on me, Brandon. Walk up in my house—late—cozy up to me and love me up and then throw down some shit like this. I won't have it." She put on her robe and went and sat on the chair. "Now. Come across or get out."

"I told you, baby. Don't get all mad. Dexter has a plan to improve our ratings. There's gonna be big changes. They're putting a lot of money in the operation."

"And."

"I told you. Part of the plan involves me . . . living someplace else. For just a while."

Sandra stared at him. Hard. "That don't make no kind of sense."

"You're right. I know. It doesn't."

She pounded a fist in a heartbeat rhythm on the arm of the chair. "Keep talking, nigger. I got all night."

He paced in front of the bed, gathering his words with care. "It's about my image, I guess."

"Your image? What's wrong with your image?"

He threw his head back, eyes toward the ceiling. "Dexter says people don't identify with my story."

"Image. Image." She mouthed his words to herself as if trying to absorb them. "Go on. Out with it."

"He has a plan to make the public see me differently."

"See you how?"

"More like one of them I guess. . . . Look, I'm not supposed to talk about this. With anyone."

"Let's go then," she said. She stood and tied her robe and started for the door. "Lots of thing I can put up with, but this kind of shit ain't on the list."

"Let's be calm, please. My business . . . Sandra, you don't know, honey. It's a war. They'll use anything against you. Any little bit of information."

"I run a damn title insurance company. Ain't nobody there gives a second thought to you or Mindy St. Michaels or Dexter Rayburn or anybody else you work with. My girls, if they ever even turn the news on, it's that Dane Stephens they watch, and I can assure you they ain't looking at him to find out the price of eggs."

"Still, you never know who . . ."

"Still my ass. You have obviously deluded yourself into believing that all I have to do at my work is sit around and talk about you and what goes on at Channel 13. I'm here to tell you, you're living in a beautiful fantasy."

He dropped on the bed and rubbed his head with his hands. "Maybe if I was more sure about this myself."

"Sure about what? Are you having a nose job? Is he setting you up some place with a wife and a ranch-style home with a white picket fence?"

Did he need his nose done, too? He ran a finger up and down the bone. It still felt okay.

As he suspected, what she imagined he would be doing was worse than it actually was. He knelt in front of her. "Promise me you will not say a word about this to anyone."

"Either you trust me, or you don't. Trust," she pointed to the bed. "Don't trust," she pointed to the door.

He sat cross-legged in front of her. "The viewers—you all," he indicated her with his chin, "have to experience my rise from the depths of the ghetto."

She laughed, "Nigger, the closest you been to the ghetto was the time you stopped on Page Avenue to get a rib tip sandwich."

"Ah, but as far as the public is concerned . . ."

"Us? You have lost your. . . . Go on. I won't interrupt."

"I'm supposed to live in a place in the inner city. Through sweeps. Do the news from there and everything."

Her expression was bemused, rolling between befuddlement and a sneer. "I don't *even* know what to say," she said.

He leaned back on the mattress. "You'd have to hear Dexter talk about it. In some psychotic way, it makes sense. This is the first time I've said it out loud. To anyone. Now, I just don't know."

"You're going through with it?"

"I rented a place. Tonight. In St. Paul."

"I guess you are, then."

He rubbed his head hard as if there were an itch there he couldn't find. "I got nothing to lose, I guess. If it works, it's the big leagues. If not, well, you can't do worse than last place."

She batted her eyes, grinned. "Well, I sure wouldn't want to throw any of those complicated terms into the discussion. You know—like pride? Or self-respect?"

"You think I lost those?"

"Sounds like a coon show to me."

"Not unless I make it one."

"You might as well put on black face and sing 'Mammy.'"

"Think of the reports I can do. On crime and drugs. On welfare reform. On substandard housing."

"You can do those anyway."

"*That* wasn't Dexter's deal."

"Then you dealt with the devil."

"Damn it, Sandra! This is what I mean about not understanding. People make compromises in my business. I thought about all that. What it comes down to is the same thing as in any business. Is it worth the price? I've decided it is. And like I said, I've got nothing to lose."

"What about us?"

"What about us?"

"Do I have to move down to 'Catfish Row?' Tie a bandanna round my head and be all fat and greasy for the camera?"

He turned away from her, "If a man said that to me I'd hit him."

"Hit me. See if I don't get a gun and blow your dick off with it."

He laughed. He stopped when he realized she wasn't kidding.

"I promise you," he said. "I will do this with ultimate dignity."

"I know you'll try."

"I will. You'll see. You have to trust me, too." He crawled back beneath the covers.

"I've always trusted you. I hope I always do. And, Brandon, I'm not having any part of this. You are on your own."

"If that's the way you want it." He welcomed her back to the bed with his arms.

"You will, of course, be watching and cheering me on."

"Nigger, I watch 'The Facts of Life.'"

Working Girl

. . . .

Nita had driven like a maniac to get home, and there wasn't even anybody around. Damn that new tenant. Tracking her down at her work—she hadn't even told him where that was or even that she had another job—and then having the nerve to demand that she give up her lunch break to let some furniture delivery people in.

"It don't work that way," she told him. "I want to keep my job, and around here you just don't come and go as you please."

"Then I'll have the movers come and get the key from you."

"I don't carry all those keys with me. I have a customer. I have to go."

"Meet them at the door on your lunch break. How long is that? Half hour? I'll give you a hundred bucks."

"You must be pretty damn eager about this furniture."

"I'm a busy man. We work fast around here. What do you say? Hundred bucks."

"Cash?"

"In your hand. Next time I see you."

She'd sighed, and, really, had wanted to say "no." But a person didn't walk away from a hundred dollars, not someone with three kids who worked as much as she had to. It was half a week's pay. "All right then, but look, I get half an hour—twelve fifteen to twelve forty-five—and I cannot be late coming back."

"Be there," he said, and hung up.

And so here she was; it was 12:25 and where was the damn truck?

"You off early today, sugar?" Mrs. Carter asked.

"No ma'am. I'm meeting a delivery truck for the new tenant."

"That must be them back in the alley. I come up here looking for you to let you know."

Damn that Brandon Wilson. He was cute — for a light-skin man — but he acted like he owned people. "I may have to ask you a favor, Mrs. Carter."

"Getting to be where 'favor' is my middle name."

Scattered around the back lot in three clusters was all of Brandon Wilson's furniture. The "Rent-A-Center" truck was open and empty. Two white men in charcoal gray stood next to it. One of them spoke to her. "You the caretaker? We arrived at — what was it, Bob? — twelve fourteen. Just like Mr. Wilson said."

"I was waiting in front," Nita said. "He didn't tell me you all were coming back here."

"Mr. Wilson insisted we use the back. You have the keys for us, Miss?"

"It would be a lot easier coming in the front. Back here you got three doors to get through, and all that basement."

"Mr. Wilson was very clear. He said . . ."

"All right then." Fuck him, she thought. He had everybody jumping to his orders today. She checked her watch. She had to go. Now.

"Mrs. Carter. Can I leave this with you?" she handed her the master key. "And you got to promise me. No snooping."

"It's remarks like that make a person want to say 'no.'"

"Thank you, Mrs. Carter. I owe you for this."

"You owe me for lots."

"Miss?" the man called. He held the end of a plastic-wrapped sofa and was following his partner and Mrs. Carter to the basement. "Please, please, let Mr. Wilson know we were on time. And we used the *back* door."

She ran to her car without responding.

"Party tonight, Nita," Sipp called out his window. She waved and pulled away from the curb, leaving a trace of her bald tires on the street.

When she came in the door at five, her house was quiet. The bass tumped softly through the ceiling.

"I'm home ya'll. Kids! Mrs. Carter!" The children's school bags were on the couch with their jackets. That was the only sign they had been home at all. There weren't any parties or after-school activities that she knew of. Nothing that would involve all three kids. Somebody must be sick. Somebody must have had to go to the hospital. She looked for a note by the phone. None. She dialed Mrs. Carter's number and got her answering machine. Where could they be?

She grabbed her purse to head for Ramsey Emergency, hesitated, thought. Realized. No. She wouldn't be. Not even that snoopy thing. Not with my kids. She hurried down to the basement. She could hear a TV behind the door. Giggling little ones. She knocked. Let her be up in here, she thought. Just let her be.

"Hi, sugar. Come on in," Mrs. Carter opened the door.

"Have you lost your mind, old woman?"

"Come on in and make yourself at home."

She saw that her kids over there on the couch had done just that. They were sunk back on that brand new brown-and-green-plaid couch, watching their show, acting like this was a cruise ship.

"Isn't this nice, Mommy?"

"All three of y'all! I want you off that man's couch and upstairs. Now. Like you got some sense. Don't *even* make me say it twice. Mrs. Carter, the first thing is, give me my damn keys."

"Listen to her. She gonna get huffy with a person." She dropped the key ring into Nita's hand as if it were a precious jewel.

"Close that door behind you, Marco!" She followed Mrs. Carter over to the chair where she was about to set herself down again.

"Oh, no you don't. You going, too." She got her by one arm and grabbed the remote control with the other. She clicked off the set. "You got no business in this man's apartment."

"That's a good episode you shut off. That's the one where Blair and Jo get into a fight over the same boy."

"Let's go."

"He *told* me to make myself at home."

"Who told you?"

"That nice Mr. Willis what has this place now. And I suggest you get your hand off my arm, especially if you intend on keeping it."

"Let's go, then. Upstairs. You ain't talked to no Mr. Willis."

"Sure have. He called when I was at your place waiting on the kids. About four. Wanted to know if all his things got in okay. Told me to go down and check for him and to call his secretary if there was any problems."

"Mrs. Carter, you do not work for that man, you hear me? If he wants to check on something, let him get his lazy self over here and do it himself." She got her out the door and locked it behind them.

"That's big words from someone ask as many favors as you. Me, I never begrudge a person a kindness when I can."

"This is different. You don't understand."

"I understand 'make yourself at home.' And I understand you was sure in a hurry to see I wasn't at home too long."

"I got to feed my kids."

"You see me standing here with my hand out."

How could Nita forget this part. She selected a bank-crisp twenty from her pay envelope and placed it in Mrs. Carter's palm. Mrs. Carter kept her palm open and stared Nita down. Nita frowned playfully and handed off another ten. "For the little extra you do," Nita said.

"Bless you," Mrs. Carter said. She pecked Nita on the cheek, then hastily, stuffed the money in her bra.

Suddenly, she jumped behind Nita.

"Hey, Nita." Sipp was on the stairs above them. Nita slipped her envelope in her pocket, almost the same way Mrs. Carter had done her money. Then she felt petty for doing so.

"You coming up to the party tonight?" Sipp asked.

"I don't think so. I promised the kids some stuff, you know."

"Just an hour. Something. Give yourself a little fun."

"I'll see," she said.

"I'll see you at eight and don't be late." He headed back upstairs.

"Walk on down that garden path, girl," Mrs. Carter said, and headed on her way.

"You kids know better," Nita lectured. She spooned a helping of tuna casserole on each plate. She hoped the tuna would taste okay. She had bought an off-brand that was on sale, way cheap.

"But, Mrs. Carter said. . . ."

"Mrs. Carter said, Mrs. Carter said," she mocked, but then stopped. If her children were going to learn to disrespect adults, it wasn't gonna be from her.

"Listen to me, Marco. You the oldest and you got to help these girls. When you get off the bus, you come straight here. There's no stopping and no playing in the streets. And no going in anybody else's house. Understand? No exceptions."

Marco nodded.

She'd have to give Mrs. Carter the same lecture, she knew.

After supper, the kids watched the Friday shows on ABC, while Nita cleaned up the dishes. Sweet Rae Anne stood beside her on a chair, drying the plates carefully and stacking them in the cupboard.

"Smells fishy in here," Rae Anne said, scrunching up her face.

"It's that tuna can. I'm gonna take this trash to the dumpster."

The tump of the bass in the hallway rattled the wall like an earthquake might. COME ON UP. COME ON UP. The only reason they wanted her up there was so she wouldn't complain, though things had really quieted down since she'd made Sipp put down that old piece of rug from the basement, and since he'd set the speakers up on some old catalogs from Penney's someone left in the basement. COME ON UP.

She raised the lid of the dumpster outside the back door. A faded brown car eased into the space next to hers—an old Dodge of some kind. It was that Wilson person.

"Like it?" he asked.

"Not particularly."

"My other car *is* a Porsche," he said, and snickered. "Really."

She didn't as much as smile at his so-called joke. "What are you doing here?" she asked.

"I live here now."

"No. I mean, what are you *really* doing here? What are you playing at?"

"I told you."

"And I want the truth this time."

He opened the trunk and pulled out two bags from Target. "I always forget this kinda stuff," he said. "Toilet paper. Bathroom cleanser. Paper towels."

"You gonna answer me?"

"Jesus, you're hot about something tonight."

She followed him through the basement to his door. He set the bag on the floor and fished in his pockets for the keys.

"I can be a real idiot sometimes," he said. "You should have reminded me." He fished five twenties from his wallet and handed them in her direction.

"It's not the money."

He dropped his hands, shrugged, turned to go into his apartment.

"You don't own this building, you know. At least not yet, you don't. Don't nobody here work for you neither."

"Fine," he said with a tight smile.

"I do my caretaking work in the evenings, on Saturday morning, and on my day off during the week. If you need something taken care of, you leave me a note under my door. I'll get to it as soon as I can. Landlord's number's up by the mailbox if you got an emergency. Unless it's something wrong with my kids, do not call me at my job. Is that clear?"

"Yes, ma'am. Anything else?"

She walked up the steps.

"Nita? That's your name, right? Can I call you that?"

She stopped but didn't turn around. "What?"

"You want this money? Nita?"

She backed down the steps and took it without looking at him.

Lying back on the couch she could almost see the ceiling pulsing with the rhythm. COME ON UP. COME ON UP. COME ON UP. A woman's loud voice broke through the drone of the beat. Feet scuffed the floor.

It was almost nine, but she let the kids stay up. Couldn't sleep no way with the racket, though back in the kid's room it was almost quiet. Almost. The kids were huddled in front of the set watching another comedy show.

COME ON UP. COME ON UP.

Who did that man think he was? Giving orders, flashing money around at people. Talking all proper. Just like them white folks who gave orders over at the store. The black ones, too, if they thought they ran anything. Must be what you had to do to get somewhere in this life. Give up who you was and act the way he did. Still, you didn't have to treat people that way. You didn't have to make folks feel like this, like they was nothing. Like slaves. That's what it felt like, cause really—what was she gonna do, tell him off? Throw him out? Not hardly. As long as he had that wallet, it was his show. He could strut around with it and buy what he wanted: a new place to live, another car, clothes, jewelry, Mrs. Carter. Shit, he'd even bought her, hadn't he. A hundred dollars. For half an hour. Like some ho walking up and down University Avenue.

The money lay fanned on the trunk that she used as a coffee table. When she had taken it from his hand it had burned like it was on fire. Oh, to be able to tear it up and throw it back in his face. To be able to ball those five bills up and stuff them down his throat. To be able to make him eat it. That humiliation. That paper—that month's rent, a month's worth of day care, food for weeks, tuition. That money. Glowing there. Money that wasn't nothing to him.

COME ON UP. COME ON UP. COME ON UP.

She should. She should go on up there. The kids would be all right. They were just watching TV. They could be alone for a bit, just like they were when she went out to vacuum the carpet or shovel the walk. A few minutes up there wouldn't hurt nothing. She might have some fun for a change. Meet some folks like her. Not like him. Might be a man up there. A nice looking man. Damn. He had to be nice looking, too, with all that money. Lighter skin than she liked, but nice features. Big brown eyes, and a cute nose. He should look like a monkey. That would be justice. But, no. He had to have everything. Money. Good looks. Nice looking light-skinned man, the kind that made jokes about girls like her. Back in school. Called you chocolate and burnt and cocoa and African. Chased after white girls and all them yellow-skinned wenches with straight hair. Wouldn't be seen with no black girls. Not if their lives depended on it.

He probably had him a white wife. Or a girlfriend. That's what he wanted this place for—so he could have a place to bring his little tramp. Some place where wouldn't no decent folks see where he liked to put his dick. A place where none of her white friends would have to see who she fucked. Let her catch him bringing something like that up in here. They'd both be sorry. She'd put all their business out in the street.

COME ON UP.

That's a laugh. Who even cared what that nigger did? She didn't even herself know who he was. Just the idea, though. The idea of him coming in here and doing his dirty business, cause wasn't nobody here he would even care how they felt about it. What were we? A bunch of hogs? We were people too, dammit. Decent folks, old folks, families. People doing the best they could, trying to make their way in this world—the world where folks like him had all the money and all the luck and all the breaks. Even them boys upstairs COME ON UP didn't hurt nobody but maybe themselves. Who was he to look down on us?

Just maybe I will go up there. For a few minutes. What's it gonna hurt?

She slipped her feet into her shoes, just an everyday old pair of loafers. She was going as is. If that wasn't good enough for em, well, too bad.

"Marco."

"Yeah, Mama."

"I got to step out for a minute, okay? I be back in before ten. Then you all will really be going to bed. I let you stay up too long as it is."

"Okay, Mama."

"You keep an eye out."

"Yes, ma'am."

"Don't you open this door for anybody but me."

"Yes, ma'am."

"All right then."

She smoothed down her jeans and then smoothed back her hair. Maybe the blouse needed tucking in, maybe not. She tried it both ways.

"You going, Mama?"

She chuckled at her son. "Yeah, baby. I'm going now."

Outside the door was a large basket of fresh flowers. There were carnations and daisies in it and some large orange flowers of a kind she had never seen that resembled baby birds.

"Will you look at this!"

The kids rushed to the door and oohed and aahed over the arrangement. She picked it up and carried it to the dinette.

"This ours?" Didi asked.

"If it's outside our door, it is," answered Marco.

"Here's a card," Nita said.

It read:

> *I guess I got an attitude.*
> *Forgive me,*
> > Brandon Wilson

"What's it say mama? Who they from?"

"Nothing, sweetie. They ain't from nobody."

Downward Mobility

. . . .

What is you always on the air with that white
woman for? You don't like black girls? I got a
niece I'd like you to meet. She's pretty. Not too
dark, either. I'll give you her number.

Mrs. Wilona Wiggs
Cottage Grove

Dexter relocked the credenza and rolled out the butcher paper on the desk. Across the paper was a five week calendar—weekdays only—and in each of the days there was a notation of some kind.

"What are we looking at?" Brandon asked.

"My man, in front of you is the secret formula that will turn your ass into a star."

"If you say so."

"Keep the faith, bro."

Jesus, Brandon thought.

"Look up here." He pointed to the upper left corner of the chart. "Up here you're settled into your comfortable tenement home, fighting off the cockroaches and rats. Your ratings are in the toilet and nobody knows you from shit. Then, in this corner," he pointed to the lower right hand side. "You're king of the fuckin mountain. You're back in your luxury digs. You're number one at five. You're on every magazine cover in town, and the networks are all over your ass."

"And in between?"

Dexter rolled up the chart. "Leave the fine print to me. Your first job is to get that newsroom shaped up."

"Why me? Isn't that Paul Erickson's job?"

"Erickson?" Dexter sneered. "Right now Erickson's only job is to check in at the unemployment office. See out there, talking to the broad." He indicated a blond curly-headed man perched on the end of Mindy's desk. "That there is your new news director."

"He's pretty young."

"He's greener than baby snot. That's where you come in."

"Me?"

"Brad Wilson. Congratulations on your new position."

"Which is?"

"Anchor *and* managing editor, KCKK news."

"Which means?

"Which means you're the guy tells junior out there how to turn this into a first-rate operation. Why you, Mr. Inquisition? Who else I got? Pretty boys, last year's models, washed-up hacks. You're the only one around here who's got the experience, God help us. You seen this done the right way, up close, all over the country."

"This is gonna be a tough job."

"And *you* ain't got much time, you and junior, that is. My chart here says we bring you home to a first-class operation. In five weeks."

"It's a lot a work for that kid."

"Hey, *he's* young and hungry. *You* know the business. You'll pull it off. Now, get out there and make nice with the big fella."

"You mentioned other jobs."

Dexter waved that off. "You find a place yet?" he asked.

"Moved in Friday."

"A god-forsaken, hole-in-the-ground trash pit?"

"Close enough."

"Listen, do us all a favor and don't catch anything over there. And if you do, don't bring it back here."

"That's it, then?"

"All you have to do is sit on your pampered butt over there in darktown and wait for the cameras."

"Nothing else?"

"Duh! You're a reporter. Or you used to be one. Start sniffing around. Get some angles, see what's going down. Sweeps starts a week from next Monday. Be ready to put some crap on — you know, some news crap."

Out at the desk, Mindy bent forward in her chair and guffawed.

"I'd never make anything like that up," the guy said. He was sitting on top of Brandon's desk, up over Mindy. The back of his blue shirt was wrinkled. Brandon wondered if maybe it was the only dress shirt he owned. Since he was just out of school, it very well could be.

"Brandon Wilson," he said, extending his hand.

The guy stood up. He was tall, something well over six feet, and thin. He said, "Of course. Mr. Rayburn's told me all about you. I'm Ted McCarron."

"Ted was just entertaining me with some stories about the U," Mindy said. Now Mindy's hair was what Brandon could only think of as a dark strawberry blonde, neither red nor really blonde at this point, and also not a hair color Brandon remembered ever having seen before on any living being except for maybe an orangutan at the zoo.

"I won't interrupt you," he told them, and then to Ted, "Lunch?"

"Sounds great!" Mindy responded before noticing the look that Brandon shot her. She added quickly, "But I am . . . darn it, I'm already booked today."

"Working lunch," Ted said. He looked Brandon straight in

the eye, letting him know that Dexter had been clear about who was the boss.

"In the lobby. Ten minutes." Brandon patted the kid on the back and winked and pointed at Mindy the same way the rest of the assholes around there did.

Brandon stood at the bathroom mirror. I don't have time to be standing here, he thought. But he stood there. Looking. The old hair was pretty solid today, for once. Ironic—he wasn't even on the air today. Mindy had been announcing that he was "off this evening," for a few days now. The plan was that he would be completely invisible for a week (according to Dexter the public had the retention of your average meat loaf) and then reemerge, broadcasting from Marshall Avenue as the host of his "Underclass in Minnesota" series.

Underclass in Minnesota. Yes, there was a story there—one that didn't get any air time, ever. No one was interested in poor people. Not here, and not at any of the other stations he'd been at. The only time the poor got on the news was when some horrible crime happened: some drive-by shooting or—better—one of those horrific Christmas Day fires where a mother and a bunch of kids got incinerated when the furnace blew up. The rest of the time they were forgotten. Brandon never pitched a story remotely related to the subject. It was pointless. The news directors didn't even bother responding. You had a better chance of flying down to Hawaii and doing a report on the resort industry or going to the Brazilian rain forest, for that matter, than doing a story about something halfway meaningful right here in your own backyard.

He told himself that it was, therefore, worth it, this publicity stunt. It was worth playing along with Dexter's ratings ploy to be able to cover an important and neglected story. It wasn't that big a deal, anyway. It wasn't as if he were Mindy and had to change his appearance. He knew people who did all sorts of humiliating things to keep their jobs. He'd worked at one station back east where the promotions people had forced the talent to make an absurd video showing them playing touch football at a picnic. It took all day to film the stupid thing. There they were in some park in rugbywear, fully made up, sweating, smiling, and chasing each other around for the cameras. It was beyond undignified. He'd known women who'd been forced to wear provocative clothing and who were taught to bat their eyes in a certain way at their male coanchors. One guy he knew sat on a specially created chair so he could be just that much taller than the woman next to him. And there was one poor woman who, unable to lose the extra pounds she'd picked up with a pregnancy, was hounded from the air—not by the management but by viewers, who sent her rude mail and teased her mercilessly on the street.

Dexter was right, the business was all about appearances. Life was tough. People worked hard and put up with plenty of garbage just to put food on the table and keep a roof over their heads. When they came home they expected to be entertained. They wanted to see a beautiful world with beautiful people in it. If there were problems with that world, they wanted to be told that they were being fixed and that someday soon there would be a happy ending. They didn't want to know about the ghetto— didn't even want to be reminded that such a place existed. Brandon could not remember the last time the news showed a picture of a housing project. Even when there was a murder they concentrated on the body and the ambulance. They did not show the homes or the despair or the hopelessness—any of the things that might have been part of the story leading up to the end of a young life.

When he was growing up, his parents never went to the city. St. Louis was a place of mystery and danger. Those other people lived there—the ones with the guns and drugs, the ones who broke into your home and knocked you over the head and stole all your belongings. Everybody they knew had a horror story. The time this one had stopped at a light on the north side and had her purse snatched right off the seat; the time that one's auntie, who still lived down there, had two of them come right into her home and beat her up and take her silverware and jewelry.

His family had even had folks in the city—good decent church-going kinds of folks, who lived down there, somewhere. "Down there." It had got so there weren't even distinctions anymore. The uncle and aunt who lived up off of Vandeventer. It didn't matter that they had a nice yard and nice neighbors who looked out for one another and no more crime than in Olivette. What mattered was that they lived *down there*. It was almost as if living there brought on some sort of disease, and if you got too close to it, spent any time around it at all, you would get it. Brandon figured that the disease was less about money than it was about self-worth and perceptions. Sometimes the people who lived in those communities were the ones spreading the word about how awful it supposedly was, people who saw all the flaws and all the malaise and who were the first to flee when their chance came to get out. The same people who might holler about trash in an alley *down there*, would ignore the stench of an open storm sewer in some worn-out first ring suburb. Whatever the reality of a given house, building, block, or neighborhood, what mattered was what people thought. If people *thought* it was bad and dangerous and mean and run-down, that was, in fact, what it became.

As a child Brandon had learned those lessons well and had never forgotten them. He had resolved that he wasn't ever going to be infected, not if he could help it. He went from the suburbs to the university, and from there to a series of jobs, being careful to find a place to live that was attractive and clean and safe and— most of all—not *there*. And so now, at thirty-eight, here he was, *forced* to live there. At least for a time. He wasn't sure how he felt about it. Yet. He had spent three nights there so far and had yet to form an impression. The first weekend had been quiet. Not much noise—certainly less than a lot of those suburban party buildings he'd lived in. Dampness had been a problem, but a good dehumidifier fixed that quickly. If he were to tell the truth about his impressions, he didn't feel any difference at all between this place and his real home, though he missed his things, and also Sandra. But, he had certainly got by with less before, covering the Olympics or a political convention. And, in some ways, that's what living on Marshall Avenue felt like so far, like staying in a hotel. Not a very nice hotel, mind you—although the rental furniture was fairly comfortable as that sort of thing went—but a hotel all the same.

The saving grace, he knew, was that it was temporary. He might not feel the same if it were for the long haul.

Like that girl upstairs with the kids, that Nita. Wasn't she typical, though? The scowling, hard face, the evil attitudes, the houseful of rug rats. The Twin Cities was full of them. It was as if there was a factory some place—maybe in some high school—that turned out these young sisters. Not a bad looking girl, that one, though it wouldn't hurt to run a hot comb through her hair now and then. In fact she might even be pretty if she fixed herself up a little and took that nasty expression off her face. The look that said it was his fault and the rest of the world's, too, that she had to live in a dump with a bunch of kids. There were plenty of opportunities out there for everybody, and Brandon couldn't imagine how she got where she was in some dingy apartment with a two-bit job to feed herself and several crumb-snatchers. Where was the father? Where were all the fathers, for that matter? A whole building in a whole neighborhood in what sometimes seemed like a whole city full of single mothers. And this Nita, she seemed sharp enough, in a back-alley sort of way. She must have had some choices along the way. With all the escape routes why hadn't she taken one?

Maybe that was the story: how girls like Nita got trapped in their miserable lives—and maybe people would want to hear it and maybe they wouldn't. Probably not. What they wanted was shoot-em-ups and all-night gunfire and random violence and chaos. They wanted to have their reasons for not going *there* confirmed so that they could feel safe and secure and good about their choices. And what if this Nita and the other Nitas and all their kids *were* the story? Well, he'd just have to find a way to make it interesting. That's what he'd talk to Ted McCarron about at lunch.

They requested a quiet table in a corner of the Vietnamese place downstairs from the station, a restaurant that hardly ever filled up even during the lunch hour.

"Tell me about yourself," he asked Ted.

"Not much to tell, I guess. Just an average Midwestern kid."

He had that air about him, too, Brandon thought, with his blue eyes and his head of blond curls. Just an ordinary kid, the kind—because of his height—who played a little basketball. He had probably been a fraternity rat. Like Brandon had been.

"How long you been out of school."

"Finished my master's last May."

"Experience?"

"Edited the *Daily* two terms. I've been a stringer for one of the wires. Freelanced."

"In broadcast?" Brandon prompted. The waitress set two orders of eggrolls in front of them.

"Produced the news on campus for a year. Did a year-long internship at CCO radio."

"In TV? Tel-e-vis-ion?"

"A month. At a college station. Outstate," he said. He didn't blink and he didn't look away. He was a gutsy kid, for sure, and Brandon was impressed.

"Swell. Just swell. What I want you to tell me is why you think a guy like Dexter Rayburn would hire someone such as yourself for this particular job."

Ted washed down his bite of eggroll with a swallow of Coke. "I figure either he sees my deep-down hidden potential or he's fixing to screw your ass into the ground."

Brandon laughed—almost choked on his food. "We're gonna do okay, you and me," he said.

"You're taking this pretty well," Ted said.

"I been in this business since I was seventeen when I interned at the NBC affiliate in St. Louis. Your first lesson is free. If you let all the crap get to you, you won't last a year. Tell me something . . ." The waitress placed a plate of hot-and-spicy chicken in front of him. "Are you organized? Can you work?"

"You betcha."

"You ready to work your ass off? We got a couple of weeks to get ready. Eighteen hours a day some days."

"Got nothing else to do," Ted said. He flipped open a notebook and pulled a pen from his pocket. "Let's do it."

"Start with the set," Brandon said.

They ate and worked through the operation. They made lists, budgets, and deadlines.

We got this, Brandon thought. We got it.

At about three Brandon pulled up behind the apartment building. If there were stories here, he'd better start sniffing around for them now.

In the basement, on the way to his apartment, he ran into the woman. Nita. She had been bent over, fishing laundry out of the washer and feeding it into the drier. He startled her.

"Excuse me," he said. "Didn't mean to scare you."

"No problem." She turned her back to him and returned to her work.

"So. You do your laundry down here."

"Don't do that," she said, not turning to speak to him.

"Do what? Speak to you?"

She threw some filmy things into her basket and straightened up. "Never mind."

"Look, if I did something to offend you, I want to know."

She punched two quarters into the machine, picked up her basket, and turned to look at him. She shook her head slowly, the look on her face more sad than evil.

"This is my life," she said. She took her basket and left.

We
Are
Neighbors

. . . .

Mrs. Carter sorted through the basket, fishing out the girls' socks and underclothes. On the TV was a story that she regularly watched, but one that Nita had never been able to get with—one of those CBS stories that had been around since before creation. Nita stuck with "All My Children" and "One Life to Live."

"So, what you think a big rich Negro like that wants slumming around here?" Mrs. Carter asked.

"Go down there and ask him yourself. Seems like you real friendly with him."

"Just seems suspicious to me, is all. Someone like that moving in here. Don't you think? Kinda cute, though."

"Watch your story, Mrs. Carter." She wasn't thinking about that nigger. What she was thinking about was getting this laundry put away before the kids got in and getting her reading done before class tonight.

"Got a minute, Nita?" Sipp stuck his head in at the door.

"I didn't hear no knocking, did you, Nita?"

"What you need?" Nita asked.

"Must be my cue to leave." Mrs. Carter rose, shoving the basket out of her way with her foot.

"How you this afternoon, ma'am?"

"Old and tired," she said to Sipp.

"You watch yourself," she said to Nita.

"All right, then," Sipp said, a toothy grin plastered across his face. "Let me get this door for you."

She looked him up and down several times, walking a wide circle around him on her way out.

"Ain't she a mess?" Nita chuckled.

Sipp pulled a pained face and shuddered.

"Sure was good to see you Friday night," he said, and asked her if she had fun.

"I guess," she said, discovering a goofy smile had crossed her face. It had been fun, too, all those hot sweaty folks crammed together up there, moving to the music, laughing, just getting lost in the smoke and the rhythm and the pulse of the crowd. She had submerged herself in it. Till well past eleven. She'd come down and put the kids to bed, thinking how good it had felt to be away, even if only for a short while. It was like being gone on vacation. Later, she had lain back on the couch and let the ghost beat of the pumping bass rock her to sleep.

"You sure move good," he said.

She sucked in her upper lip and focused on her laundry basket.

"Look at you, all shy and stuff. Don't be shamed."

"You needed something?"

"Oh, yeah. You get me so I forget myself. Let me see. Uh . . . you got any, uh . . . writing paper. Yeah. That's what I need."

"Writing paper, huh? Yeah, I got some over there with my school stuff. Hang on."

While she shuffled her stack, he took a seat on the couch. She crossed her arms and sneered at him. Nerve of a nigger, she thought, come and sit up in my house, big as life, uninvited.

"Them Zig-Zag papers work a lot better than this. So I'm told."

"How you know I don't got some important writing to do?"

"You can write?"

"Ow! Damn, girl, you do know how to put the hurt on a man."

"Something else I can get for you?" As enjoyable as teasing this boy was, tonight she had a big test in her English class. She had to look over those stories once more at least, and she wasn't having her grade pulled down on account of some foolishness like this. Even if he did be looking awful cute today, in his camouflage pants and with that big grin of his. She held open the door and waited.

"Glass of water might be nice," he said, leaning back with his hands behind his head.

She filled up a teacup with tap water and handed it to him. "You can bring that back when you're done." She opened the door again.

"Won't even sit and talk to a brother for a minute? That's cold."

"I got work to do."

"Five minutes?" he begged.

She closed the door and sat in the chair across from the couch. "Talk," she said. They sat quiet, staring at each other.

"Nice day," he said.

She laughed and he laughed with her. She started toward the door, beckoning him to follow her. "Let's go," she said.

"Hang on! Hang on! Okay, tell me. You lived up here all your life?"

"You mean in St. Paul? Yes, born and raised. How bout you?

"Me? Itta Bena, Mississippi. Just out from Greenwood. Just down the road from this college where my mama and daddy worked."

"Teachers?"

"Kitchen, grounds crew."

"You come by your name honest, then?"

"Amen."

"So how'd you wind up here?"

"Got a cousin. Over in Minneapolis. Came up for a visit. Liked what I saw. Here I am."

"You go to school?"

"I did. Not now."

"So what *do* you do? Sides have parties, that is?"

"This and that. Take care of my business."

"What's your business."

"You know. I'm into a few things."

She hardened her face, stared him in the eyes. His grin changed to a smirk.

"Yeah, I do. I do think I know what your business is," she said. "And I told you. We got children in here. Children. And old people, and . . ."

"You got nothing to worry bout, Miss Nita. I know. I know my business." He tried to charm her with his smooth, million-dollar smile.

She opened the door again. "Time for my work."

"On my way, then." He rose, smiled some more, walked slowly by her. He dipped one knee at each step, passed close enough so she could smell the Jovan Night Musk he had sprayed around his neck. "Y'all don't have nothing . . ."

"You just make sure of that," she said. She pushed him out with the door.

"See ya," she heard through the wood. The notebook he came for lay where he set it on the trunk.

After supper she opened the anthology for one more look. Her teacher had assigned a dozen stories for this test, and she'd read each one twice. She liked the one about the lottery by a woman named Shirley Jackson. She really bought the idea that people drew straws to see who was gonna get it. That's how people was. Happy to throw rocks, as long as it wasn't them getting hit. She kinda liked the one about a man swimming his way across town through all the pools, even if the story was a little fancy for her taste. She wished they'd been assigned more stories by people like her, but apparently wasn't a lot of black folks wrote this kind of thing. She figured she'd do okay on the test. She'd written down all the professor's opinions, had memorized them, and was ready to spout them back. Which is what he wanted. One time she'd taken a risk and raised her hand and offered the opinion that this Flannery O'Connor story was about how, when you got right down to it, there was really more freaks out there than anything else and that people worried too much about what normal was. Professor King told her and everyone else that the story was about how Flannery O'Connor was Catholic and how her religiousness was all she ever thought about. He made it clear that, though Nita's idea was interesting, his was the one counted on the test. Fine. In fact, better. It was a lot easier spouting back what he wanted to hear than to come up with something of her own. All there was to taking most of these tests, then, was getting yourself there and staying awake long enough to play back the lectures in your head and record them with your pencil. She was up to that much.

After supper there was another knock at the door. Tap tap ta tap tap.

She hated a cute knock, but at least the nigger was learning some manners.

"I'm on my way . . . Oh. It's you." Downstairs.

"You got a minute?"

Everybody wanted a minute today. "As a matter of fact I'm on my way out the door." Not that she had time for a fool like this, anyway.

"Walk you to your car?" he offered. "I just want to ask you something. Can I carry those?" He held out his hands as if he was accepting a gift from her.

"No thank you," she said. Hadn't nobody carried her books for her since André back at Ramsey Junior High. She locked her door and started down the corridor toward the back entrance.

"Start talking," she said.

"You're direct," he said. "I like direct."

"You come all the way up here to tell me that? Thank you."

"You gonna cut me some slack, Nita? I came to ask you if we could have a fresh start."

She set her books on the roof of the car. She sorted through the ring for her car key. "I try not to get too familiar with the tenants," she said.

"Fair enough." He grabbed her books and handed them through the window. "Just wanted you to know I'm downstairs if you need anything. Any time."

"Thank you, Mr. Wilson." She said. She kept her eyes straight ahead to keep from seeing the snotty look she'd like to slap off his face. Bastard. As if there were a thing he could do for her she hadn't been doing for herself—for years.

She cranked the ignition. Nothing.

Shit.

She cranked it again. Nothing.

She wanted to pound on the steering wheel and scream and grab her hair, but he was out there, watching her. Maybe if she sat long enough, he would go away.

He tapped on the windshield. "You got a dead battery," he said through the glass.

Damn kids. Always leaving the dome light on and playing the radio while she ran into the store. And this bastard here, look at him. Standing there waiting for me to ask him to help me. If it wasn't for the damn test . . .

"You think you might be able to . . . ," she started to say. She wouldn't look him in the eye or smile. She couldn't even get the whole sentence out.

"Hell, I'm not doing anything. Got me this new ride over here."

"No. I just thought if you had some jumper cables or something . . ."

"That's what triple A is for. Let's go. Where you headed?"

She let him open his car door for her. She felt froggy and relieved at the same time.

"Metro State. Down on Seventh Street."

His Dodge started right up. Of course it would. He rolled down the alley and out onto Oxford Street. "This is a nice little old car," he said. "It'll be a classic in a few years. If I hold onto it."

"Shoot," she said, pounding on her notebook.

"Something I said?"

"I *need* that car. For work tomorrow."

"It's taken care of. Don't worry."

"I can't let you . . ."

"It's taken care of," he said. He patted the seat beside her in time to some music that must be in his head.

She looked out the window. There was the part of her that wanted to hug him and then another part that didn't want to be owing nothing to no one.

"I'll pay you back," she said.

"If you want to, but it's not necessary."

"Yeah, it is."

"If you insist."

"I do."

"Just being neighborly. Neighbors look out for each other, don't they?"

"I don't know what kind of neighbor you are, Mr. Wilson. I don't want to offend you or nothing."

"I'm your neighbor that lives downstairs."

"You know what I mean."

He snorted. "I guess I do. All I can say is, I'm not a bad person, if that's what you mean. No, I haven't announced my business up and down the street, but that's because that's what it is: *my* business. It's you assuming it's something evil."

"A person can't be too careful these days, Mr. Wilson."

"A person can accept help when it's offered."

"Comes at a price. Always. Nothing's free." She bit the inside of her lip. She'd said too much to this man. He was one of those has a way of getting you to talk when you'd just as soon not. Had all of that confidence and poise, so much so it came off as stuck up, like he had the big head or something.

"Where would you like to be dropped off?" he asked.

"That door there. Middle of the block."

"What time do you finish?"

"I'll catch a ride."

"It's no big thing. I don't mind."

She gave him an evil, hooded-eyes look. "I can get home. Thank you anyway, Mr. Wilson."

"Suit yourself. You got my number." He gave her a smile that could melt steel.

"Good night, Mr. Wilson."

All through the test she saw that smile. That ain't-I-the-cutest-thing-you-seen-in-a-long-time smile, that Eddie Murphy nasty-joke smile, that smile boys had been using on her since seventh grade, and men on woman probably as long as there had been men and women. André had used it, and she'd even seen her Marco practicing it on his sisters, and on her. Must be a built-in thing, must come with your regulation man—with a dick and some balls you got one of them smiles to use as needed.

What was she frettin for? So, the man helped her out, saved her from having to stand over on Selby waiting for the damn 21A—which never came—and then riding downtown with all them thugs. Wasn't no crime there. What was he supposed to do, leave her standing in the alley with a dead car? Here she's gonna act all ugly cause a brother did the right thing, for once.

And he was right. *She* was the one assumed he was up to no good down there. How'd she know? It could be perfectly innocent, a man like him renting an apartment in a run-down building.

Naw, see that was the part didn't make no sense. Why was someone like him—a person who could buy the damn building if he wanted it—renting that dump? If it wasn't something illegal, it was something not quite right. If it was innocent, wouldn't be no secret. Not that it was anyone's business. Which is what he said.

Shit, why was she spending her time thinking about that fool anyway? Wasn't even her type. She never did care for them light-skinned men. They thought they was special. Thought they was pretty. And they never did have the time of day for a brown-skin girl like her. Lot of em came right out and said it—said they didn't want to be with no dark girls cause they didn't want to have no chocolate-colored babies. That shit hurt. She'd been hearin it all her life. No, she hadn't heard it from this one, but why should he be the exception?

He would have to be cute, with his yellow self.

She managed to focus on finishing the test. She'd aced it, she knew—could have written the damn questions herself. That Professor King. So lazy. She was one of the last to finish, and most of the others had left as soon as they turned in their papers. Which meant there weren't too many to ask for rides. She didn't know any of the ones who had straggled like her to even speak to. She fished through her purse to see if she had quarters for the bus. She belted her coat, and just as she went out to Seventh . . . No, it couldn't be. There were a lot of old blue Celebrity wagons still on the road. She just caught the back end of it. He wouldn't. Couldn't. Not even somebody like him. She hadn't even given him the key.

She supposed she could stand there and see if he circled the block.

And, then what if it wasn't him? Here she was, standing there expecting some nigger to pick her up, and it was just a damn fantasy.

And what if it *was* him.

She walked toward Robert Street. If he did, she'd just have to have the nigger arrested for unauthorized use. Or she'd kiss him, or she'd . . . Oh, hell.

Just as she crossed to the bus stop on Sixth, he pulled up and honked. He leaned over and unlocked her passenger door and gave her one of them Howdy Doody waves. Smiled that damn smile, too.

She shook her head, waved back, and got in.

In the Ghetto

. . . .

*My friend Xenobia and I were wondering
whether or not you had a fan club and if
you didn't we would make one for you. Please
send us a hundred dollars to get us started.*

> *Your fan,*
>
> *Doretha Welters*
> *Minneapolis*

Ted McCarron turned out to be a pretty smart boy, and a lot
tougher than his "Minnesota Nice" exterior let on. Brandon had
prejudged him as being one of those simpering feel-good types,
but he'd been out there giving orders and slamming down the
phone as if he'd just stepped off the plane from New York instead
of off the bus from Roseville. Brandon had turned over to him
all the cosmetics and the nuts-and-bolts stuff, like creating a
halfway decent set and getting them the latest technology (and
some people who could run it). Things were coming together.
They might just make it.

Dexter had been laying low, focusing on, or pretending to
focus on shaping up the other parts of the day. He'd been trying
out three or four different talk shows of the "Cross-Dressers with
Eating Disorders" variety and had somehow managed to steal

"Jeopardy" from across town for the afternoon lead-in. He hadn't said anything to Brandon at all lately, only winked at him and pointed his finger at him as if it were a gun. Pointing and winking, just like the rest of them. He supposed he should be glad Dexter was steering clear, glad he had no one over his shoulder second-guessing him, asking that things be done some other way. At the same time, he knew that if it didn't go just so, it would be his ass and nobody else's.

For the most part everything was under control. Everything, that is, except for the "news" part. He hadn't a clue yet what he was supposed to be reporting from his new home. He had tried the housing-code angle—the basic rats-and-roaches and substandard-construction stuff—but that only worked if you caught some scumbag building inspector collecting bribes or came across a blatant slumlord. Those kinds of stories called for an investigative team, something KCKK didn't yet have. And, anyway, to her credit, Nita kept the place fairly presentable, considering what she had to work with.

There was the street-gang angle, but that story'd been done to death. And all he'd seen around here so far were some loud teenagers screeching around the block in mufflerless cars. There were the garden-variety high-school dropouts, and the fourteen-year-old mothers, and, and, and. . . .

And he needed something fresh, or at least something shocking.

Where were the crack houses and the prostitutes and the welfare queens folks talked about? People didn't make that shit up. Where were the imported LA gangs? Where was the despair? There had to be a story around there somewhere. It was time to put on his reporter's hat and go out and find it.

He grabbed the bouquet he'd picked up at Bachman's and headed to the second floor. Might as well start with a little background.

"Afternoon, Mrs. Carter."

"Mr. Willis. How nice of you to drop by. Come on in."

"Wilson," he corrected her. "And these are for you." He handed her the flowers. "Just a little something to thank you for all the help you've been in getting me settled."

"Thank you so much, you know, I don't usually like carnations, but these are sure pretty enough. Let me set em in some water. You all have yourself a seat."

He dropped himself on an old-fashioned love seat, the kind with an exposed wooden frame, just like the one his Aunt Telma used to have. The small warm room had a cozy feel to it, everything within easy reach: the remote for the tiny TV, a magazine rack, some candy jars, and a nice hassock for putting your feet up.

"You all settled in that basement?" she called from the kitchen alcove.

"Yes, ma'am. All moved in."

"Kinda damp down there, ain't it?" She brought out the flowers in a large plastic cup from the Taste of Minnesota celebration. She set them on a cluttered butler's table, full of magazines and coasters. "I usually like the daffodils or a rose," she said, "but these'll do for now."

"Mind if I ask you something? How long you been in this building?"

"Going on seventeen years. Since after my husband passed. We had us a big house, just back there, over on Dayton, but I didn't feel like messing with it, the yard and all. I found this place here."

"You know the area pretty well."

"Whatever's worth knowing. Why? You down here snooping on somebody?"

"Can I trust you, Mrs. Carter?"

"Like you trust your own mama. I'm right, ain't I? You down here on some big story. You can tell me."

"It's something like that." He smiled, leaned forward as if to share a secret. "You know how you never see anything on the news at all about *us?*"

"You mean you and me?"

"I mean folks like us. Folks that live here in the city. The news never talks about us. All the stuff we have to put up with to survive."

"I guess we must not be news."

"You have to give me your word you won't tell a soul what I'm about to reveal to you. We are in an extremely competitive business, and I can't risk having this story scooped."

"Like by that Dane Stephens."

"Yes, ma'am"

"He's awfully cute."

"Yes, he is."

"I watch his show all the time. He's so cute he makes you just want to pick him up and hug him."

"We do an excellent news show, too, you know."

"What time is you all on."

"Five o'clock. Live at Five."

"That's when "The Facts of Life" comes on."

He swallowed. Hard.

"Anyway, Mrs. Carter, what I need your confidence on is this. Starting next month, I'll be broadcasting the news from right here on Marshall Avenue."

"Hush your mouth."

"From right downstairs. Right out front sometimes, too. I need your help to put the show on the air."

"You want me to be the weather girl? I point just as good as most them gals. I point to New York up here and Florida down here and . . ."

"I need you to help me find the news around here."

"The news?"

"The news. What's going down? Who-shot-john? Anything you think people might want to know."

"I ain't in the habit of gossiping. I think folks should mind their own business."

"No one is asking you to gossip." He leaned back on the

love seat and covered his mouth while he thought. "Look, news is about people. People just like you and me that something happened to. All I want you to do is tell me what's going on in the neighborhood. What are people thinking about? How are their lives going? That's all."

"Give me a for-instance."

"Okay." He closed his eyes to think. "For instance, somebody gets broken into and gets their stereo stolen by a drug addict. What about that?"

"Go on," she prompted.

"Or, let's say a mother finds out her son is hooked up in some street gang. How does she deal with it?"

"That's all just everyday life round here."

"That's what I want."

"And what you want from me is?"

"Introduce me to folks. Get them to talk to me."

She leaned back in her chair, studying him through one almost-closed eye. He met her gaze. He leaned further forward, calling her to the challenge.

"What do you say?" he asks.

"Nita says you up to something."

"I am. I just told you about it."

She held up a finger. "I tell you what. I'll take you around, introduce you to some folks. But you got to promise me something."

"Anything."

"Won't be no embarrassing of folks. I won't be involved in no humiliation."

"You have my solemn word. All I want is to make things better around here."

"Cause I'm telling you—you mess folks around down here, you get hurt. I might look like an old woman, but I got ways of fixing folks."

"I'm sure you do, Mrs. Carter. I'm sure you do."

He bet she did, too. These tough old sisters, you really didn't want to mess with them. She reminded him of his great-aunt Sarah, back in St. Louis, a feisty old gal, survived forty years teaching typing at the business college, and she'd just as soon slap you as say good morning if you looked at her the wrong way.

Mrs. Carter came out of her room, having put on her "swinger" wig, the kind of hair he remembered Julie Christie wore in the movie, *Shampoo*. She told him they were going on a little walk around the block.

Though parts of the block were a little run-down, for the most part Marshall Avenue didn't impress Brandon as particularly distressed, not compared to some of the places he'd seen. On a comparable street in St. Louis, half of these houses would be boarded up or burned out, or every other one would be completely gone, torn down, spaces left as prominent as the gaps in a six-year-old's mouth. Here, most of the houses looked sound, looked like all they wanted for was a little paint and a few boards nailed back up. And why was it black folks couldn't get this lawn-care shit together? What was the big deal in putting out a little grass seed, keeping it trimmed, and not letting a whole lot of garbage accumulate? Maybe we had had enough of that through time—working in massa's field, breaking our backs on some plantation. But those times were long gone, and he swore he could always tell where "we" lived by judging the state of the yards.

"Pretty quiet around here," he said.

"Usually," she responded. She hooked her arm through his, almost strutting along beside him, he thought. She peered around. He figured she was checking out if anybody noticed who she was walking down the street with. He put up his shield, became incognito—dark shades, street clothes, as opposed to his usual suit. Not that he'd seen too many folks who'd be noticing either of them.

They circled the block on Dayton, where it was more of the same—more almost-presentable houses, more shaggy lawns. Then they headed back to the building.

"Don't see many stories," he said. They lingered on the slab in front of the apartment door.

"Stories all up and down this block," she said.

"Nothing I can see."

"Right over there, that house the porch done fell off. Woman up in there, she got nineteen kids. Lord knows how many grand-babies. They keep her a place on the bench outside juvenile court. She down there regular, getting one or the other them heathens out of trouble.

"Back around there on Dayton, that pretty house with the bird bath on the lawn? Well, the dog that lives there been messing with his own two daughters since they was this big. Don't care who knows about it, neither."

Brandon studied the old lady. She crossed her arms, put her fingers on her lips, and scanned up and down the block, a gleam in her eye, deciding, he imagined, whom she should tell on next.

"You know em all, don't you Mrs. Carter?"

"Come on back inside. It's getting chilly in this wind." He followed her down the steps to his door.

"Just want to see what you done with the place," she said.

She went inside and made herself comfortable on his sofa. "Can I get you anything," he asked her.

"No thank you, sugar. It's about time for me to be meeting Nita's children." She looked around the room. "I never did like this place, but you sure made it livable. Better than most."

"Thank you."

"You get anything you can use today?"

He sat across from Mrs. Carter and lowered his head. "I appreciate your time. I really do. It's just that, I expected . . . I was looking for something more . . ."

"You wanted to see some niggers carrying on."

He started to protest.

"It's hard to say when they's gonna get started. You never can tell."

"Mrs. Carter, what frustrates you? Don't you get frightened sometimes?"

She stared at him. "Life's frustrating," she said. She started toward the door. "I hear them kids on the walk. Hang on up there you all!"

He heard the thumping of the bass from the second floor. "What's the story up there?" he asked.

"Now that's scary," she said. She followed the kids up to Nita's place.

"On a cold and gray Chicago mornin', a poor little baby child is born, in the ghet-t-o-o-o," Sandra sang. She sang it as she rode up and down on top of him.

"Don't make me laugh, woman," Brandon said, his breath husky and heavy.

"And his mama cries," and Sandra cried out, too.

He grabbed her around the waist, laughing, rolled her over and put himself back inside her. "I warned you."

She squealed.

Later, when they were still and she had nestled herself behind him, he heard her humming some more of the old chestnut.

"Silly," he whispered.

"My man," she said. "Soon you'll be the Elvis of local television." She ran her nails gently up and down his back.

"I got no story," he said.

"Nothing?"

"Zip. Hardworking poor people. Decent folks, just trying to get by. Maybe a little trouble now and then."

"What did you expect? The wild, wild West? Somalia?"

"I don't know. You've seen the crime statistics. You've heard the rumors. I guess I figured . . ."

"Use your head, Brandon. Can't everybody in the city be a criminal. If that was true, wouldn't be enough jails on earth to deal with them."

"Some of those people are just trapped there."

"A lot of those people *want* to be there. You and me came up a different way. Out here in the suburbs is what we like. People out here do all the same stuff those people down there do—drugs, stealing, you name it. We just have a better-looking backdrop."

"Where'd I learn this . . . this loathing, this fear?"

She squeezed him tight around the chest and laughed into his back. "You're not serious?"

He swallowed his shame. "The more fool I, huh?"

"The hustler buys his own rap."

"So, what now? Now that I've got myself into this."

"You tell the truth, is what."

"Life in the big city. Where folks are just doing the best they can," he said in the stentorian tones of the announcers reading the between-show teasers.

"If it was news to you . . . Brandon, I told you going into this how dumb I thought it was. But maybe not. Maybe you can turn it into something important after all."

"A month's worth of feel-good news?"

"Why not?" She again wrapped herself around his torso, nestled her head against his side. "Why not spend a month letting people see that everyone down there isn't a hoodlum or a drug addict? We've been getting the other side of the story the whole rest of the time. Why the hell not?"

"Cause it's not good TV. I can just see Dexter . . ."

"I thought this was your gig."

"It is."

"Then you go in there and tell him what you're going to do and why you're going to do it. And then you do it."

"Just like that?"

"Just like that."

The next day, just before lunch, he knocked on Dexter's door.

"Brad! Long time, no see. What it is." Dexter had a pile of

videocassettes on his desk that he was apparently popping in and out of a small combination TV/VCR. "You wouldn't believe the crap people produce. I'm looking for something to nuke Oprah's ass."

Brandon sat in his usual chair and waited for an opening.

"This one here," Dexter held up a tape. "It's one of those 'Love Connection' dating deals, except they make all the contestants go out on one big date, and then back in the studio they do a half hour of group sex and orgy jokes." He tossed the tape in the trash.

"We're ready to go," Brandon broached. "The new 'Live at Five.' We're all set to premier from the heart of the Summit/University neighborhood."

"That a fact? Say, and not a minute too soon. Old Mindy out there is killing us. She's giving up shares like a drunk coed gives up nooky."

"That's a charming analogy."

"Thanks. Your boy, though . . . what's his butt?"

"Ted. Ted McCarron."

"Yeah. He's great. One tough little motherfucker. Reminds me of me at his age."

Brandon wished that were comforting. "I wanted to tell you about our series," he said.

"You mean *your* series."

"My series. 'City Life,' we're calling it now. Promos start tomorrow."

Dexter said nothing. He picked through the pile of videotapes, looking them over as if to see exactly how they worked.

"Heavy on the human interest," Brandon continued. "I'll be profiling some of my neighbors. Have them talking about their trials and triumphs."

Dexter gave a big yawn and fished absentmindedly around his desk for God knows what.

"Of course, we'll get all the breaking news in, as well. Whatever comes up."

Dexter stared right past him. "Hand me that disk," he said.

Brandon handed him a 3½-inch floppy and then rose to leave. "Just keeping you informed," he said, and turned for the door.

"Yeah, yeah, yeah, thanks, bro. Close the door on the way out." Dexter waved his hand in dismissal.

"Oh, and one other thing, Brad. The thing that's so fucking pathetic about that 'City Life' shit is that you know better." He looked him right in the eye.

"Don't you, Brad?"

Brandon didn't answer.

Ice
Cream
Dreams

. . . .

Thank the Lord for small favors, Nita thought. Didi's birthday was coming up, and Mama had picked up the kids at school and taken them to shop at Rosedale. And on her day off, no less, giving Nita a good three hours on her own. It seemed there was never time just for her. It was the kids or school or her job or the building. It was always something. Well, for three hours at least she planned to lie on her butt on her couch and do absolutely nothing. A little nap, a little daydream.

She played out her favorite fantasy, where she has hit the Powerball and has retired herself to a tropical paradise. This rich bitch spends her days sitting under a beach umbrella while a fine nigger in one of them tiny swimsuits serves her strawberry margaritas and potato chips. The kids, well, in this particular fantasy they have suddenly grown up and left town to start their own fabulous careers. And as for men, well, the current problem is how to get Wesley out of town before Denzel comes in and catches him. Yeah, she should make a choice, but she can't bear the idea of breaking hearts, and they were both big boys, and what was it gonna hurt them if she took her time deciding?

She lay on her couch and willed her body to be still. And more still yet. The fantasy made her breathing even and calm. She felt lighter and her mind floated and swam through her body, almost as if she were high. I'm here, she thought, completely here, but then not here at all. This is what it feels like to own me. She floated that way for what felt like forever.

She surfaced to a knock at the door.

She opened the door to Sipp, his face hidden behind a notebook. "I got my own paper now," he said, dropping the pad, revealing his grin. "And," he tore a sheet from the front of the book, "I *do* know how to use it." He handed her the paper. On it she read what appeared to be a poem:

To Nita

Wanted to say
That I never met a girl like you
Special, sweet, fly
My dear, you are a man's dream come true
When I see you
My life lights up inside
Sunshine, blue skies
Gone are the tears I've cried

She held the paper in front of her face to hide her expression — the crooked smile she wished weren't there, the glow she was sure he could see on her cheeks. He danced around in front of her and plopped himself down on her couch.

"I'm rusty," he said. "But I'm gonna get back in shape."

"You trying to embarrass me?"

"Naw, Miss Nita. Sit yourself down here." He patted a place next to him on the couch. He sprawled back, comfortable, on *her* couch, and she wanted to tell the nigger to remove his hat, but the way he wore it turned to the back with a big X across the top, was kinda cute. She sat down, but at arms length from him.

"You always write poetry?" she asked.

"Back in high school, I did. I was pretty good, too. They used to put my stuff in the newspaper and shit. I'm out of practice, though. You got to work at it all the time in order to stay good."

"This is fine. Really sweet. It's been a long time since somebody wrote a poem for me."

Actually, she couldn't remember anyone ever writing her a poem. She read the words over and over, shaking her head. She felt his eyes on her, saw them out the side of her own. She thought she saw a leer on his face.

"You're staring at me," she said.

"You're awful fine. You know how fine you are?"

She walked away from him, to the front window.

"I ain't playing with you. You are one fine woman. My whole posse thinks so."

He tickled along her arm with his fingers. Part of her was glad she didn't sit closer, the other part would like to feel those nice, long fingers on her neck and down her back and . . .

"I bet you run this play all over town," she said.

"Pretty, pretty, Nita. What that short for? Anita?"

"Bonita. My great-grandma gave me that name. Means 'beautiful' in Spanish."

"That's you, then."

Damn, she thought, the nigger was smooth. She decided to put him out before it went too far.

"I got some stuff to do," she said, standing and straightening her pants.

"That's the other thing I like."

"What?"

"You not one of them sit-around bitches. Can't stand me no woman sits around wasting time."

"You mean like you do."

"Ow! That cold-blooded tongue again."

She reached toward the door, then changed her mind.

"I got dinner to get," she said.

If he wanted to leave, fine. If not, well it wasn't hurting nothing to sit and listen to his B.S. a while.

She removed a skillet from the broiler beneath the stove where she kept the cooking pots stored.

"What we having tonight?"

"The kids and I are having some pork steaks. I don't know what y'all is having."

"I know what I'd like to have."

She cut him a look. She took out a large onion and sliced off the ends before chopping it up. "Tell me about Mi-ssi-ssip-pi," she prompted.

"Down home? You know about down home, don't you?"

"Closest I been to down home is South St. Paul."

He sputtered at her joke. "You'd like it down home. I know you would. I'll take you one of these days."

"Is it like hills or mountains? What's it like?"

"It's the delta. You heard of the delta, I know. Just as flat as it can be. And hot. You don't want to be out on them summer days down there.

"What makes it nice is the people down there. All the relatives and them. Everybody know everybody and they all take it pretty easy with each other."

"Is it like what they say about down there?"

"What they say?"

"With the white folks, and all that."

"Crackers? Got them same crackers up here, ain't they? Matter of fact I like it better down home. Folks down there don't play all that mess they play up here. But, you know, that shit be the same wherever you be."

"Why'd you leave?"

She set the onions to simmer in some bacon grease, started a pan of rice, and reached down a can of applesauce.

"Wanted to see something different, I guess. Fore I settle in. A little excitement."

"Then you going back?"

"When I get me a little money, yeah."

"Money?"

"Ain't no jobs down home. Not a one. A person got himself a little stake, though, he can do all right for hisself. Get all kindsa things going."

"Such as."

"Get a truck and do some hauling. Start a little catfish farm. You heard about fish farming ain't you? Don't laugh at me, girl. That ain't no joke."

She recognized in his eyes something she hadn't noticed before, some kind of hard honesty.

"You're serious about going home."

"Serious as a heart attack. Can't figure the game up here. A person can't make it—or make it legit, at least. A man can't even find the damn doors up here. Back home, like I said, *if* you got a stake, *if* you can hustle, you on your way."

"It's school up here," she said, surprised, not expecting to have found herself in a conversation like this with a man like this. "You want to get in the door up here you got to have that degree."

"I see you got them accounting books over there. How much longer you got?"

"Year or two. Depends on how much of a load I take. I'm finishing, too. If it kills me, I'm finishing."

"Go on, then."

She found herself just looking at him, and him just looking back at her. She couldn't believe how comfortable it felt. How good and how safe. Every few seconds his lips parted to reveal his even, pretty teeth. She didn't say anything, didn't feel like she had to.

"Would you ever go with me, Nita?"

She looked down.

"You don't like what I do. Ain't that right?"

"I don't know what you do."

"Yeah, you do."

"It's your business."

"To a point."

"I don't want to talk about it. I don't want to know."

She got up to turn the pork and add some tomato paste to the onions.

He came up behind her and put his hands on her shoulders. "You do know. And I want to hear what you got to say about it."

She slammed the lid onto the skillet.

"All right, then," she said. She slid from beneath his touch and sat in her chair. "It makes me sick. I hate it. Everybody knows what that stuff does to folks. And I warned you bout these kids up in here. I ought to call and . . ."

"I don't *do* my business here. I don't. Not in my home. I ain't that stupid. And it's dope and a little blow, and I sell it to them rich white boys over at the colleges, and it ain't hurtin them one bit. You tried it, ain't you."

She remembered some parties here and there. How it hadn't seemed like a big deal. She remembered a little buzz, a little thrill, a little excitement. Nothing she hadn't gotten from a Miller. Hardly worth the money, as she figured.

"So, I tried it? So what?"

"You still here? Still taking care of business? Folks like you and me, we too smart to get sunk down in that shit."

"What about folks who ain't?"

"There's a few of them out there. Like them crackheads down the block here. But, most folks, you know, it's like a playtime thing. Get a bag, just like you get a fifth of scotch or what have you. Same thing, really. The fiends, you stay clear of them. They ain't good for the money no way."

"You make it sound simple. Like it was selling popsicles or something."

"That's all it is. A business. You provide the product and people pay you for it. That's the American way."

"Still don't make no sense."

She went back to the skillet, though the onions had barely cooked. Her bottom lip had pushed out and she was afraid she was pouting, childish looking.

"What don't you understand?" he asked.

"I don't understand why somebody would . . . why somebody like you would risk so much to get involved with . . ."

"Cause. That's why. Cause I make as much in a week as I make in six months at home. If I could *get* a job back home. Cause I got plans, and I'm in a hurry and cause fifteen more causes, and the point is this ain't gonna be my life, Nita. Like anything else, you put the risk on one side and the payoff on the other. You weigh up, and you make your choice."

He spun a gaudy gold ring on his finger, the only spoil Nita could see from all this so-called money. Maybe it *was* all going into the bank.

"Besides," he added, "can't everybody do it your way."

"If *I* can . . ."

"You're special. A special lady. I knew it the first time I saw you. I'ma ask you again. Would you go with me? Could you?"

"I don't know."

"I been looking around for somebody like you. I have. We'd be good together. I'd treat you right."

Her brain muddied the way it did when she had been up all night studying. The words blurred together and nothing seemed clear. She found her way to the door. "Kids are coming," she said, opening it.

"I don't give up easy," he said. He kissed her gently on the cheek. "You know that."

"Be careful," she said.

"S'my middle name. See you, sweetness."

It sounded like a stampede roaring up the steps. The kids charged into the apartment, vibrating with excitement from their shopping trip. Her mother ran behind them, puffing and blowing.

"They worn you out, Mama," Nita laughed.

"Don't talk, child. Just get me a cup a water."

"Sit down. You kids take them things on in back."

Marco stuffed handfuls of cheese popcorn into his mouth.

"We getting ready to eat here. You done spoiled these kids' supper. I shouldn't have even cooked."

"I got em a treat. Stop fussing," she sloshed down the water. "I gotta run."

"Sit a spell. We don't hardly get to visit."

"A minute," her mother said, dropping into a seat. She pushed a wave of silver-gray hair behind her ear and held the cup up for a refill.

"You look tired, Mama."

"I'ma slow down one these days. Always so much to do."

Arnelia Curtis was the busiest person Nita knew. She belonged to three or four clubs, including her neighborhood council. A bunch of her social friends had regular doings, and she had church activities, and a part-time job down at Dayton's. She also had a big fat lazy husband who loved her to death and who let her wait on him like he was the king and she was the hired help.

"I appreciate you taking the kids today."

"These my favorite grandbabies."

"Don't let Brenda's boys hear you say that."

"Them heathen boys? They got up to that teenage stage where you know I can't stand em. Glad I didn't have me no boys. I'da killed em."

"We wasn't always easy, Brenda, T.C., and me."

"You know the old saying, 'boys be the devil I *don't* know.' Still, after all these years . . . which reminds me—you got a daddy lined up for that Marco yet?"

"You see me looking for one?"

Damn, she thought. Mama didn't never give up on that daddy for Marco shit. Find a daddy for Marco. Find a daddy for Marco. As if that was the only thing she needed a man around here for.

"Kids tell me you got a new tenant. Nice looking light-skinned fellow. That's what they told me."

"You want him, he lives right down there in the basement."

"I tell you one thing, you won't be catching nothing with that funky attitude."

"Mama, what you think, I spend all day every day worrying about whether some man's gonna come along and improve my life? I got too much on my mind for some foolishness like that."

Her mother rubbed at her feet before snapping her heels back in place and gathering her purse and gloves.

"You make it sound like there's something wrong with having a nice man around."

"Did I say that?"

"Before I go, my angels was wondering if they could sleep over on Didi's birthday. I'll have that Sheena from next door and Miss Kinney's grandbaby. You keep that Marco here."

"I guess so. If you want."

Mama always got to the girls' parties first. Oh, well, she could have another little cake for Didi at home afterward.

"I want you to stop fussing at me about men, Mama. I could be one of these women . . . but I'm not, and I try to . . . and I don't . . ."

Her mother rose and patted her on the back and gave a little hug.

"Calm down, sugar. Didn't mean to upset you. Put it out of your mind." She started toward the door. "I'm gonna let you get on with your evening. Smells good. What you fix?"

"Just some smothered pork steaks." Nita hugged herself and tried to remove the frown from her face.

131

"It's fried-chicken night at our house. See don't I stop over here on University at the Colonel's. I ain't cooking or washing one dish for the rest of this day."

"Take it easy, mama."

Nita set the table and called the kids in for supper.

They picked at their food. Rae Anne confessed that Big Mama had bought them all hot dogs at the orange juice stand, and Nita figured there had been other treats that even a big mouth like her oldest daughter knew better than to reveal. She packed most of the dinner away for later in the week. It would all keep; the meat, as a matter of fact, would taste better on the replay.

Everybody dropped in front of the TV, playing with their new toys. Bless her heart, Mama didn't mind spending on the kids, spending for the kinds of things wasn't never in Nita's budget: the little spinners and doodads the kids always came home with. Didi had something on a Day-Glo elastic string that bounced and made a whirring noise. Mama was smart about toy shopping. She knew how to steer the kids toward the flashy stuff that didn't cost too much but wasn't so cheap it fell apart on the way home.

More than a few yawns drifted around the room.

"Big Mama done wore you all out."

Hallelujah, she thought.

"Everybody can get to bed a little early tonight."

Seven thirty. They'd be out cold, fast, and here she'd have another bonus: just a touch more time, all to herself. She scooted the kids down the hall and started them on their preparations.

Damn, she thought. Who would be out there worrying the door at this hour. She checked the peephole. Him again. She cracked open the door.

"Got a minute?" he asked.

That fool downstairs.

"I just put my kids down."

"I bought a treat. We'll be real quiet," he whispered.

He pulled out two containers of some of that expensive ice cream she could only drool over up at the Rainbow.

"New York Super Fudge Chunk and Cherry Garcia," he says.

"You got a problem downstairs?"

"No. Can I come in?"

"You want something?"

"I want to talk to you. A couple minutes. I'll be real quiet."

She stepped aside slowly, opening the door for him to pass.

"Some bowls and spoons?" he asked, holding up the containers.

She retrieved one bowl and a spoon from the dish drainer.

"I'm not hungry," she said.

"Suit yourself." He pried the lid off one of the containers and shoveled right into the pale pink mixture. He apparently wasn't studying no bowl.

"This stuff is sinful," he said, chewing and talking at the same time. "I'd eat two of these a day if I didn't know better. Try it?" he offered, extending a spoonful.

"No thank you."

"Put that other one in the freezer for the kids. Keep me from eating it."

"That's nice of you," she said.

She took the ice cream to the kitchen, stood across the room watching him pick through the frozen cylinder. He was scraping here and there in the pink, picking, as if hoping to find a diamond or the secret prize.

"You wanted to see me about something?" she asked.

"Yeah, I did." He set the container in the bowl, popped the lid back on it. "Got to let it soften a bit," he said. "Can we have a seat?"

He sat, not waiting for the offer or refusal.

"Please don't be uncomfortable. I don't bite. A lot of people think that when you're on TV or you're a little bit famous or something that you're different, but really, I'm just regular folks."

"I'm not uncomfortable."

"You seem nervous."

Go to hell, she thought. This kind always had something to say about her so-called "attitude," always expected you to smile and be pleasant, always left her feeling like there was something wrong with her cause she didn't act like he was God's gift to sisters. He was one of those who when they were boys back in school didn't have the time of day for girls like her. Boys who lived in nice houses over in Highland or up in Roseville and who had all kinds of money and clothes and what have you and who couldn't even be bothered to look at a poor girl like Bonita Sallis.

And don't say nothing about a poor girl who was brown skinned. Or darker. All them boys had the white-girl fever, every one of them, all the way through school, and those white bitches couldn't get enough of em. Traded around them stuck-up muthafuckers like they was baseball cards. Walked around talking all tough and hard, like if they acted ignorant enough folks would forget what color they was. Go downtown and St. Paul Center was full of them wenches, every afternoon. Acting all ignorant, treating folks just as rude as them thugs and heathens they hung out with. And a lot of these nigger men didn't grow out of it neither. You still saw them driving around with their blonde whores—always blondes. Nita couldn't stand to see no black man with a white woman. It was like a slap in the face. It said basically all you black bitches can kiss my ass. You see *I* don't need you. Well, fuck them dogs—she didn't need them neither. One thing, if he valued his life, her Marco had better never show up around here with one of them pale-ass bitches. Be his last day on earth.

Yeah, she knew his type. Walk around thinking they better than folks cause they got a little money or advantage, and here she got to sit up in her own house and worry was she speaking proper and do he think she's common.

"Naw, I ain't nervous," she said. "It's getting late, and I'm tired."

"Eight o'clock? Oh, well. I won't keep you long. Just wanted to check out a few things with you."

She raised her brows to indicate she was waiting. He continued eyeballing her, circling her face with his eyes, adjusting his head as if to get a better angle.

"You gonna stare at me all night?"

"You remind of this girl I used to know. I worked in Indiana a couple years. You could be her sister."

She tapped on her armrest. Waiting.

"You're not related to some Hubbards, are you?"

She rose and crossed her arm.

"All right," he said.

He got up and put his hand on her as if to guide her back into her chair. She dropped her arm from his reach.

"I'll get to the point. I'm only trying to be friendly. We're neighbors, after all." He leaned back, all comfortable, put an ankle on his knee and started in.

"What I wanted to let you know is that the TV station—KCKK, the one I anchor for—some people, a technician and a camera man, a producer or two, . . . we're gonna be around here for a few weeks. We'll be doing the news from here. Parts of it at least."

"From here?" Now she knew he was crazy.

"Right here. Downstairs. Out front maybe. I wanted to let you know, being the caretaker and all. There might be a bit of commotion. Not too much, I hope."

"I don't know about this." She wondered what Skjoreski would think. He might not be too crazy about having some cameras snooping around his investment. Such as it was.

"Is there a problem, us being here?" He opened his hands when he asked, the same way Professor King did when he was explaining some stupid-ass point no one hadn't heard of but him but he figured they all must already know.

Despite her reservations, she wasn't gonna let him think she had to answer to somebody—even if she did—but figured she better throw a little bit of brake on this train. "This is people's homes here. Not some movie set."

"This is my home, too."

While you need it to be, she thought.

"It's just, you know how it is when the camera comes around. You got all kinds of folks come around clowning and carrying on. I don't want to be living in the middle of a circus."

"I've been in this business half my life. Believe me, we do everything we can to avoid circuses. We'll be very discreet."

He said "discreet"—pausing for emphasis, drawing it out—like one of those people just learned a new word and wanted to see how it sounded on their tongue. She shook her head.

"Hey, we might even get you on the air."

"Put that right out your mind," she scoffed.

"You're a natural." He framed her up with his fingers, like he was a movie director or something. "Perfect," he said.

She yawned. "My bedtime."

"So?" he prompted.

"Yeah?"

"So, it's okay we work here?"

She walked to her door and opened it. "Won't be no problems," she told him. "That's all I'm saying."

"Great. Great." He stood up tentatively, as if he'd forgotten something, brushed himself off. "Look, come on down and watch us work. Look around. Ask all the questions you want. Hey! Bring the kids. Let me know if there's any problems. Anything at all."

"I'll do that. Good night, Mr. Wilson."

"Good night. Enjoy that ice cream." He winked, nodded toward the table and then slid out the door like a dancer.

136

She picked up the container and opened the lid. She expected it to have melted, but discovered it at a temptingly soft and silky stage, like a perfect milk shake. She scooped up a finger full and closed her mouth around it. The ice cream on her tongue felt cold and creamy, rich, sweet and shocking, luxurious. Just as she always imagined it would.

Transformation

. . . .

*I am writing on behalf of the ladies at my
church. We would like you to come and speak
to us about being on television. Please answer
the following questions. How much do you get
paid? Do you like your job? Who does your
hair? Please come to our meeting on Thursday.
Lunch will be served.*

Mrs. Rev. Arthur Jackson
North End, St. Paul

"People live this way?" Mindy remarked. She cringed and minced
around the apartment as if she were afraid something would
crawl out and bite her.

"Have a seat," Brandon ordered.

She hovered tentatively, "This is silk," she said of her suit.

"It's clean. I'm the only one here."

She eyed him suspiciously. "It's plaid," she said.

"Which automatically equals dirty?"

"That's the thing about plaid. You just can't tell."

"Sit down."

"Really, Brandon," she said. "Isn't this all a little . . . over the
top? This place? You said it was a dump, but *this*?"

"It's not so bad," Ted said. "I lived in worse when I was at the U."

"There are worse places than this?"

"Come on, Mindy," Brandon said. "You aren't that much of a princess."

Actually Brandon believed she just might be. And she was certainly that naive. She existed in a narrow circle that encompassed the TV station, a house on a lake, and a few trendy bistros and stores. She was of the school that believed that the best solution to social problems was beautification—the interior-design school of social engineering. She'd been working with a group of "community leaders" for a year on a plan to build a new social-services center for the indigent, locating it to a more "secure" part of town. He wasn't sure that she even knew the real agenda, which was to move the shelter to a place where its clients would be a lot less likely to mingle with the professional types taking their lunch in Rice Park. She meant well, but that was Mindy— right causes, wrong motives. Or vice versa. Sure, she did plenty of charity work, but that mostly consisted of going to pricey banquets with bad food, or maybe being videotaped dishing up a couple of turkey dinners at the soup kitchen on Thanksgiving. An apartment like this was so far from her ken she didn't even know the categories into which to stereotype it.

"You should see some of the places I didn't move into," Brandon told her.

"I am fully serious. If I heard one of the sponge sisters moved into a dump like this, I'd place her under house arrest."

"I lived in one place," Ted said, "over off of Fourth Street where there were six or seven of us sharing. You never knew from day to day how many. In the morning you'd get up and there'd be whoever got picked up the night before or whatever other strays happened to wander through. The toilet was always stopped up, and there was stuff in that refrigerator you wouldn't believe. We didn't need a light bulb because the food glowed in the dark."

"And anyway, what do you expect is gonna happen here, Min? I'll be carried off by roaches? I'll get "poor" germs on me?"

"Can we get this meeting started, please," Ted implored. "I got some guy coming in from the coast with a new character generator."

Brandon had brought Mindy and Ted to the apartment to discuss the series, to begin the following week. He felt it was important for them to get a sense of the place where the other half of the broadcast would be originating. He also wanted to pick their brains, see if looking around here gave them any bright ideas that just might make the series work. Mindy, whose hair was now the color of peaches, was still stuck on the surface issues.

"You know, for all the trouble this place is, we could have hired a set designer and built it in a corner of the studio. Who'd know?"

"I'd know," he said. "And this place is no trouble. That's its main problem."

Mindy sighed. She picked at the fabric of the couch as if looking for insect life.

"What do you think, Ted?" Brandon asked.

"I'm thinking that it's like a cliché almost, this place. You follow?"

Brandon shook his head.

"Think about stock footage. You need a shot of New York, you get your standard panorama—from the Island, never from Jersey, downtown on the left, midtown on the right. Or Chicago—always from the lake. This place is your stock footage of your lower-income home."

"And what I want to know," said Mindy, "is why is it that poor always equals bad taste? Why does inexpensive have to mean ugly? Plaid, for God's sakes."

"Plaid is what they have at those rental places," Brandon said.

"No, see, I know I've been sort of carrying on about all this, and, yeah, I know I'm spoiled. But seriously. If you surveyed a thousand people and asked them to pick the ugliest thing on a page, 99 percent of them would pick this brown-and-green-plaid couch. Regardless of income or background or education or any of that. This is a damn ugly couch. Yet you drive by one of these discount furniture places—like that one over here by the freeway entrance—what do they have a window full of? Plaid. Right underneath the 'Public Assistance Welcomed' sign."

"So?"

"So there's a story here, Brandon. Think about it. How could it be cheaper to cover a sofa in this hideous plaid than to cover it up in a neutral color like beige or gray, or even a tasteful print?"

"Did it ever occur to you, Mindy, that maybe, just maybe, there might be people out there who like plaid?"

"So now what you're saying is that lower-income people have bad taste."

"I'm saying that maybe they don't share *your* taste."

"There's a problem with my taste?"

"You have wonderful taste. You're a regular Martha Stewart. And this is a cheap-ass sofa I rented for three months, and I don't know or care what kind of taste poor people have. Can we drop this?"

"Don't patronize me. You dragged me over here. At least do me the courtesy of listening."

He raised his palm for her to proceed.

"I know I'm not saying this clearly," she said. "What it has to do with is, there's got to be something more going on other than where people shop or how much they pay for things. I mean, why is it that I would automatically associate this kind of furniture— these colors and these styles—with poor people?"

"Because you're a classist snob." He laughed, put his hand up for a high five from Ted. Ted declined.

"Go to hell," Mindy said.

"Sorr-ry. So touchy. It's only a little joke. You were saying?"

"Forget it," she snapped. She leaned back on the couch, angry, sulking.

Ted squatted in a corner, framing the sofa, then moved himself to another corner. "This is good for two, maybe three remotes down here," he said.

"Because of what she was saying?"

Ted waved his hand. "Just in general. A couple shows, maybe. No more."

"I don't understand," Brandon said.

"Well, it is some of what Mindy's talking about."

Mindy sneered at Brandon.

Ted said, "After people see you down here a couple times, they've got the idea. Any more than that and people get antsy. It makes people uncomfortable to look at this crap."

"Nothing wrong with a little discomfort."

Ted shook his head.

"There *is* something wrong with a little discomfort?"

"It's like when you got on underwear that bunches up. People don't like to be uncomfortable. For a while—a short while—yes. But the minute you can reach down there and fix it, you fix it."

"You sound like Dexter."

"Thanks."

"I'm not sure I meant that as a compliment. You're telling me I moved into this dump for nothing."

"Of course not. It's a symbol, you know. I thought you understood that? It's like people hollering about Chelsea Clinton not going to public school. People don't care about that kid's education. It's just the symbol they wanted to see."

Brandon shook his head in amazement. "More like Dexter every minute."

Ted stared up at the windows. He walked over and pulled a curtain aside. "I'm thinking what we need to do here is a low-key kinda thing. You know what I mean?"

"Go on."

"There was a show on when I was little called 'Real People.' Remember it?"

"Piece of shit," Brandon said.

"That 'piece of shit' had dynamite ratings. Everybody watched it."

"Which is why it went off the air, right?"

"There's plenty of stuff just like it still on the air, and a lot of it is always at the top of the ratings. Those funniest-video shows and, hell, even Oprah and Phil and all those guys. It's all the same thing—people aren't happy just watching the news, they want to *be* the news."

"So I become the host of a trash TV show. Live from St. Paul! Brandon Wilson presents Minnesota's Most Vulgar People. What do you think, Min?"

"I'm not speaking to you."

Brandon answered a knock at the door. Mrs. Carter sashayed in past him.

"Heard some noises and thought I'd better to check," she said.

"We're fine," he responded, holding open the door.

"A person can't be too careful round here. You likely to get cleaned out."

"We're fine. If you don't mind, we're sort of in the middle of a meeting."

"Don't mind me." She stepped around him and perched on the couch next to Mindy. "Over on the next block where my friend Arlene live, she had heard someone in the apartment across the hall, and she didn't pay it no mind cause she knew the girl what lives there was usually home. Well, it turned out that the girl had stepped out to the store for a minute and that the noise Arlene heard was the robbers in there stripping the joint. Girl wasn't gone five minutes, and when she got back they had taken everything wasn't bolted down."

"No!" said Mindy.

"Yes, ma'am. You can't be too careful around here. I'm Mrs. Carter from upstairs." She stuck her hand out to Mindy. "I'm helping to produce this show."

"Isn't that sweet," Mindy said. She turned and simpered in Brandon's face. "Mindy St. Michaels. How lovely to meet you."

"I thought I recognized you," Mrs. Carter said. She beckoned Brandon with her finger. "Has she come down a few shades? Her hair I mean."

"You'd have to ask her hairdresser."

"Is he anybody?" Mrs. Carter pointed to Ted.

"Ted McCarron. Producer." Ted bent to give her his hand.

"We'll be working together then."

"She's great," Ted whispered to Brandon. Brandon, who faced away from her, shook his head in exasperation.

"This is exactly what I'm talking about," Ted continued. "Mrs. Carter, who do you love to see on TV more than anyone else?"

"Well, I am partial to that Dane Stephens. He's awfully cute. And of course this Mandy here."

"It's Mindy."

"Bless your heart."

"Can we get her out of here?" Brandon whispered.

"What I mean, Mrs. Carter, is don't you just love it when you get to see your neighbors on TV? Ordinary people, like yourself."

"You want to put me on the air? I knew it. I got up this morning and I said to myself, I said, 'Cora, this your lucky day.' What you want me to do? I told that one over there I could be the weather girl, though he didn't seem too partial to that. I figure I'd wait and talk to someone had more authority down to the station. Someone knew what he was doing. You want me to sing for you? I do 'Am I Blue?' and 'Do Nothing till You Hear from Me.' Or I can do a gospel number . . ."

"This is the news," Brandon shouted. Ignorant old woman, he thought, seething.

"Stand over here a second," Ted ordered. He placed Mrs. Carter by the window with some more of that Dexter framing shit. She smiled, coquettishly.

"I don't know," Ted said. "I got a pretty big assignment for you. You think you can handle it?"

"He's really good," Mindy mouthed to Brandon. Brandon put his hands on his forehead and exhaled loudly.

"You come to the right woman," Mrs. Carter said. "What you need?"

"All I want you to do is come on the air and have Brandon over there interview you."

"Him?"

"He's a pretty good guy."

"What's he gonna be talking to me about?"

"Your life. What goes on around here?"

"I guess I can do that."

"Look," Ted said, walking her to the door. "Why don't you go on home and make a list of what you'd like people to know about you. We'll work out all the details later."

She rubbed her hands together in glee.

"Ten more like her," Ted said to Brandon, "and we got ourselves a monster. We do it here and right in their homes. From their living rooms, to the city."

"I won't disappoint you," Mrs. Carter said.

"Before you go, Mrs. Carter," Mindy asked. "Can I get your opinion on something?"

Mrs. Carter gave Mindy an impish smile, "Anything, sweetie."

"What do you think of this couch?"

"This ugly thing? You wouldn't catch me dead with it in my house."

Mindy flashed Brandon a triumphant smile, though what she'd been vindicated of, he really couldn't say.

A royal blue silk dress, a deeper color still in the amber light of candles, lent Sandra's creamy brown skin the rich warm tone of freshly risen bread. Her eyes in that light were gray-green crystals and, here in a restaurant named for a horse, in a downtown office tower, Brandon basked in the warmth and the light.

"What are you leering at?" she asked him.

"You really are the most beautiful woman in this restaurant."

"You been looking at these other bitches?"

"For product comparison purposes only, my dear."

She took a sip of her wine. "Tell me something. When you were growing up, did you imagine some day you'd be all dressed up and sitting around some fancy joint like this?"

"Trés glamorous."

"Trés."

"I used to go up to this little movie theater by where my cousins lived, back home, and watch those James Bond movies," Brandon said. He stared wistfully out beyond Sandra as he spoke. "James was tough. He'd be standing around some casino. He always had on that white dinner jacket, a martini on the table, some beautiful woman next to him. Now for me, that was the ultimate in glamorous."

"So, I'm your James Bond fantasy?"

"Boys don't have that kind of fantasy."

"You're lying."

"It's true. Boys have two fantasies. First one: you're at the plate, Busch Stadium. Game seven, World Series, bottom of the ninth. Cardinals are behind by two. Two outs, bases loaded, full count."

"Of course you knock it out of the park."

"Actually, that's the whole fantasy. It's like sex. Just before you come. You know what's gonna happen. But you linger there, in that moment. Forever, if you can."

"So that's what that shit's all about."

"What do you mean?"

"Nothing. Go on. What's the other fantasy?"

"That's the easy one: cars."

"Cars?"

"Yeah. Any nice car. Preferably a convertible."

"And what happens?"

"It's one of those nice, LA kind of days. Sunny and warm. Palm trees along the boulevard. You get in your car and you put on your shades. You ride around and people look at you."

"That's it?"

"Uh huh. Oh, and did I mention it's best if the car's red? And there can be a pretty woman in the car, if you want."

"Red, huh? Well, this is some deep shit here."

She rubbed her nose with a finger and gave him a bemused look. He had always suspected that she was smarter than he. He always wondered if he was entertaining her or just playing the fool. She manifested what might be a disarming combination of 1990s female-macho toughness and old-fashioned feminine wiles, the kind he associated with classic film noir starring people such as Barbara Stanwyck, the kind where the man always wondered as he was being seduced if there wasn't a knife hidden beneath the pillow.

"What do girls fantasize about?" he asked.

"Used to be the dream house with the white picket fence, but we're changing that."

"Is that really what you used to think about? The husband and kids and the whole package?"

"Part of me, yes. And I think any woman tells you she didn't is a lie."

"It's genetic, I guess."

"Maybe. But it's not the reactionary bullshit you're thinking of. What it is, see, is women haven't lost touch with what the program is, the reason we're put here."

"Which is?"

"So we can take care of one another."

"The woman's job is to take care of people?"

"That would be how a man would turn it around. I didn't say woman. I said 'we.' Your psycho male dreams are all about 'I' and . . . a car. A thing. You all have completely missed the point."

"Yeah, yeah, so we're dogs. What did the other half of you dream about?"

She set her wine on the table. She got a far-off look in her eye, looking at a place beyond his head, as if she were looking through the wall.

"I used to fantasize about being white," she said, her voice like fine china. "I didn't run around with a yellow dishtowel on my head, or anything like that. I just used to think sometimes about someone who was as smart as I was and who had parents like I had and the advantages I had. I'd think what would happen to her if she were white.

"If you were to ask me to make a list of things—bad things— that happened to me because of the color of my skin—you know, things like I wasn't allowed to join a club or somebody didn't give me a grade I had earned—I bet I couldn't come up with more than three things. In my whole life. You were brought up about the same way I was, so you know what I mean."

She was a Moore, from a solidly upper-middle-class clan down in Nashville, people who'd built comfortable luxury homes and had had their kids welcomed at the finest schools their money could buy. By day shuttled off to this academy or that one, in the evenings she and the other scions of her class were folded into the arms of an insular community of like-minded people, and they were watered and nurtured and raised to take over as the princes and princesses of the New South.

"You may not believe this," she continued, "but the only 'Whites Only' sign I actually saw with my own two eyes was on a documentary. And I was in the heart of the South, the home of country music. Oh, I got called out of my name enough. Nigger, and what have you. But Momma and Daddy taught us that that was just bad behavior, and that it didn't have anything to do with us.

"I can't tell you where it came from. I even have a hard time saying exactly what it is. It's not like an inferiority complex, because, believe you me, the Moores were not raised to be inferior to anyone."

"It's doubt," Brandon said. He took her hand from the table, massaging it.

"Yes. That's it, I think. It's like you always have this nagging suspicion in the back of your head that . . ."

"That if your skin were a different color, life would be perfect and all your problems would disappear."

She laughed. "Yes, but it's more subtle than that, isn't it? Because, you know, I've been around them all my life, and white people are no mystery to me. I know their lives are far from perfect. I have no illusions. I'm not fascinated by them, and I don't think I'm too prejudiced. I really don't think about them much at all. As white people. You know what I mean?"

"They're just there."

"Exactly. Still, I get these fantasies."

"Get?"

She shook her head, confused.

"This isn't about way back when, is it? This is now."

She lowered her eyes.

"Damn this shit. It's like some weight we bear our whole lives. Whatever we do, wherever we go, it's with us."

"It makes me furious," she said. Her eyes lit up with the rage. She could hardly look at him. "It makes me sad, too."

"Let's not ruin our evening."

"Made my mind up a long time ago—wasn't letting this shit ruin my *anything*."

"Good girl," he said, rubbing her hand.

He thought about all the vows he'd made to himself: that he was above that, that he wouldn't be bothered worrying about what a bunch of ignorant honkies thought of him. The games he'd played with himself, telling himself that they weren't talking about him. They were talking about *them*, those other folks, the loud and wrong ones, the ones who committed the crimes, the ones with the low morals. It was *them*. And how he really believed—had been taught to believe—that if you spoke a certain way, made a nice appearance, followed all the rules, you'd rise above it. And then the times when, despite all those mind games, there would be confirmed what he knew all along—he was just another nigger. The same cab that wouldn't stop for *them* wasn't stopping for him, either. Same suspicion, same nasty looks, same withering distrust.

"One of these days," he told Sandra, "I will get beyond it."

"You got some magical powers the rest of us don't?"

"Maybe."

"I'm listening."

"It's hard to explain. When I'm out there in front of that camera none of this shit matters. It really doesn't."

"I don't know what you're talking about."

"You know. There's me, here, and then there's that other me. The one on people's television sets. We aren't the same. It's almost like I become something else. All of us do. I look in that red light, into that lens. I put myself inside it and give myself to it. Something happens. I don't know what it is. It's not me that comes out the other side. Not this man, this black man, Brandon Wilson. It's someone else, something else."

"And what might that be?"

"I don't know. I don't think anyone does. We send out those sounds and those pictures. Who knows what happens to them when they come back to earth?"

"They don't teach physics at journalism school?" She walked her foot up the leg of his trousers. Her shoe cooled its heel beneath the table.

"I just know there's a difference. That's all. And I know it means something."

That night in bed, late, her fingers circled a figure-eight pattern on his back.

"You think I'm crazy?" he asked.

"Depends on what you mean."

"Things. About television. We don't understand. We aren't ready for yet."

"I guess not."

"Someone like you, even. It's powerful, Sandra. More than people know."

"I know. You go on to sleep." Her nails gently raked his shoulders.

"Power," he said, drifting away, images of himself sifting into the air with something like a warm current moving above him, around him.

At the Zoo

. . . .

Somehow, everything was askew, the day had gone misplaced. The sun warmed the air like June. Only the still-bare trees said it was spring, just turned seasons within the month. The park was full, the zoo part of it at least. Herds of day-care kids dressed in matching T-shirts trailed out behind adults on fluorescent-colored ropes like ducks behind a mother. Lots of folks playing hooky from work. There was a whole other life that wasn't the women's department at Wards or some apartment building on Marshall Avenue. You just had to go out and get yourself some of it. Still, Nita felt frivolous. She picked a few kernels of popcorn from the box Sipp offered. She nibbled them guiltily.

"You not hungry?" he asked.

"No, not much," she answered, but it wasn't true. She'd like to snatch that box from his hand and gobble the whole thing down, and then get another. She had had an appetite these past few days like she couldn't remember ever having. She had fixed elaborate casseroles with noodles and meats and cheese and made tuna salad and such to snack on in the evenings. She got this way, she remembered, just before Didi was born. And also once, a year or so back, when there were rumors about closing down the store. Eating nerves, her mother called them. Damn them.

"Here, hold out both hands," Sipp told her. He dumped from the box into the cup she formed.

"Boy!" She shuttled the corn back and forth like a Slinky, trying to figure out how she was going to be able to hold it all and eat it without grazing out of her hand like some kind of cow. She opened her fingers a bit and managed to get most of it in one big mitt, catching the spillover with her other hand and dumping it in her mouth.

"Little popcorn ain't gonna hurt you. Besides, I like me some flesh on my woman."

"I'm your woman now?"

"Any time you want to be." He danced around her, eyeing her either with a leer or in admiration. He followed her eyes around with his head. She was trying not to look at him and not to smile.

She plopped herself on a bench across the walk from the monkey enclosure. A large crowd had gathered. The primates were performing today, as happy as everyone else to be getting out after the long winter. Sipp strolled up to look, turned around and headed back, exaggerating the length of his arms in imitation. He took a last big handful of popcorn and handed her the box, telling her to finish it.

She couldn't eat this man's food. And what was she doing here in the park with him in the first place? Stuff back home needed doing. Errands to run. Studying. Here she was, big as life, wasting her day, chillin in the park with some nigger she didn't hardly know. Who did she think she was? She wasn't no woman of leisure.

"I got to get home," she said.

"Sure nuff a beautiful day," he responded. He dropped an arm across her back.

"Yeah, it is, but I got a lot to do. You know?"

"I know you need to take some time for yourself. Otherwise, you blow your stacks."

"Blow your stacks." Nita sputtered a chuckle. "My stepdaddy says that."

"He must be from down home."

"I believe he is, as a matter of fact. You won't see him blowing his stacks, though. Sit on his big booty and let my mama run for him all day long."

She felt his arm drop a little more, his hand squeezing her shoulder. She should tell him to move it — all kinds of nerve this nigger had to put his hands on her. She wriggled her shoulder and felt the hand loosen. It stayed where he put it, though.

"This a nice little old zoo, here," he said. "Friend told me about it. I didn't even know it was up in this park."

"Me and the kids come out every once and a while," she said, though she knew it was mostly a lie. Every once and a while was maybe twice. They'd been to Como Park more times with their school than with her. She shivered at her little fib.

"Sit still, Miss Nita. I brought you here to relax."

She released a long sigh and her muscles let go. She allowed her face to be pleasant and soft. She smiled. To please him.

"That's better," he said.

"Still got a lot to do," she said, and he drew her closer. She let him, reluctantly, fighting the urge to lean her head against his shoulder — too familiar. Like the popcorn. Like his arm. Like being here at all.

"All that will keep. Come on, let's walk down here and make faces at them bears." He stood, holding a hand out to her, which she took. He kept her hand, held it in front of him in two of his, as if he owned it, as if to show everyone in the park it belonged to him. She should smack his old hands, smack him. But she didn't. She walked with him, was led by him. She held her face up to the sun and let it heat her right through to her spine.

"Feels good, don't it?" he said.

"A person forgets sometimes."

"Not me. Never let myself get where I can't appreciate all the good things in life."

"I'm jealous."

"Of me?"

"Seems like you do what you want, when you want. Come and go as you please."

"Naw, baby, you mixed up now. You talking about two different things. Look at this black muthafucker up here. This bear." He indicated a large male in the center of the compound, hunched over, pawing something beside a rock. "What's he got to do all day but sit here and soak up the sun and have folks bring him food."

"Just like you," she said. She smiled, opened her eyes wide, daring his response.

He laughed, loud and deep. "That's where you confused. See, a girl like you thinks she got to get with the whole program. Do all this work, jump through all them hoops. Thinks if she relax, or take a little something for herself, she'll be out something. It don't work that way."

"How's it work then? You know so much."

"What me and Smokey here know is you do what little you need to do to get by. And if they want to feed you and take care of you, you let em. Meanwhile, you lay back and enjoy the fresh air and sunshine."

"One problem with that."

"Yeah?"

"You might not have noticed, but this here bear is locked up."

"Look at him. He's doing pretty good."

She walked away toward the giraffes and toward the exit. "Some of us got responsibilities," she said.

He followed a few steps behind her. "You make responsibilities sound like a bad thing."

She stopped and turned toward him, staring, angry, unsure what he meant.

He said, "You talk like you got this shit on you that you can't stand. You love them kids? Don't you?"

"You know I do."

"I'm saying enjoy em. You got to enjoy what you got to do."

"And I'm saying you ain't got nothing to do. That's why you got all this time and all this joy you spreading around."

Wasn't this boy just too much. The ignorant, lazy fool. Didn't do a damn thing all day long, then got the nerve to tell her she got to enjoy life more.

He grabbed at his heart as if he'd been stabbed. "Got to get you out of the sun, Miss Nita. You done got cranky on me."

"What you got to do is get me home so I can get the hallway vacuumed before the kids come in."

He pulled his car into the Dairy Queen on Lexington Avenue. Before she could protest, he hopped out and sauntered over to the window. When he returned he handed her a cone. He was already eating the one he bought for himself. She bit at the cone, pouting. She hadn't said a word to him since the park.

"Didn't mean to make you mad," he said.

"I'm not mad, really. It's just . . . I don't know. You think I like to work this hard? You think a person wants all this on them?"

"You ain't hearing a word I say."

"Yeah, well, talk is cheap."

"Sure, I take it easy. Do my little business and lay back. What I say is, you figure how much it's gonna take you to be comfortable and get what you want out of life. That's how hard you should work. No more. You spend your time chasing after shit and never take any time to enjoy yourself, before you know it, life's over. What's it for if you don't get to enjoy it?"

She shook her head. "Well, I guess someday. Maybe."

When she got her degree.

Maybe.

Got a halfway decent piece of a job.

Maybe.

Got these kids grown.

Maybe.

"It's a long road," she said.

"And someday may never come." He took a massive bite from his ice cream.

She watched him eat, the creamy white of the ice milk a shocking contrast to his lovely dark brown skin. Something about him glowed, a glow that resonated from somewhere in his middle and came out on his face. When she'd first seen him she thought it was arrogance—that quick warm smile full of teeth and those sparkly eyes. But it was a real and down-to-earth thing and always there. It was some kind of wholeness, some fullness of spirit. Something which resisted her anger and her frustration. It was something that drew her to him, beckoned her closer.

"So you don't have big dreams?" she asked. Damn the time. Let him talk some more. Just a little more.

"Dreams as big as the next one. Bigger."

"Well, dreams take time and work."

He popped the last of the cone in his mouth and chewed. She watched his throat expand as he swallowed. "Man like me, black man from Mississippi, poor, no education—lot of folks say I got me a nerve having dreams in the first place."

"That sounds like an excuse to me."

"Come on, Nita. You know it's real. You know you up against the same stuff yourself. Point is, when the table's tipped against you, you got to do a little something to tip things more to your favor. You know what I mean?"

"I guess so. If you call trifling around with that shit you mess with turning things to your favor. Me, I call it something else."

"Ah, Miss Nita, you really won't give a man a break."

"It's just that it seems like a big risk for a person to take, just so he can waste all day sitting on his ass in some cheap apartment in St. Paul." She smiled at him, slyly, happy with her point.

"You think I'm stupid," he said. He looked away from her, out the windshield toward the SuperAmerica station across the street. She could see the glow fading from his face. She reached out a hand to his arm. He looked at it.

"Folks see a black man and the only thing they think about is what he can't do or what he won't do or what he gonna do to them. Won't nobody let you prove yourself. You try and you try and you get to the point where you say 'fuck it.' Nita, I'm be twenty-two years old this summer. By my age a lot of us have just give up. Me, I ain't one of them quitters."

"I know you're not." She felt a hand cover the one she had kept on his arm.

"Naw, I ain't doing this penny-ante shit forever." He parted his lips, a grin full of contempt crawling across his face. "Make enough to get by until they throw your ass in jail. Not this nigger."

"So what you gonna do then?"

He turned back to her, looked at her hard, searching all around her face. His face warmed again to its glow. His lips parted again, this time revealing a welcoming smile. "I'm in on a big one, baby." He said it in almost a whisper.

Her brows knit with a question. She turned her head slightly.

"*The* big one," he said. "Remember I told you I was putting me together a stake. Going back home and set myself up. Live the way I like. Well, I'm talking about enough to do all that and two or three other dreams, too."

"What if . . . ?"

"Naw, baby, don't "what if" me. I thought through that shit. All of it. I got to take my shot. Then I'm out."

"Out?"

"Out and back home. With you. Maybe?"

It was her turn to look away. Here for the first time was someone offering her something. Something different anyway. André, he'd never offered her anything, except some excitement, a few thrills, and a chance to get away from mama. These days André didn't have a thing, and there hadn't been anyone much else interested in her either.

Maybe he was just flirting. Maybe not. Maybe he was one of

those men fell easy and hard and fast. Saw the woman for him and went after her.

Maybe he was just playing her.

"I do got to get home. Kids coming soon."

"That's cool," he said. He pulled out onto Lexington. "You help me, Nita?" he asked.

"What?"

"I asked, would you help me?"

"Help you what?"

"Can I trust you?" Another whisper.

She didn't respond.

"I feel like I can trust you," he said. "So I'm gonna tell you something. Ask you something."

Something gnawed at a corner of her brain. A bead of sweat rolled between her breasts. She wiped her brow.

"This little deal," he said. "I'ma let you know something. First and last time I'll ask you."

"You said *big* deal, remember? And I won't have nothing to do with that shit."

"You don't need to touch a thing. I just need a place."

Her anger boiled in her stomach like soup. She could hardly get the words out.

"Using me," was all she can say.

"I would never . . ."

"I should have known. A goddamn fool." Him and her both.

"Look, you got me wrong. All wrong."

"I'm wrong, am I? Tell me this. Did you or did you not just ask me to get involved with your damn drug deal?"

"I asked you to be my partner."

"Bullshit."

"No, Nita. I mean it. I want you to share all I got."

Nita's breath came hard and fast. "I warned you, nigger. I did. Bring me out here. Talking your bullshit talk."

He pulled the car around the corner by the high school and stopped.

"Take me the hell on home."

He reached for her arm. "I'd never hurt you. I wouldn't."

"Fine. I'll walk." As she opened the car door, he started up and did a U-turn. She hung onto the handle, fuming with rage. When he pulled up in front of the building she yanked back on the handle to jump out. He grabbed her arm.

"Let go of me," she said.

"I didn't have to tell you any of this. Not one thing."

She stayed facing the building, the grabbed arm pulled behind her. She wanted to wrench free, but she didn't. She wasn't sure why.

"I got one shot," he said. "The only one I get, probably, my whole life."

"You know how I feel."

"This shit was going down here whether I told you about it or not." He let go her arm.

"So why are you telling me now?"

"Cause I care."

"Fuck you." She started out the car and he grabbed her back again.

"I do. Think I'd risk my business over any old bitch out here? I didn't have to tell you nothing. I'm doing this for us. I told you cause I trust you."

"Maybe you shouldn't."

"I do." He let go the arm.

She rose from the car, turned and looked back in the window. "I warned you about this shit going on up in this building with my kids in there." She tried to look fierce, but was deflated by his glow. His face was open, his eyes soft and wet.

"Send them away," he said. "It'll be one night. Then we're out. You and me. And them, too."

One night. Could it really be as simple as that, as simple as one risky night. And then maybe — maybe — something else. Something good. Or better, at least.

"When?"

"Friday, week. You're with me then?"

"Didn't say that."

"Yeah, you are." He started the car. "Dream large, sugar. See ya." He screeched away from the curb, waving and grinning, a hot smokey gray cloud from his tailpipe covering his back.

The hallway outside her apartment was cluttered with coils of thick cable and metal boxes and trunks with hinged lids and lights on stands and various white men she had never seen standing around, seeming to belong to all this mess and . . . All this just what she didn't need right now.

"Excuse me," she said. "Excuse me. What the hell is going on in here?"

There was no response.

"Excuse me!" she yelled into the group of men.

Out of the mess, here he came.

"Good afternoon, Nita."

That Brandon.

"Today's the big day."

"Have you lost your mind?"

He looked at her as if he didn't understand what she'd said. "On the air at five. We might just make it."

"People live in this building."

"Coming through," a man behind her said, a big man, tall and thick, carrying what looked to be some kind of camera hoisted on his shoulder, straining with the weight. She pressed herself into the wall to let him pass.

"No, no," another one said, a thin, tall young one. "To the basement with that. Only Minicams up here."

"I need to see you," she said to Brandon.

"Hope you can walk and talk at the same time, cause I got to keep moving." He flew down the steps, two at a time, to his apartment.

"Look, who do you think . . ." She chased him down and followed him into the apartment. "Didn't nobody agree to . . ." He met her at the door, pulled her into the apartment with a hand on her back.

"Everybody! I want you to meet Nita. She's the caretaker here." The several folks around the room looked up from whatever they were busy with and waved and smiled.

"Help yourself, here," Brandon said. He pointed to a table full of sandwiches and doughnuts and drinks.

"Molly, I need to see those scripts sorted by segment first. Then we'll decide. Did you patch that mike to the director's booth?"

"Hey!" Nita said, pulling on his sleeve. "Stop a minute. Now!"

He walked her to his bedroom. "Okay, go ahead, but you've got to hurry." He checked his watch and then gave her this look as if she were some nosy child.

She shook her head. "I . . . I can't believe you."

"What?"

"All . . . this."

"What do you need?" He smiled, put his hands out as some sort of offering.

She didn't even know where to begin. He checked his watch.

"All that stuff up there . . ."

"If something's in your way, let one of those big guys know and it's out of here."

And what if it was all in her way? "I was going to vacuum the hall," she said.

"I'll vacuum the hall. Tonight after the show."

She looked at him skeptically. He checked his watch.

"I will. What else? It's crazy time here."

"Umm . . . the . . . the kids."

"Great. Come with me. Let's go." They headed out of the apartment. "Ted, you make sure that back-up line to Vince is working and you tell him I want somebody on it through the whole broadcast. Him or somebody—I don't care who.

"You ever seen a television broadcast before?"

"No." Closest she'd come was when there was a shooting down the block and she got to watch the cameras and out the window. She had been afraid to leave the children to get a closer look.

They followed a cable up the stairs to Mrs. Carter's place. Inside where Mrs. Carter usually had her TV table was now a bank of four black-and-white televisions. Mrs. Carter's color set was perched on top like some kind of exotic bird. On the coffee table was a contraption with switches.

"When we start you'll be able to monitor everything that goes on from right here. Number 1 is my camera, down in the apartment." He flipped a switch and she could hear the sound of those people down there rustling around. "Number 2 is Mindy. You might catch her picking her nose if you watch carefully. Number 3 will take the Minicams, and number 4 is always what's on the air at the moment. You still with me? I got to talk fast. Back here in the kitchen, we got pizza for you and the kids. I didn't know what you liked, so I got four different kinds. There's pop and ice and some cookies for dessert."

"What have you done with Mrs. Carter?"

"Mrs. Carter! You ready yet?" he yelled.

"Here I come," she yelled back. She paraded down the hall, circling the two of them. "How do I look?" she asked.

Nita's mouth dropped open. Mrs. Carter hair had been pressed with care and then combed and shaped around her face. She was wearing a lovely navy blue suit and a white blouse. Her usually ashen complexion actually had some color in it. She'd never seen the old girl look this good. "You look fabulous, Mrs. Carter," she said.

"Thank you, sweetie. Now, can I count on you and my kids to wait for me up here after my interview? I'm gonna need somebody to sit with me when we're done. Help me get calmed down."

Nita gave Brandon a crooked smile and shook her head. He was a slick one. "Yeah, we'll be here."

"Great!" Brandon cheered. "Mrs. Carter, you have a seat up here. We'll be up to get you about a quarter till. Just relax." Then to Nita he said. "Come on back down. Look around. Ask questions. If somebody asks you to pick up a cable, consider yourself in the union."

She pointed at Mrs. Carter and mouthed the word "later" on her way out the door. She followed Brandon down the hall. "You thought of it all, ain't you? You know, that's not my apartment back there."

He turned and grinned at her. "Yeah, well, I thought about setting all those goodies up in your house. But since I didn't have your permission, I thought again."

"Using that poor old woman."

"Hey, believe it or not it was her idea to have you come up and sit with her. She's producing this show, you know."

"I'll just bet."

"Besides, couldn't very well have a bunch of kids running around on my ceiling during the first show. Got enough else to worry about. Know what I mean?" Another grin and he bounded down the steps.

Bastard. Really did think of all of the angles. She should just let those kids in there, feed them some sugar, and put on their tap shoes. That would serve him right.

She stood in the front door of the building, waiting for her children, watching the commotion. She'd give him this—all the coming and going was through the back, and the trucks were unmarked so there weren't a whole lot of neighbors snooping around. There was nothing worse than a lot of folks standing on the lawn gawking. Around here the littlest bit of ruckus would bring folks out. All that would change, she guessed, once the word got out, once this got on the air. Assuming anyone watched Channel 13.

"Can I see you for a minute, miss?" a man asked her. He was a blond man with a tool belt around his waist.

"Sure."

He beckoned her to follow him. "Wilson says you're in charge around here. I wanted to show you this." She followed him to the basement. "Right here," he said. He indicated where the fuse box used to be. The old box was now a jumble of wires and metal on the floor. In its place was a shiny new junction box. "Had to pull that thing out. Kept overloading on us. You own this place?"

She wished. "Just the caretaker."

"Tell the owner I wired back into this new box and checked everything out for him. Tell him that, for the most part, his system here is pretty sound for an old building. No permit, so this is off the records, right?"

"Right."

"Hope this doesn't cause you folks any problems, but you ought to do fine with circuit breakers. Tell everyone to reset their clocks."

"I'll do that," she said. The electrician saluted her and took off.

How long had she been campaigning to get that fuse box taken out? What a little money and power wouldn't do.

She heard someone shout "Clear these halls!" and she headed back up to investigate.

"How do I look?" Brandon asked.

He leaned into the front door frame, dressed in some khakis and a light blue polo shirt.

"I thought you people wore suits and stuff."

"We're casual down here," he said, pulling on a lightweight jacket.

We are? she thought. His leather jacket might be casual, if you were the kind of person got the money to drop on something that fancy. "You look okay, I guess."

"Can't believe we're ready. Can't believe we're even doing this."

"How long's this going on, if I can ask?"

"Couple weeks. Believe me, today is unusual. It gets much less hectic once we're set up and running. You won't see most of these people around here again. Just me and a small tech crew." He squatted on his haunches in the door, looking out at the street. It was the usual scene. She couldn't imagine why Marshall Avenue merited such attention.

"Every night's like opening night," he said.

"You nervous?"

"I used to think it was nerves. You ever in a school play?"

"I sang in the choir."

"It's that feeling you get just before you go on to sing. I been doing this so long, nothing scares me. Still, when you're on live anything can happen."

"Like what?"

"Power goes out. Somebody drops a cue. I was on the air one time back in Wisconsin and somehow this man got on the set. He came and stood behind me at the desk. I'm reading a news story about Ronald Reagan and Contras and here's this crazy guy standing behind me."

"What did you do?"

"Kept reading. Some grip crawled over and tackled the guy and dragged him out of there. I said something like 'Seems to be a little commotion on the set.' Then I cued a commercial break. It gets pretty strange sometimes."

"Sounds like you enjoy it."

"Yeah, I do. How bout you?"

"I just work. Nothing exciting about that." The most exciting thing that happened at Wards was when they caught a shoplifter. Particularly a dumb one. One time a girl came into her department in a store smock. Nita knew the girl didn't work there. She called security and watched while the girl pretended to be rearranging merchandise on the racks. Every few armfuls she'd stuff one or two dresses into a big satchel she had. Just as bold as she could be. Nita just stood there and watched the poor simple thing. She wondered if she should tell him this story, like he told her his. Not that he would care. He was just making small talk. It was nerves.

She crossed her arms and leaned against the glass framing the door. She could feel him looking at her from where he was crouched. His eyes on her made her uncomfortable and she suppressed a shudder. She should ask him what the hell was he looking at? She wondered what he saw. Was he judging her? And, if so, on what basis and what gave him the right? What could a man like this possibly think about someone like her? A salesgirl. A single mother.

"I think you know these folks," he said, pointing down the street. He indicated the kids, barreling up the block, Marco leading the way like she'd asked him to do.

"What's all this, Mama?" he asked.

"He's on TV," Rae Anne said.

"Yeah, there's gonna be a TV show," she said. "We'll get out of your way now."

He stood and held open the door.

"After the show you guys get a big tour. You can see the cameras and the rest of the equipment. What do you say?"

"Can we, Mama?" Marco asked.

"We'll see. Good luck, Mr. Wilson."

"Thank you," he said. His eyes shone and that television grin was plastered on his face. Some of those large men hauled boxes and spare parts down the hall. She took the kids up the back steps to Mrs. Carter's to watch what happened next.

Let It Snow,
Let It Snow,
Let It Snow

. . . .

*Where have you been at? The girls in my club
and me don't have nothing to laugh about with
you gone. We getting bored. Hurry back.*
      Julie Marie Daniels
      St. Louis Park

This had better work. That was the main thing Brandon thought standing there in the doorway waiting for his cue. Here they had hauled this crap to the ghetto and disrupted people's lives and rewired a whole damn building even. It had better work.

"Hear me okay?" Mindy asked in his earpiece.

"Just like you were here. You me?"

"Loud and clear. Nervous?"

"Naaah," he lied. "We got it covered. Long as they don't pull the plug at the power plant."

But he had this knot in his gut and a flush of perspiration across his back. Not that he could tell you what there was to be nervous about. According to Ted it was even better if it looked a little rough — give it some of that raw, street edge. People liked that spontaneous look, liked to see the camera jerking around and to hear background noise. Gus was using the hand-held out front, as if this were one of those real-life police shoot-em-up shows. If something unplanned happened, it just could make the series.

Make the series. Can't think about that now, he thought. Got to be blank, clear, calm. Don't worry this to death. Just B.S. with Mindy. Shoot the breeze. That would do the trick.

"So today was the final rinse," he teased her. "How's the hair?"

"Red as Lucy's. You'll die when you see it."

"Can't wait."

"Hate to interrupt this scintillating personal conversation," Katy Tannenbaum, the new director said in his earpiece from back in the studio, "but I need you in place now, Brandon. One minute."

"Looks clear out there," he said. They'd waited in the vestibule so as to avoid drawing a crowd.

"Hurry," she said.

"Keep your drawers on," he snapped. He heard Mindy giggling across the wires.

"Thirty seconds. Everybody looks terrific. Have a good show."

Brandon took a deep breath. The street was still clear. A car went by, but ignored them.

"Fifteen."

A window opened upstairs. Out sailed tiny bits of torn-up bathroom tissue. It drifted down delicately, littering the trees. Pieces landed in Brandon's hair.

"Shit."

"Ignore it! Five . . . four . . ."

He picked his hair as if it were on fire, at the same time careful as always, picking through to grab all the scraps and patting down at the cowlicks.

"Cue the opening! Get your hands out of your goddamn hair! You look fine."

In his earpiece he heard the martial, new-age theme they had commissioned. Above him he heard guffawing. From that place. Those thugs upstairs.

"This is Mindy St. Michaels from the studios of KCKK in downtown St. Paul."

"And this is Brad Wilson, reporting live from here in St. Paul's vibrant but troubled Summit/University neighborhood."

What was that noise? That thumping?

"For a while now I've been living right here in the heart of the community, in the humble, but comfortable building you see behind me. I've gotten to know the neighbors and the neighborhood."

That thumping. Not on the wire. The damn stereo upstairs.

"Over the next few weeks I'll be introducing you to some of the people and places that comprise our interesting community."

Damn them. Maybe it didn't carry.

"You'll meet my neighbors. You'll hear firsthand about their challenges and triumphs. We hope you'll learn something, we hope you'll be informed, and we hope you'll be encouraged to find out more about the city we call home."

Loud stereos were not the kind of spontaneous event that made a career.

"In a moment I'll introduce you to a lifetime resident of the community—a woman who has an interesting perspective on how Summit/University has changed over the years. First, back to Mindy for today's top stories."

"Thanks, Brad."

"You're clear!" Katy shouted over Mindy's reading of the latest from the Balkans.

He swung open the door and met Ted coming down the steps. "What's that shit," he said indicating the bass from the speakers.

"I know," Ted said, holding out his palms to calm him. "I just came from up there."

"Well?"

"They won't answer the door."

He started up the steps but was blocked by Ted. "No time. Get down there with the old lady. Hold her hand. We'll deal with this. It's very faint down there anyway."

"Shit." Wasn't there always something you forgot about, something you couldn't plan for?

What was that bastard's problem, anyway? He'd only seen him around the building once or twice. Hadn't seen him at all today. They were typical. Choice, grade-A, died-in-the-wool lowlife. The kind made folks roll up their car windows and lock their doors when any of the rest of us walked past.

"About three minutes, Brandon," Katy said. "Mindy's just cued the student-walkout story. There's two other short pieces and then it's you."

"Thanks."

Didn't seem to work at all, their kind. Probably got some sort of general-assistance check—from *his* tax money.

"Is it time? Is it time?" Mrs. Carter said. She was trembling and as fluttery as a baby bird. He put his arm around her.

"You are terrific, you know that?" He hugged her to him, giving her a reassuring shake. "Come sit by me. Sit right here, and we'll do it."

The kind that probably took advantage of sweet old things like this. Snatched her pocketbook, made her unable to leave her own home after dark.

"I look okay?" she asked.

"Let's see. Hair, beautiful. Clothes, beautiful. You got your mike on, and your face is just perfect. Perfect. Take a deep breath."

She did and the lens of the camera lowered toward the sofa and flashed its red light.

"Stand by," Katy said.

"Look at me," he told her.

"And now back to Brad Wilson, at his Summit/University home."

"Thanks, Mindy. And sitting here with me is one of my neighbors, Mrs. Cora Carter, and when we come back from the commercial she'll be sharing with us her lifetime of experience as a community resident. Stay with us. We'll be right back."

"Clear."

He dashed out the door. He had exactly one minute and fifty seconds. There was no way he could focus on talking to the old woman with that . . . annoyance—that's all it was. It was like a minor toothache or a lump in a mattress. You could ignore it, but you didn't expect to concentrate on anything as long as you were aware of it. He bolted up the steps and pounded on the door.

"Turn it down!"

"Brandon!" Ted called after him. "Man, what are you doing? There's hardly a minute."

He pounded on the door again. He saw Nita coming down the hall.

"One minute!"

He shook his head at Nita and pointed to the door, pleading with his hands before charging back down the steps. He snagged a heel on the bottom step, turning his ankle. He limped over and sat down next to Mrs. Carter."

"Thought I was gonna have to go on without you," she whispered, chuckling.

"You'd do a fine job, too."

"Back in ten . . ."

"Yeah, I would."

"Look at me again," he said, ignoring the throbbing in his leg. "Cue Brad."

And just then the drumming of the bass ceased.

"Back with Mrs. Cora Carter. Mrs. Carter, how long have you lived in Summit/University?"

Damn, I'm cool, he thought. Just as calm and together as if this were a cocktail party.

"I was born here. Been here all my life. You don't want me to tell my age, do you?"

"Now, we'd never ask you to do that. Tell us how you've seen the neighborhood change over the past fifty or so years."

"Let's see," she said. She looked down thoughtfully, but only for a second. Like most folks these days, she knew dead air was a killer. "Well, for starters there's a lot more people here now than when I was coming up. Back then you knew all your neighbors. Everybody looked after each other."

"And it's still a rather close-knit community. Earlier today Mrs. Carter took us on a tour of her neighborhood."

"Cue tape. You're clear, Brandon."

The old lady collapsed against him and giggled.

"You're doing fine," he told her. Ted gave them the okay sign. Brandon had gotten so he didn't even have to count a one-minute-twenty-second tape. There was a certain rhythm you got into. He hoped the montage of faces and images was not too facile, would encourage some people out there to tune in again.

"Ten, Brandon."

"Yeah. Here we go, Mrs. Carter. Just a short talk here and we're done for now."

"Cue."

"It's a wonderful part of the city, as you can see. Now, Mrs. Carter: you have basically lived right around this block your whole life?"

"Back a ways most of us were clustered together by where the freeway came through. Street called Rondo Avenue and a couple of blocks either side of that. That's what really changed things, putting the highway through."

"How did it change things?"

"Folks moved away. Scattered. More and more new folks come in. Then it got where you didn't know your neighbors and didn't nobody care. People got to look out for each other."

"So, you'd say that what makes a community work is people looking out for each other."

"Yeah, I just said that."

"Okay, Mrs. Carter." Brandon laughed his TV laugh. Feisty old thing. They'd *better* love her out there. "Tell us what the biggest problem is you see around here these days?"

174

"It ain't nothing new. It's these wild kids and young folks don't got no manners or sense. They the ones make the trouble. I imagine they got em all over town, though."

"I imagine you're right about that. Our community here faces a lot of the same problems as the rest of the city, only, as Mrs. Carter says, compounded by poverty and race. We'll have some closing thoughts at the end of our program. Back to you Mindy."

"Brad?"

"Yes, Mindy"

"Tell Mrs. Carter she looks fabulous for her age."

"I'll do that."

"And, we'll be back with the weather right after this."

"Clear."

"How she know how old I am?"

"She's just being nice, Mrs. Carter."

"And where did you hear me say anything about race and poverty? I don't recall no such thing."

"Well . . ." Well, she hadn't, but he had to say something. He beckoned Ted into the bedroom. "What a piece-of-crap interview."

"It was fine. The old lady was perfect. Perfect."

Brandon was incredulous. "You really believe people out there want to hear some crone reminisce about the good old days? Dexter's in his office shitting a brick right now. We're all fired."

"Calm down. We're building this thing, remember? This man-of-the-people stuff. You got to soft peddle at first. If you start off digging in garbage cans and hitting too hard, it turns people off. The old lady's perfect. Trust me."

"Son, you better be right. And I'm telling you, Dexter will be all over our ass tomorrow."

"We'll handle him."

"Or he us. Look, I got to lay down—my ankle's killing me."

"Want some ice?"

"Nah. Just go out there and keep Grandma happy. Give me till two."

Brandon leaned his head back on his special bolster pillow, the one he had found that was perfect for protecting his hair at moments such as this. There was nothing worse than pillow hair, except for maybe hat hair. Some more shit black folks had to worry about. He knew people who slept in various bizarre kinds of elaborate head gear to keep their hair looking good—helmets, styrofoam shields, plastic bags. People who looked like they just got off the spaceship from Mars. Men and women. And don't even talk about winter. Some folks would freeze their ears off before they wore a hat that might mash their "do" down. Probably why there weren't too many black folks up here in the first place. One thing black folks wouldn't put up with was hat hair.

Maybe dreadlocks were the thing. Dreadheads didn't seem to need to do nothing to that mess. But somebody else would have to cross the dreads line on TV—be the first. Maybe Bryant would do it and then it would clear the way for the rest of us. Nah, never. We'd all just continue with the same old nappy mess, Bryant included.

Maybe he should just be bald, like Montel. That would work. But no, he had one of those funny shaped heads—boxy, and with a big forceps indentation in the back where the big monster got stuck coming out of his mama. He was gonna be worrying after this nappy mess the rest of his life.

In his earpiece he heard the new weather guy teasing and jiving about a possible late-spring snowfall. Perfect. Slush in the middle of chaos. You could never imagine a winter so long. Starting in November, sometimes October even. Lasting until April, occasionally longer. Half the damn year. No, it wasn't always hundreds of degrees below zero, and no, it didn't snow every day. It was just so . . . unendingly brown and white and sterile, so empty and dead.

Old Man Winter had made him crazy, had already driven most of the natives nuts—in a harmless and endearing sort of way. It was the kind of crazy like the crazy aunt every family has. The loud aunt who wears inappropriate colors and gaudy hats, the one who flew by herself to Vegas two or three times a year to play the slots, the nosy one who everyone hoped would behave herself at Christmas dinner. Up here crazy folks did things such as build little houses out of plywood, complete with beds and appliances, and set those little houses out on the lake and then drill a hole in the lake and sit around a space heater, fishing. In January. When it was fifty below. People did that. And they had a big festival in the middle of winter called the "Winter Carnival" with a parade and everything, and if you could be even remotely considered some sort of local celebrity, you were expected to ride in an open convertible. At night. In a blizzard. Waving to the crowds. People expected that. And then the first day the temperature went above forty degrees, out people came, shirtless, pasty white, with the barbecue grills and the frisbees. They did that, too. It was some sort of mass psychosis this climate produced. This craziness transcended boundaries of race and class. When the snow fell and the wind blew thirty-five miles an hour off the north pole, you were nothing but a Minnesotan. Like any decent natural disaster, the climate drew folks together. It was something everyone could talk about, something everyone could share. Shit! They had to share it. This Dexter wanted to exploit the differences between people. But in the good old U.S.A.—a country founded on the belief that some people are superior to others and therefore had rights that others don't have—wasn't the real story the similarities between us, the common ground, the things we all suffered together? Such as the fact that skin—any and all skin—froze in mere seconds in a sixty-below windchill. For too many people that was still news.

"Two minutes," Katy said.

He twisted up from the bed. "Katy."

"Yeah, Brandon."

"Dexter on the floor?"

"Three o'clock, ten feet."

"How's he look?"

"Blank as slate. On the couch, fast. Mindy's early."

Mrs. Carter extended her arms as if to a lover. "Let's go, sugar."

He took her hands.

"It'll be over soon," he said, not sure whether he was comforting her or himself.

"I could do this every night."

Fat chance, he thought.

"For some closing thoughts, back to Brad Wilson on Marshall Avenue. Brad."

"Thanks Mindy. You know, a neighborhood like Summit/University is a microcosm of the entire metropolitan area. We have rich and poor and people of every different ethnic and religious background. This is a strong community, facing the challenges of the nineties. I want to invite you to stay tuned over the next few weeks as, with the help of my good friend Mrs. Carter, we'll be getting to know Summit/University and its people. What's the best thing about living here, Mrs. Carter?"

"Oh, the good people, I guess."

"Good folks like you." He clasped her hand between his and shook it. "You'll come back and see us again?"

"Any time."

"Any last comments for the folks out there?"

"Yes, I want to say to the crooks and thieves and drug pushers to stay out from up in here. We not gonna have that no more. That's all."

"That about says it. Thank you, Mrs. Carter. That's it for today. Wishing you a pleasant good evening, and we'll see you here tomorrow, live at five, on Newscenter 13. Mindy."

"Brandon, you're clear."

"See you tomorrow, Brad. And from New York, here's News Around the World."

"Cue network feed. Aaaaannnd . . . we're out. Nice job, everyone."

"Thanks."

Brandon plucked out the earpiece and dropped it down his shirt. He sat forward so the technician couldn't thread it from his waist. "Thank you, ma'am," he said to Mrs. Carter. He patted her on the knee.

"What's this," she said, reaching up and pulling something pink from his hair. She handed him a piece of that damn tissue.

"Could you see that? Was that there?" He wanted to scream. This was supposed to be a new start, and now there would be another sackful of letters about his hair.

"Excuse me," he said. He stormed out the door and up the steps. The damn ankle slowed him down. He pounded on the door at the top of the steps.

"What's going on?" It was Nita, come from Mrs. Carter's door.

More pounding. Sipp opened the door.

"I believe this is yours," Brandon said. He tossed the pink confetti into Sipp's apartment, then felt like a fool watching the tissue dance in the air before fluttering to the ground.

Sipp sneered at him. "You want something?"

"Yeah, I want something. I want to know what your damn problem is."

"You the one pounding on doors. That makes you the one with a problem."

Brandon rubbed one hand around another which had made itself into a fist. This was one of those ignorant black ones. One of those thought they were hot stuff with their gaudy gold jewelry and gold teeth and nasty attitude.

"I'd appreciate it if you'd keep some of this damn noise down when folks are trying to work and sleep and live."

"I don't hear no noise. Afternoon, Miss Nita. You hear some noise, Miss Nita?"

Ape grinned at her like she was some street tramp he was trying to pick up.

"They turned it down right when I asked them to. Thank

you, Sipp. We appreciate it," she went around Brandon and took his arm.

"It's disrespectful," Brandon said. "Somebody ought to . . ."

"Ought to what? I pay rent here. What you gonna do?"

"Look, boy . . ."

"Boy? Boy, you say?"

"Come on Brandon. Sipp, I'll see you later. Let's go. Now." She dragged Brandon to the stairs and down to the first landing. He held the bastard's glare all the way.

"Yeah, I'll be seeing you, Nita." Sipp pointed at Brandon. "Later."

She opened the door to her place and guided him inside.

"All that was unnecessary," she says. "With all else, I don't need feuding in the building. I won't have it."

"I'm sorry. I lost my temper. Fool threw a bunch of garbage out the window just before we went on the air."

She laughed.

"It's not funny."

"Well, actually it was. Kids and I cracked up. You should have seen yourself batting at that mess."

"That could have ruined the show."

"But, it didn't. It was fine."

"Really?"

"Really. I only seen y'all a couple times before, but it was like a whole different show today. And Mrs. Carter . . . boy."

"She did okay?"

"I felt like she was speaking for everybody around here. She was so dignified and calm. Sure made me proud."

"So you really think it was okay?"

"I said that, didn't I?"

"Thank you. Means a lot coming from you."

She was animated in a way he'd never seen before. Usually there was something hard and cold about her, but today she seemed excited, almost bubbly. This way she was much prettier than he'd first thought. She had beautiful eyes. The black, black kind these dark-skinned girls sometimes had. When her face opened up this way, her eyes shone out like jewels. Nice figure, too, with a little flesh on it. A cute, broad smile she had, but not even now, happy, was she gonna show any teeth. She wasn't bad at all, really. Not bad at all.

"I didn't mean to cause trouble. I just get hot. I don't like people messing with my work." Or my hair, he thought.

"I'll take care of them. Won't be any more problems."

"They don't bother you? It doesn't worry you, living downstairs from that?"

"They're not so bad. Just young and foolish. You know how that goes."

"They seem like some tough customers."

"I can handle them. Don't you worry."

"You'd do that for me?" He smiled at her, raised his eyebrows. He saw what he thought must pass for a blush on a girl her color. She turned away from him, walked down her hall. She returned wheeling the vacuum cleaner.

"You got work to do," she said.

TV
Guide

· · · · · · · · · · · · · ·

She hated to admit it, but there was something kind of exciting about all the TV stuff. The equipment, the hustle and bustle. Even though they put on a show every day, it seemed as if there was always a crisis, always something unexpected going on. Despite herself—though she knew she had better things to do—she found herself hanging around to watch them set up. She admired the way, despite the craziness, everybody seemed to keep pretty cool about the whole thing. She'd watched one of the big fellows drop a lamp of some kind yesterday as he pulled it from a van in the alley. The shattered glass had spread across the asphalt in tiny shards. He and another guy had had a good laugh and talked about how it would be coming out of Brandon's paycheck. It would be nice to be able to laugh about your job. At the store, during Christmas rush or during a good sale, folks just got nasty and testy, and she got so that she didn't even want to come in with the temper tantrums and carrying-on. These TV folks seemed to enjoy what they did.

Still, she had doubts about them being around. Not because of Skjoreski. She had been worried about him being mad, but he told her that he loved the whole thing. You'd think it was him they had on the air instead of this old raggedy building. He'd been hanging around every afternoon trying to see if he could find a way to get into the picture.

Something, though, just wasn't right. The TV business gave her an odd feeling, like that déjà-vu thing people always sang about. The feeling that what was happening had happened before. She would be sitting up in her place or up at Mrs. Carter's watching the television, except what was on the television was going on right in her basement or right outside the front door. She'd actually sat in her front window looking back and forth from the television to him and back to the television. She remembered being confused about which was real. And which was better. And she wondered if because she was seeing both was she seeing something different than others got to see. Or something more. Did she know something that other people did not?

More than that, there was a . . . discomfort, a queasiness in her stomach she felt when she thought about the folks she'd seen on TV this week. Tuesday he did a story about the pick-up basketball games over at the rec center, and on Wednesday he had talked to the Reverend and some of the members over at the church on the other side of the freeway, on Aurora. He was talking to folks she saw every day—at the store or walking themselves up and down the street. Folks she went to school with. Suddenly they were all on TV, part of the news, talking like they had something to say. She'd always thought the news was supposed to be about people in trouble or people who were more important than anyone else. These was just plain folks. Like her. And she wished she could put her finger on what bothered her about watching them. Something was up. These TV people were smart folks with a lot of money. They wouldn't just come to Marshall Avenue and waste it for no reason.

She wrapped the sweet potato pie in foil to carry up to Mrs. Carter. She'd been nice enough to let them watch her monitors during the broadcast. A little sweetness would pay her back. The TV people had left the sets there, and Mrs. Carter really thought she was the producer, too, the way she was carrying on. Nita figured they put the toys up there to keep the snoopy wench busy while they were getting their work done. Bless her heart. She loved all the attention, and she'd been good about letting the kids sit with her. Nita had figured, what the hell, why even try to keep the kids quiet, might as well get with the program. It wouldn't kill them to be out of the apartment an hour or two for a few weeks. They liked Mrs. Carter. They loved helping her direct the show.

Nita surprised herself. She would have guessed that she would be furious, thought she would have been down there asking that man and them people who in the hell did they think they was, disrupting her children's routines like this? But there was something fun about all this—something like when the carnival came to town and everybody acted wild for a few days.

Sometimes she tiptoed down and peeked out her apartment window to catch a glimpse of what was going on. Or she sat quietly on her couch to listen to what she could hear from below. Despite her misgivings, she was attracted to the fun. Today at work she actually found herself looking forward to getting home, to seeing who would be interviewed tonight, what the story was going to be.

She handed Mrs. Carter the pie, telling the kids there was one for them downstairs after they'd had their supper.

"This fool on camera 3 plays around too much. We gonna have to replace him."

Nita laughed. "Let's get Marco that job. He's ready to work, aren't you boy?"

Marco nodded his head vigorously. Mrs. Carter had him keeping count of something on a piece of paper with tally marks. The girls played Barbies on the floor.

"Who's on today," Nita asked.

"We got this girl what runs the children's theater over here on Selby. You know where I'm talking about?"

Nita knew the place. Rainbo, they called it. She wanted to see about the girls going over there, but she'd been afraid to ask. It might cost too much and there was no money in her budget for such frills.

"Should be sort of interesting today. We gonna try interviewing her out back. Just up the alley a bit where Miles got those evergreens. Little different background for a change. Was my idea."

Nita rolled her eyes. "Mrs. Carter, let me ask you . . ."

"Shhhh, we're on. Play my song!"

While the theme pounded away Nita watched the fast-paced, jerky little movie of Brandon and that ugly Mindy St. Michaels and some of the other white folks that worked there. She didn't know who this Mindy thought she was kidding with that red dye in her hair. Should have spent the money on a mask. Nothing in the little movie lasted more than a second. The whole thing was no more than a half minute long, and they had Brandon running down the street and snatching a paper from somebody and laughing at somebody's joke and just smiling. She figured it was supposed to make you see how busy he was, but judging on what she'd seen around here, he was the least busy of them all. The folks with the cameras and the lights were the only ones she saw running. Mrs. Carter threw more switches than he did.

While the film was flashing, on the other monitor the folks sat facing the cameras with their faces blank and dumb, looking like animals do just before you run over them with your car.

The camera moved in on Brandon in the basement and suddenly his face changed to excited looking. Like someone had flipped a switch on him. Good thing he got rid of the polo shirt. Folks didn't like to see us looking *too* casual. Think we're the caddy or the gardener or something. Today he wore one of those nice-looking crewneck sweaters—they had those at a good price at Wards—$19.95—but she bet this one didn't come from there and probably cost a lot more than that. His pullover, a little lighter than a navy color, looked nice on him, too. It brought out his skin tones good. He had that kind of beige colored skin that had some red in it—around his cheeks particularly. Her mama had always told her that meant you had Indian blood in you somewhere. Rae Anne, she was even fairer than Brandon, but Marco and Didi were dark skinned, like her.

She hoped that Rae Anne wouldn't get the big head about being fair. Already folks would pet her and tell her how pretty she was and ask her if she was a mulatto, her sister sitting right there beside her being ignored. Didi was every bit as cute—cuter in fact—with her big dark eyes and those long lashes around them. She was an ebony jewel, and it made Nita sick that folks looked over her to her white-looking sister. Was gonna be a mess balancing this out—building Didi up while keeping Rae Anne's feet on the ground, convincing both girls that what was special about them didn't have nothing to with the fact that folks had a thing about skin color.

"Here's that Merline," Mrs. Carter said. "I sent them over to her, you know."

"They're lucky to have you, honey."

Just like Mrs. Carter had said, Brandon was interviewing the drama teacher out in the alley in front of the pine trees. Their faces caught the late afternoon sunlight and a slight breeze waved the tree branches behind them. They could be at a resort instead of in an alley behind some dump in St. Paul.

"All right, let's cue up the tape," Mrs. Carter said, and Nita wondered who she thought she was talking to. On the broadcast, children full of energy sang pop songs and danced like they were on a music video. On monitor 1 Brandon smiled at the woman and moved his fingers around on her arm. He must be encouraging her, Nita thought, and trying to keep her calm. Or maybe he was just feeling her up, she couldn't tell. Mrs. Carter had turned the sound to the broadcast and Nita was afraid to ask her to flip it so she could eavesdrop, afraid she might sound too interested or nosy. Brandon and the teacher looked like characters in a movie, animated and happy, or at least he did. The woman, pretty and artsy, carried a head full of wild, free-looking hair, wound in a beautiful scarf. She dressed in flowing and flattering clothes, but somehow looked out of place on the screen. He, on the other hand, looked as if he were born to be there. Here he was beside this beautiful woman, and it was almost like she couldn't even be seen. Everything about him seemed made to be viewed, the way his body was placed, the turn of his head, the way he moved.

"Cue Brandon!" Mrs. Carter said.

"Mrs. Carter, where did you learn all this TV mess."

The old lady gave her a dirty look.

"I was just asking. You don't need to get an attitude."

She flipped to monitor 2. "Does she look like she's ready to you?" Mrs. Carter asked.

Mindy tossed her new red hair back and forth and sang "I'm gonna wash that man right out of my hair."

Nita was annoyed. She wanted to hear what Brandon was asking the teacher, maybe hear the clue as to why they were down here in the first place.

"You're on!" Mrs. Carter shouted, and, as if she'd heard her, Mindy turned instantly calm, professional, and appropriate. It really was like they had switches attached to their brains.

"There," Mrs. Carter said, letting out a big breath, slumping over.

"We did it," Marco said.

Nita felt the relief too, but she didn't know why.

"You probably didn't hear me when I told you I brought you up a pie."

"Did you? The boys and I will share it later."

Nita guessed that the boys must be some of those men downstairs. "Tell me what you really think about this mess going on in our building."

"I'm having the time of my life."

"I don't mean this stuff and your . . . advice. I mean what you think about them being *here*. Showing *us*."

Mrs. Carter sat back in her chair and gave Nita the once over. "You ask that like it bothered you."

"No . . . well . . . you know, I'm not sure. I think that's why I'm asking."

"I guess I don't see a problem with it. Wouldn't be doing it if I did."

Nita searched around the room with her eyes, searching for some words. "It's just . . . I don't understand what's so interesting to them. I watched TV my whole life. Why all of the sudden are they interested in what goes on over here? It's like they just landed on a new planet and discovered black folks."

Mrs. Carter laughed. "I know what you're saying. But you're looking at it the wrong way. Way I see it is, they never been here before, and I have lived long enough that I can tell you I wouldn't be waiting for them to be back any time soon. Not in my lifetime or yours."

"So?"

"So they're here and we got our chance and we'd best take it."

"Don't you worry they may be up to something?"

"Does it matter? Up to something or not, I got a chance to put on my best suit and go on the television and let them know people in this community stand for quality. Didn't cost me a red cent, neither."

"But they're making it seem so . . . easy. People work *hard* around here to try and keep it decent. Why aren't they showing them?"

"You got a story? Go on down there and tell him. He'll put it on if he can."

"Maybe I will."

She ought to. Ought to go on down there and tell him what to put on. Get some of her ideas out there.

"Sign off in two. Go on down there."

Nita started down the stairs. She felt rather foolish, the same way she felt back in school when she was trying to do something such as get on the teacher's good side by erasing the boards or watering the plants.

"Nita!" Sipp said. He lay on his couch, bare-chested, the door open for all to see. Like he'd been waiting for her.

"Ain't seen you hardly at all this week," he said.

"Been busy. How about you?"

"You know how it be. Just being me. Say, you still ain't told me what this mess is I'm supposed to be quiet for."

"Just some TV stuff." She hadn't remembered seeing a set in his place.

"What kind of TV stuff? Sit down a minute. Come on."

"I'm kinda busy. You want to know so bad, go on down there ask yourself."

"Let that yellow nigger get in my face again, only question I got for him is how far he wants me to kick him in his white-looking behind."

"You'll do no such thing. Not in my house." She said it flirtatiously. Any bit of charm to keep the peace.

"Sit. Sit."

She perched on the arm of the couch, the only furniture in the room, aside from some empty bright-colored milk crates. And that huge stereo.

"You still mad at me from Monday?"

"What I got to be mad about?"

"What I told you. What I'm gonna do." His eyes seemed to pierce her. "Well?"

"Well. You told me. You're gonna do it. What else you want from me?"

"I told you what I want."

"Look, I can't help you. I won't. That's final." She made the words into a hammer, a brick. She pushed them out hard. She headed toward the door.

He came up behind her, draped an arm across her shoulder, brushing her breast. "Come with me, then."

The arm drew her toward him. He was warm, moist, sweet smelling.

"Where?"

"Home."

He pulled her around to face him and tried to kiss her. She turned her head away and felt his mouth graze her cheek and her ear. She pushed him away.

"I don't hardly know you."

"I know you. I know what I want."

She wandered over to his front window and peered at the few curious folks hanging out to get a glimpse of the show. Old folks and little kids for the most part.

"You act like nobody ever loved you," he said.

"It's too fast. You confusing me."

He threw his hands up, a mild surrender. "No more pressure then. Offer's good. Stays good. Take your time. Think."

"And that other mess?" she asked, facing him again, tilting her head, daring him.

"I should have kept that apart from us. My mistake."

"But you didn't."

He lay back on the couch.

"Go on," she prompted.

"It's on. Friday week. Like I said."

"And . . ."

"It's in and out of here. I collect my cash. I'm done. Gone."

"Just like that."

"Just like that."

She lowered her head. "I was on my way to do something." She opened the door.

"Nita."

"What."

"Think of yourself for a change."

"I always do." She stared at him for a minute and then started downstairs.

Fine. Just fine, she thought. What was she supposed to do about some shit like this? Was it even serious? What if the man really did want her, kids and all? Wanted to take her some place and build a life together, wanted her despite everything? Where in the hell did this come from in the first place, out of the blue, and why now? Maybe she was just part of some game he was playing. What did she even know about him except that he was from Mississippi?

. . . drove an old beat-up piece of a Ford. Liked funk and blues music. Liked to take it easy. Had been kind to her, always. Told her he liked her, loved her, wanted her, and here she hadn't even put nothing out for him. Was warm and firm and black and beautiful.

. . . and he could be anyone. He could have a girl like her with a bunch of kids in three different states. He could be wanted for murder, AWOL from the army, hiding from the police.

. . . was a dealer. He had told her that. Told her, knowing she could destroy him with that information. That meant something. . . . Anybody loved me, he'd wondered. And me, anybody? How did that feel? Like this, this burning in my chest, this attraction, this fear? Maybe this was just about wanting something else, about wanting away from here. Maybe I should wait for lightning to strike. Or however that feeling was supposed to feel. She could wait the rest of her life and that might never happen. Maybe this would be the last offer she got.

"Nita."

"Huh? Oh, hi."

"Hi." Brandon smiled, showing her his bright white teeth. She blocked his doorway, mind gone blank, and remembered somewhere she had a reason for being there. Some reason.

"I enjoyed the show," she said softly.

"Well, thanks. I always appreciate a fan."

She lingered, addled, eyes roaming around.

"Anything else? You all right?"

"Oh. You know, I was thinking. About your show, I mean."

"Yeah?"

"Yeah, well, I was wondering if maybe you ought to show some other stuff around here."

"Such as?"

"I don't know. I was thinking there are a lot of folks up and down here spend a lot of time making sure folks are taken care of. You know what I mean?"

"Social services? Sure."

"Welfare? No, that ain't happening. I mean ordinary folks."

"You know someone like that?"

"I know this lady over on Selby. I work with her niece. She runs her own little food shelf right out her house. If folks have trouble feeding their kids, she has stuff for them. You just go over there and knock."

"That's a great story, Nita. We'll do it. Tomorrow. Ted! Get out here."

Ted stuck his head out the door of the bedroom.

"Bump the professor to Monday. We got a live one."

Nita couldn't believe it was so simple, that this was how you get on TV.

"You working tomorrow?" Brandon asked.

"Yeah?"

"Get off early. You'll be on the news."

"No, I couldn't do . . ."

"Don't worry about the money. Okay?"

"No, it's just, I'm not the kind who . . ."

"Think about it, then."

Nita wasn't sure she wanted or needed one more thing to think about.

"Can we go meet this lady now?"

"She's usually there."

"Let's go. Introduce me. And, that's all I want you to do on the air tomorrow. Introduce us. That's all. You can handle that, can't you?"

"I . . ."

"Sure you can. You're gonna be famous all over town. Just leave it to me."

The
Brothers
at
Five

. . . .

Who was that shriveled-up wench you had
on last night. I know her. She ain't nothing but
an old heifer. You want a person of quality,
have me on. I sent you my phone number and
picture. I expect to hear from you tomorrow.

Hattie Conaway
Maplewood

"Don't be nervous," Brandon said. He gave Nita a hug. These
ordinary people responded to a little physical reassurance, being
hugged or petted before the cameras rolled. They wanted you
to reach out and fix a lapel or remove a piece of lint. They appre-
ciated a laugh or a joke before the interview. He preferred just
to stand there, saving his charm for the camera, but when you
worked with nonprofessionals you had to do everything you
could to make sure they didn't fuck things up. Once, on location
at a school-board meeting, he had snagged one of the members
for a reaction. The poor guy could hardly speak, he was so nervous. Brandon had to make most of his statement for him while
the guy stood there and moved his lips.

Nita was as nervous as anyone in a long time. She was breathing
deep and fast, in and out—he hoped she didn't hyperventilate—
and he could feel her trembling. Perhaps this had been a mistake,

talking her into this. But she was telegenic—in that "real people" sort of way—and her presence had really helped to put Miss Eva at ease.

They had set up on the screen porch of Miss Eva's house on Selby Avenue. At the cue he would introduce the piece, and then Nita would ring the doorbell and present him and the viewers to Miss Eva. The woman's name was Eva Phillips, and as much as Brandon insisted on calling her Ms. Phillips or Mrs. Phillips, she wouldn't allow it. She said everyone in the neighborhood called her Miss Eva, and if she was going on TV that's how she wanted to be known. Brandon hated calling folks Mr. Tom and Miss Carol and Miss Eva. His father had told him that that habit was one of those left over from the way black folks in the South talked to each other and that it marked you as ignorant. But if that's what the woman wanted . . .

"Hope I remember my lines," Nita said. She waved her hands around as if she had just finished some kind of exercise routine.

"This isn't a play, and there's no right way to do it. Ignore the camera if you can. Pretend like I'm a friend and you're introducing me to someone you know. Do it just like you did when we came over here yesterday."

"You make it sound so easy."

"Shhhh. That's the secret. It *is* easy and the more plain and simple you make it, the more *they* like it."

He pointed toward the viewers out in television land. He put on his most reassuring face, the one he'd used at the end of the Gulf War and during the Midwest floods and the California earthquakes to assure everyone that things were under control. She bought it, or her face betrayed that she did. It was only a little lie. Yeah, you kept it simple, but anyone who thought that sitting out there every night trying to appear trustworthy and as if you knew what you were talking about was easy, or that boiling an enormously complicated story such as the federal deficit down to a thirty-second news story required just a pleasant demeanor and a friendly voice, was a fool. People had this idea it was just glamour and being cool, and for some of them—like Mindy—it was. She dolled up, you handed her some news to read, she sounded good, and everyone was happy. But when you really tried to do the job, you worked your butt off. You could never predict where the pitfalls would come even in a simple assignment like this one. It ought to be a cakewalk—a sharp story with a lot of human-interest appeal, a snappy backgrounder already in the can. The only live feed was the teaser, a quick set-up, and a couple of interview questions either side of the tape. Still, anything could happen. A ringing phone. A bulletin from New York.

Miss Eva was another natural—warm and friendly and straightforward. More and more that was the case. People these days had had something bred into them, some new sixth sense that told them how to act in front of the camera. They knew not to smile too much, and to look at the person they were talking to and not at the camera, and to keep it short, and not to do something uncool like say hello to your kids. Nita was the first one in a long time who threatened to not make it. On what could have been a smooth ride, she was the shorted-out cable, blown lightbulb, the low-flying plane over an open mike.

"Keep doing that," he said of her flailing hands. "As a matter of fact, do more. Jump up and down. Run in place. Shake out all your limbs."

"I can't," she said. She averted her face in embarrassment.

"Come on. No one's looking." He thought it best not to mention that back in the control room and on that old console he'd dumped up at Mrs. Carter's, any number of people could see and hear everything.

She started shaking and jumping and running.

"That's right, burn it up. The excess energy. You know, when we work we're running all over the place anyway before the telecast to make sure everything's ready. That eats up the nerves. Keep going. Looking good." She did look good, too. She'd pressed her hair or something so it wasn't as unkempt as he'd seen it, and she wore a lovely crimson dress and a matching scarf. Red wasn't the best shade for the camera—it was going to swallow up her face, particularly with her complexion—but it dazzled him in the afternoon light. He delighted in a woman who knew what made her look good. Sandra was one of those women. She had one of those color charts hanging in her closet that told her what her best shades were, and she loaded up on all kinds of products advertised in *Essence* and on BET that were designed specifically for black women. Nita had a ways to go in that department, but she did pretty well with what she had. It cost a lot to keep up with a woman like Sandra.

"Okay, in about two," he said, pressing his earpiece in further.

"Oh, God." Nita raised her eyes, appealing to the heavens for assistance. The last of her energy filtered from her fingers, and they were still. He hoped she didn't go rigid. That's another thing amateurs did.

"Let's go through it one more time, quick. I'll talk, introduce you. Then *you* say?"

"Uh . . . I want to . . . I'd like to have you meet one of my neighbors who does so much for the community."

"That's perfect." Without the stammer he prayed. "And then you introduce us the same way you did before."

He came and stood beside her, laid an arm across her shoulder.

"Got us?" he asked the cameraman. "Relax, now. We're almost ready. Now when that red light comes on I want you to remember who you are. You are Bonita Sallis and today you are making yourself a beautiful gift to the world. Okay?"

"Okay," she said, and her face opened up with one of those looks of exterior bravado that the brashest kid in the school play puts on opening night. You saw one thing, but your radar told you something else. Hang in there, girl, he thought. Just hang in there.

He convinced her to celebrate at a fancy cafeteria on Grand Avenue. The place was six blocks from her house and he couldn't believe she'd never seen it. She acted awed and a little intimidated by the designer salads and soups.

"You can get a plain ham sandwich," he'd told her, and though she seemed irritated at his advice, that's what she got, along with a cup of gussied-up tomato soup. She appeared satisfied with her choices.

"You were wonderful," he said, toasting her with his apple juice.

"I don't think I ever been that nervous. I can't believe I let you talk me into that."

"First time's always the hardest."

"My first and my last time."

"No! I think you got a career ahead of you, young lady." He framed her with his fingers. "Did you enjoy it?"

"It wasn't too bad. Yeah, I had fun."

"Good. It's no good if you don't enjoy it. You gonna finish that sandwich?"

"Why, you want it?" she laughed. Then, "No. I need to get back. You know."

"Mrs. Carter can watch the kids for a while. Finish up. How often do you get to go out on your own?"

A shy downcast face served as his response.

"Go on. Finish up."

"Actually, it's just Marco. Mama has the girls. It's my Didi's birthday coming up. Mama wanted to have a little thing over at her house."

"I kept you from that? Why didn't you tell me? I'm sorry."

"No, no. This is Mama's little thing. She's having a sleep-over and I'm happy for the break. I'm gonna have my own party for Didi later on."

He observed something around her eyes—a relief or a release—that let him know it was true—she was happy for any break she could get. What a life this woman led. Working hard, going to school, kids. Especially the kids. With everything else in life, he didn't know how anyone dealt with adding kids to the mix. A few of the fast-track reporters and anchors he knew were dragging kids around, from market to market, from one year to the next. He'd seen more than enough of those marriages crumble, often enough because the wife just put her foot down, wasn't moving the family another inch. And he'd seen enough up-and-comers turn down a key post because they had a daughter in the last year of high school or a kid who had finally found a school that worked for him. He'd decided ten years ago he couldn't do that, to himself or to a child. More and more, lately, as he looked around at his siblings and at their broods, he had to will away a trickle of anxiety that flickered through him, a ripple of jealousy. He had a nephew, Roderick, of the most loving and gentle nature, and it was sometimes unbearable to visit his brother because there was a part of him that wanted to snatch the child away, to have him for his own. He wanted his own. He and Sandra had discussed it. Maybe, they'd said. If they could make it work. If he landed where he could stay a while. Maybe. Together the two of them could do it. Maybe.

"You have my admiration," he said.

"Cause I said a few words on TV? Thanks."

"No. Because you have a lot on your plate and you seem to handle it pretty well."

She dropped her eyes again, masking an expression he really couldn't read. Was it pique or just weariness?

"Did I say something?"

"No. It's just . . . It's not like it's what a person would do if she had a choice. A lot of days I feel like I'm digging my way out of the same hole as the day before. You never get anywhere."

"That's what I admire. Lots of folks give up. Or go on the fast fix. They wait for the lottery to save them or something. You're not one of those."

"You know so much about me?"

"I know what I see."

"What you see is one tired sister. That's all."

"And strong. What I see is strong. I like strong." He reached across the table and touched her arm.

They found Mrs. Carter pacing outside the building.

"Where you been? Something's happened." She wrapped her arms around Nita, smothering her. "Wasn't my fault," she sobbed. "I just left for a minute. I thought it be okay."

"My baby! Where's my baby!"

"His arm, that's all. Was an accident. I was just gone a minute. That Sipp was here."

Brandon untangled the old lady from Nita. "Where is he?"

She gasped for air and sobbed.

"Calm down and tell us where he is."

"Ramsey. Wasn't my fault."

"Let's go." They abandoned Mrs. Carter and headed to the hospital, breaking every traffic law in St. Paul. At the emergency room they saw the one from upstairs that Nita called Sipp. He was sprawled on a chair, drinking a Pepsi. She ran to him and Brandon went to the desk.

"Been looking for you all," Sipp said, loud enough for anyone to hear.

"Where's my son? What you do to my son?"

Brandon waited while the nurse on duty looked up the name. Sipp bent to Nita's ear and whispered something. Brandon guessed he was pleading his own case.

"Better not be!" Nita yelled.

Brandon watched Sipp hold his arms out in supplication and watched Nita push him away.

"Nita." Brandon signaled her to follow him and the nurse.

She said something to Sipp and he went away.

"Baby," Nita called. Clearly wanting to scoop him up, but not sure where to touch him, she petted him the way someone might pet a newborn chick. Marco was perched on a gurney, fresh plaster wrapping his arm, a big square bandage on his forehead. He was sucking something on a white stick.

"Look—orange," he said, pulling the sucker from his mouth. Brandon laughed. Kids, they were made out of rubber and steel. This little guy always had seemed to him the kind who could take on a tank.

"Mr. and Mrs. Sallis?" a woman said, poking her head in.

"I'm Ms. Sallis. This is my son."

Evidently Brandon was not to be introduced.

"Dr. Meier," the woman said, offering her hand. "Good strong boy you have here."

"Is he gonna be all right?"

"He'll be back hanging out of windows in no time."

"Hanging out of windows? Marco! I ought to kill you."

"We was just playing."

"I'd like to keep him tonight. That's a nasty break and he hit his head hard. I'd like to check everything again in the morning."

"I get two more suckers, Mama."

"Not if you don't lay down," Dr. Meier said. "I'll look in on him before I go. Nice meeting you all." She gave Brandon a look. Brandon wasn't sure whether it was because of who he was or who she thought he was in this situation. Whatever, he didn't care for being dismissed.

"Can I stay?" Nita asked in a quiet, almost pathetic voice.

"Through visiting hours, sure. We'll move him upstairs for you."

They stayed with Marco through the evening. He was brave and funny even, for a while, and then the pain reliever wore off. The nurse brought him another pill of some kind—which didn't do much good.

"It's gonna hurt, guy," she said. She was one of the brusque, efficient kind who brazened through the ward and saw her smart answers and snappy manner as a kind of sweet medicine.

"Suck on this," she said. She pulled out another lollipop.

Marco seemed to respond to something in the woman, seemed to forget his pain while she stood there harping at him.

Nita sat stroking her son's brow. Brandon could feel the tenderness flow from her fingers, a kind of nurturing and caring that made him weak inside. There was nothing for him to do—nothing he could think of to do—except stand there, sit there, move around the ward, watch. When he offered a lame joke or a silly anecdote, they responded with tolerant smiles. This was not his woman, his child, his family. He wasn't really needed at all. Still, he stayed and watched.

She sat there for two hours, hardly moving, caressing her child with a touch like velvet, cooing. This tableau, this painting, this frozen frame from the end of some movie, it touched some place inside him that he rarely had contact with.

After the nurses assured her they would check him diligently, after he had gotten her away—felt he had wrenched her away—he told her that she was beautiful with her child. She collapsed against him with heaving sobs. By the time they pulled into the alley, she had cried herself out but was still crumpled against him, breathing deep and slow. He helped her from the car and to her apartment. She fished for her keys, stepped inside her apartment and stopped—her open purse hung from her arm the way a toddler drags a doll. He waited. His arms wanted to reach to her, and they began to, and then dropped.

"Can I get you something?" he asked. "What can I do?"

He came around in front of her. Molasses-slow tears coursed her cheeks. She wore the sad, blank face of a person who had nothing left to lose. She took his hand and walked him down the short hallway to her room.

This? he thought.

She sat on the bed and he sat beside her. Her arms went around his waist and she leaned into him. He nuzzled her neck with his nose, brushed it with his lips.

Was this how this went? He hadn't thought of this.

She pulled his face around, finding his lips. She kissed him deep and hard. Her hands roamed his back, tugged at the hem of his shirt.

If she needs this, he thought.

When he entered her she recoiled with a spasm and he thought he had hurt her, but she surrounded him with her hips and pulled him down into her with her hands. She alternated sobs and moans, kissed at his collar bone, whimpered.

She fell asleep wrapped around his body as if he were a large doll. He was uncomfortable, her warm body draped across him, a hand clasping his arm, though not quite relaxed, her legs here and there. Still, he held her there, let her sleep and was at last overtaken himself by sleep.

In the morning she was gone.

He thought about her in Dexter's office, Monday morning. One of those things, he guessed. Maybe? He didn't know what to think. But she was there with him. At the meeting.

Dexter riffled the ratings book, heaved exasperated sighs.

"Not enough," he said.

"We're up," Brandon said. "We're out of the cellar, at least. Right there with the big three and closing fast." Brandon didn't want to be dealing with this crap. It had only been a week. What did Dexter expect, miracles?

Dexter had insisted on the meeting. He'd kept his hands out thus far, but now, Brandon guessed, came the time for tinkering.

"Watched you all last week," Dexter said.

"Yeah?"

Dexter sighed again. "You know what I wish right now. I wish more than anything I could tell you that what you did was complete horseshit. Really, like that would make my day more than you could believe."

Brandon just stared at him.

"Instead, you, you and this . . . what's the name of the tall prick we hired?"

"Ted."

"You and this Ted put together a first-rate operation. You got a world-class set, top-of-the-line equipment, cracker-jack staff. You even put some life into that cunt, Mindy."

"I'm supposed to say thanks, I guess."

"So, I don't get to ream your ass the way I'd like. I'll have to do something else for kicks today—hey, maybe I'll cancel those fucking 'M*A*S*H' reruns. That shit always got on my nerves."

"Get to the point, Dexter. I got work."

"Let's see . . . the point. Oh, yeah, the program still sucks."

"How so?"

"Well, it doesn't exactly suck. Much. It's just a little . . . I don't know. . . . It's like it's got some sort of a giant stick shoved up its ass. You know what I mean?"

"No. I have absolutely no idea what you're talking about."

"It's like this. You got most of the ideas in there, but you're missing the main deal somehow. Can I say something to you? Promise you won't get offended?"

You offend me by being on this earth, Brandon thought. He signaled him to proceed.

"See, here's the problem: you got too many black people and not enough niggers."

Brandon doubled over laughing. He didn't know where it was coming from. This guy. Just when you thought you'd heard the worst.

"You know what I'm saying. You got all these decent hard-working black folks. Salt-of-the-earth types. God love em—they're boring as shit. If you want 'The Ghetto Hour' to be a hit, you're gonna need to get yourself some niggers."

"Stop saying that word, man," he said through his laughter.

"You know what I'm saying, though?"

Brandon threw up his hands.

"Some of those Def Comedy Jam types. Some people got some edge on them. I told you, Brad, people have to see what you came from."

Brandon rose, shaking his head. There was no use saying anything to this guy. About anything.

"I'll see what I can do," he said.

Dexter waved his hand absentmindedly to dismiss him. He was already lost in the reports, circling this and highlighting that.

"This week," he muttered. "The brothers at five. Don't disappoint me, man."

The
Big
Payback

. . . .

Nita ran her fingers around Marco's head, touching him softly so as not to wake him. He was cool and dry, the same way he always was when he slept, even when he was the smallest baby. How fast that time had gone. Eight years, smooth and seamless, an almost graced childhood, this the first really rough road they'd hit. And he would come through it okay. They'd told her at the hospital that she should check for a temperature now and then and look in on him every hour or so and ask him where he was and if he felt dizzy. But he would be fine. The arm would heal and the bump on his head would subside. The hardest part, the doctor said, was that he would have to be patient while the arm knitted back together and she didn't want a whole lot of running around or roughhousing. She knew kids, this doctor. Getting Marco to be still would take plenty of effort, but so far he was the model patient. He'd never had a lot of pampering— lying in bed and having Mama bring him some chips or a glass of juice—and he had taken to it like he was born to it. He slept a lot. The doctor said that was to be expected; she'd even given Nita a few pills for the weekend "in case he got restless," but there were no plans to mask the pain. After telling Marco that what he was feeling was just his arm remembering the hurt, she'd told Nita that it was a good idea for him to get used to a little discomfort.

"People expect they can take something so they don't have to feel anything. Sometimes you can, but even so, a lot of times it's better not to. He's better off if he learns to live with a little pain. Next time it'll be easier."

Nita had nodded at her, passively. The words sounded awfully cold to her—how could it be good for you to feel pain? For a child particularly. For her child. If there was something she could give him to make the hurt go away, she'd do it and not think twice. Or to make it not have happened in the first place. Maybe the doctor was right, though. Life was gonna be tough. Maybe the sooner he got used to it—the sooner he learned to live with pain—the better for him.

Was a dangerous world out there. She didn't even like to think how bad. The things people told her that folks did to children— sometimes folks in the child's own family. And strangers! These fools out there, driving up and down the streets with their pants undone and that sort of mess. Sometimes she wished she could lock her children away, put them someplace safe until they were old enough to fend for themselves. If there were such places. And when would that time come?

Problem was, even if they got to where they could take care of themselves, they could never do it alone. Nita sure didn't. She had Mama. If Mama hadn't kept the girls another night it would have been awfully hard to look after her son. And Mrs. Carter, the poor old thing felt so bad and so guilty. Had spent her whole Saturday night and the next morning up there baking cookies and fixing other goodies for the boy. Drove herself so crazy Nita finally had to sit her down and tell her not to blame herself, though there was another part of her wanted to hold it over the old sister's head until she needed something from her. Make her feel good and guilty for running up the street for some catfish dinner she'd gotten word of. Naw, she couldn't do that. Look at how much Mrs. Carter did. Really. And she wasn't even no kin. The accident could have happened to anybody. Nita knew that.

And then there was him. Brandon. Damn him. He would have to do it right. All of it. Damn him. He would have to be there when she needed somebody, ask the questions she couldn't ask, get her to where she needed to be gotten to. He would have to stand around when what she needed was someone to do just that, and be quiet when she needed quiet, and hold her when she needed to be held. He would have to do all that. Damn him.

You just couldn't figure, could you? He didn't look like the type who gave a damn about anybody but himself. His type— these pretty boys, they were the kind that when things got tough, they headed for the hills. Left you standing there on your own, left you to figure it out by yourself. You just couldn't figure. What was in it for him? His kind didn't do nothing unless there was payback on the other end. He didn't have nothing to gain by helping her through this. She certainly didn't have anything to give him. Still, the man had spent his day off cleaning and vacuuming and getting groceries. Never had so much food in the house. Didn't ask, just did. You couldn't figure on a man like that. It didn't fit in with the program.

Everyone knew the program. The talk shows were full of it, and the radio and her girlfriends had it on their minds. One woman had written a whole book about it—about these doggish men and how you had just better not expect nothing from em. When you sat down with another black woman the conversation would sooner or later switch around to my man and how he done me wrong. Nita had her share of stories, too, of that lazy, crazy old André. She used to have the ladies shaking their heads and cooing in sympathy when she'd tell them about the time she had just given birth to Didi and the nigger had the nerve to bring this other hussy he was running around with to the hospital with him. He came in the room with a bunch of balloons, all lovey-dovey, and she'd known something was up, cause he was acting suspicious. He almost got away with it, too, but what happened was the nurse opened the door real wide to bring in a machine for the girl in the next bed, and there the hussy was. The ho had the nerve to stand right outside the door where anybody could see her. Fortunately, at the time, Nita had already decided she was through with André. The bitch could have him for as long as she could hold onto him, and good luck to her. She told André to go and wave at his little girl on his way out and then to keep on going. Every one of her girlfriends had a story like that one. And her mama's girlfriends, and her mama, too, probably, but Mama wanted to pretend like she didn't, though why she should be any different, Nita didn't know. Instead Mama just talked about how much her husband liked to sit around and be waited on. Which was the same thing, really, but don't tell Mama that. There wasn't nobody talking about this kind of man. The part of this man, this Brandon, that she had just seen.

What would it be like to have something like that to yourself? She didn't even know where to begin imagining. She thought about the stuff she had to deal with on her own. First thing, she guessed, was that he'd help out with some of that. Maybe, like, instead of moving this heavy piece of furniture by yourself would be somebody there ready and willing to pick up the other end. And you wouldn't have to be making a list of what needed doing. Somebody would have eyes of his own, and he would see those dishes in the sink and do them without being told. He would have some initiative. And there would be surprises, too. You would come home to your little house—the one with the garden out back—and the dining room would be papered with the pattern you liked, the off-white paper with the tiny pink roses. And there would be a necklace for you one day, and it wasn't even your birthday. And a hug. Just because. And I would do for him, too. Little things that I could. I would make sure there was his favorite cereal in the cupboard always, and I would buy for him the kinds of things a man doesn't want to buy for himself, like bubble baths and other things to make his skin feel soft and smell good. We would go dancing and on long trips out of the city. Places on those rich-and-famous shows, with waterfalls and palm trees. There wouldn't be a thing for us to worry about, but if there was, it would be okay because we'd come through it together.

She tucked the sheet around her son. The cast was right where the doctor asked him to keep it, resting on top of the covers. Keeping her arm in one place would drive her crazy, but Marco had that kind of head on him, saw a task such as holding something a certain way as a kind of challenge, same as beating your best time on a mile run, or saving money for your own bike. She went to answer the door.

"Got a minute now, Nita?"

She had put Sipp off long enough. He'd come down every couple of hours, tapping on her door. Yesterday she could barely look at him. Not even them pathetic hangdog eyes were doing a thing for her. But, if it was gonna be done with she'd have to deal with him sometime.

"Come on in," she said.

He sat on the couch, straight backed, hands on his knees. None of his usual mannish slouch on him. He sat for a while as if he had lost his words.

"I wanted to explain . . . ," he began.

She waited. He wouldn't even look at her. The light around his face had been replaced by a kind of hot heat. Maybe that's what shame looks like, she thought.

"Well," she said.

"We were playing. That's all."

"You were playing with my son and he fell on his head and broke his arm."

"I would never do anything . . ."

"What exactly *did* you do? I want to hear the whole thing start to finish."

He cleared his throat, looked her in the eye for the first time. His own eyes were watery and veined. "Mrs. Carter, she asked me to look after him for just a minute, and I was happy to cause

I want to be close to your kids. I want to have some of my own. One of these days?" He cocked one eyebrow as if that were a serious question.

"Go on."

"We was wrestling around. Playing. Boys like that. My daddy used to toss me around and I loved it. I wasn't hurting him. We were teasing and tagging. I told him if I caught him I was gonna dump him out the window."

"So you did."

"I was playing with him. I had him by his ankles. Just playing. I thought most his weight was inside. He was squirming and the next thing I knew, he was gone."

"You dropped my child out the window."

"I'm sorry." He lowered his eyes to the floor. He was as stiff as a politician caught in a lie on one of those sixty-minute shows.

"My child could be dead, and you're sorry." She stared at him with her arms crossed. Let him melt. Let his sorry butt melt right into that sofa.

He had frozen. He didn't say a word. When he did move, it was to rise and walk to the door. He touched her arm on his way past her. He closed the door and left.

She hugged herself harder, pulling against her rage. She trembled with it.

A mistake, she told herself. Remember, a mistake. There was planned evil and then there were mistakes. This was a mistake.

So what? Wasn't the result the same. Someone throws her child from a window or someone drops him by mistake. He was still hurt. Or worse. Didn't think of that, did he? The fool.

She went to the refrigerator. It was full of stuff she never bought: melons and squares of cheese and thin-sliced lunch meats wrapped in white paper. She peeled off a piece of salami, rolled it up and started eating.

Just a foolish simple country boy. Probably didn't even have second-story windows in Itta Bena, Mississippi. She'd have to cut him some slack—being stupid didn't make you a bad person. She would have to stew a while longer, and enjoy it, too, but then she'd have to let him off. All in all, he was okay. Just young and simple. There sure wasn't any law against that.

She felt like a person just cleared the tracks before the train came through. She'd really considered it, really thought that just maybe she might go with him to Mississippi. He was awfully cute, that shiny black skin and that grin. And kind, too, and funny. He'd probably do all right for himself. If he was careful and if he was lucky, he would. Some place down the line, he'd settle in and make a go of it. He'd put together a nice little life for himself, with a ranch home and a passel of kids. Put together "a little hustle" as he called it. God, she hoped that happened for him. He deserved it, with his simple self. Some girl down home would be mighty blessed. But it sure wasn't gonna be her. She knew that. There were other possibilities for her.

Her anger filtered away like cigarette smoke. She lay back on the couch and stared at the ceiling. Other possibilities, for sure. The one downstairs . . . huh. She wasn't kidding herself with that mess. Not in her life would she be reeling that in. Sure was fun to think about, though. She'd sure know what to do with him if she did catch him. And these bitches around here would fall down dead if she hooked up with something like him. But that was just a nice dream. In terms of the long run, at least.

For now—well, he was around for now. Where was the harm in spending some time with him? A little casual thing. A lot of folks did that. Nobody got hurt. God, it was so good. Had been so long, and she'd never been with anybody but André. André was always fine, but this was . . . different, somehow. She didn't even have the words to explain this new thing. It was like sex with this man was new, and the main thing she knew was she wanted some more. Why not? Whose business was it? She was a grown woman, doing what a lot of these other women did every day, getting herself a little good loving. He'd be gone in a few weeks and that would be that. Then she could get to work on those other possibilities. She didn't even know where to begin, but she knew now that they were there.

Monday she invited Mrs. Carter to supper. When she thought of how bold and silly her plan was, she had to laugh, and then she had been shocked when it worked. She had made a big supper out of some chops and beans Brandon had left and then sat everyone up in front of the TV. She'd poured Mrs. Carter a glass of brandy that André had brought over one Christmas. As the kids fell to sleep she bundled them off to bed. After Mrs. Carter nodded off, she left her a note saying she had stepped downstairs for a minute.

He had answered the door in his stocking feet, a handful of papers at the end of one arm. He wore glasses—she'd never seen glasses on him.

"Hi," she said. "I made you this. To say thanks. Again." She handed him the pie.

He peeled back the aluminum foil and sniffed.

"Sweet potato?"

"Only kind I know how to make."

"My mom makes these, too." He took another big sniff and closed his eyes in bliss. "Let's eat."

He had gone into the kitchen to serve up the pie. Though she wasn't hungry, she took her piece and a fork. She ate it—eating with him was part of the plan, as well. And when she found herself lying beside him on his bed again, on her belly, running her hand around his chest, she was not sorry. For the pie or for any of it. His chest was hairy, softer than she imagined. She had always wondered what it would be like to be with one of these men with fur—fur like some kind of animal. André was as smooth as a baby all over.

"I should be getting back," she said, but she didn't move. She didn't really want to leave at all. She wanted to stay there forever.

He stilled her hand with both of his. "I should tell you something," he said.

"You don't have to."

"Yeah, I do."

"I ain't asked you for a thing. And I'm not going to. I'm here cause this is what I want."

"That's pretty casual, coming from you."

"It is. It's like on TV, though. Grown up folks like us, they can do what they want."

"Consequences be damned?"

"My mama says, you gonna give a dance you got to pay the band."

"Seems like you thought of everything I didn't."

"You sound guilty."

"Does that surprise you?"

"Yeah."

"Why would that surprise you?"

"A man. A famous man."

She didn't add rich man. Light-skinned man. Stuck-on-himself man.

"So men are just guiltless pigs, taking on every little piece they see." He rolled back and rose over her. "And famous men, so much the worse, huh?"

She couldn't believe he could do it again, but he just tickled her. She giggled. "That's what they tell me."

"Shouldn't believe everything you hear," he said, relaxing to his back again. "You're just another surprise," he said.

"Another one, huh. And what did *you* expect?"

"Don't know. I never knew a woman like you before."

"A black woman?" That figured, she thought.

"I know lots of black women. You're different from them."

She cast her eyes up and down her body. "Where?"

He laughed. "You know what I mean."

"Tell me. Now. Fore I hurt you." She snatched at him, teasing.

He batted her hands away and asked her to quit. Then he rolled on his side with his head on his elbow, facing her.

"The women I know had advantages you didn't."

"That make them better?"

"I didn't say better. I said different."

"Go on."

"I'm talking about the kind of girls who always had whatever they wanted, who never had to fight for anything. You see those sisters walking around, and they're not afraid of anything. They act like they own the world."

"Just for your information, Mr. Wilson, there's not much scares me, either."

"I know that."

"So you still ain't told me how I'm different."

"Maybe that's the thing. Maybe that's the surprise. You're just as strong. You got everything those women got. Except the leg up life gave them."

"So you feel sorry for me, is that it?"

"Hardly."

"So what is it then, boy? I'm losing patience with you. I gots to go soon."

"You are too much, you know that? I'm gonna tell you something. Promise you won't take it the wrong way. Promise?"

"Promise."

"Men like me and those women I was talking about, black folks, those of us who got out of here, we take a look down at a neighborhood like this and we don't even have a clue what it's all about. When I moved into this building, I had a lot of expectations. I can tell you I was sure wrong."

"What was you expecting?"

"All kinds of things, I guess. Maybe I thought that everyone would be hard and angry. I had these ideas in my head that because a person didn't have much money, somehow they were . . .

I don't know. Stupid. Or lazy. I'm almost embarrassed to say this. You know how you and I talk different?"

"Yeah, you all stuck up, and me, like normal folks."

He looked away and she wondered whether that was something she shouldn't have joked about.

"In my business, in the world I live in, this is the way people speak. Everybody does. It doesn't matter what color they are. My parents taught me to talk this way from the time I was born, and you know what? I'm glad they did. They also taught me—or someone did—that I couldn't even have a conversation with someone like you. According to them, you and I would never even meet."

She rolled back on her pillow. She guessed everyone had stuff like this they carried around. She had her share. She had always heard you had to be careful around those little Asian women— Hmong, they called them. That they were dirty and carried disease. Someone was spreading around that they were killing and eating the squirrels in the city. Folks believed that mess, too, but who knew? She didn't know any Hmong ladies she could ask.

"You know what else?" Brandon continued. "I was scared."

"Of us?"

"Yeah. Thought there'd be murderers and thieves in every house. That's what they tell you."

"I got news for you, Mr. Wilson. You *is* us."

"I am and I am not. For some folks, yeah—your basic redneck sees one nigger the same as another. But to a lot of folks, black and white, because I got out, I'm different. I *am* something else."

"And just what might that be?"

"I don't know. People think that the kinds of problems poor people have are like in a slide show in a church basement. They think there will be pictures with captions underneath that say things like 'hungry' and 'welfare cheat' and 'drug abuser,' and that if you walk down the street in a place like this you can pick out those people just by reading their signs."

"You didn't find what you were looking for?"

"I look around here and what I see are folks doing the best they can. Like anywhere else."

"But that other stuff is here, too. The drugs and the folks that don't take care their kids. A lot of it. Right in this building, even."

"Hungry people?"

"Yes, sometimes."

"Drugs?"

"Yeah. Whole bunch coming in."

"Right here?"

"Yeah."

"Where? When?"

She looked away, to the ceiling. She wondered whether Mrs. Carter had woken up yet. She had said too much.

"Where in this building?"

She shrugged.

"Tell me."

She shook her head.

"It's those boys. It's that Sipp, isn't it? Come on. You can tell me."

"Look, I don't know nothing, hear. And if you know what's best for you, you'll leave them fools alone."

"Think he'd talk to me?"

"I gots to go." She left the bed and started gathering her clothes.

"I knew there was a story here."

"Don't," she said.

"You want this stuff coming in here? In your home? Oh. I get it. That's why I can't get a story down here. When it comes right down to it, you all don't want any help."

"I have to live here. You don't."

"Not like this, you don't."

"They'll be gone soon."

"So they said. You believe that? Do you? Nita, I've done stories about their kind my whole life. Those kind of people will tell you anything they think you'll believe to get you to go along with them. To get you to turn a blind eye. Next thing you know, you're right in the middle of it."

"Not me."

"No, not you. I know that. But what about your kids? What about your son? Think they wouldn't use him? Think they wouldn't send a package with a little boy? Nobody suspects a little boy. That's why they use them."

She rolled away from him. A modesty came back to her, one she knew had never really gone. She pulled her top over her head and turned to face him again. She wiped away tears she wished weren't on her face. She grimaced.

"Come on, Nita. There's already been one accident." When he said accident he waved his fingers in the air to single out the word.

Yeah, accident, right. She must have been out of her mind to listen to that smack. Her kids here. All these other folks. Maybe this was a way. The only way maybe. He didn't mean anything to her anyway, that other one. Not anymore.

"Friday. After three, it'll be here. A lot of it, I think. That's all I know, and you have got to promise me you'll be careful. I'm trusting you to get us through this."

"I will. I'll do my best."

She straightened her clothes, ready to leave. There on the bed, his beautiful coffee-with-milk-colored body had stretched out, his eyes gone far away on some scheme or other. He glanced up, startled, it seemed, seeing her there.

"Nita," he said, a low rumble really. That look in his eyes. He smiled at her. "Nita . . ."

"Don't say anything, please. I don't want nothing, and I ain't asked you for nothing either."

An Emmy, at Least

. . . .

You're doing fine. We are all so proud of you out here. And I'm glad they bought you a suit finally. Kind of embarrassing you out there looking like a bum.

Sister Carlotta Robeson
Lexington/Hamline, St. Paul

She had insisted.

He'd come up with a half dozen reasons why this visit was a bad idea: the area wasn't really safe, he had too much to do, there was a movie they should go see. To no avail. Sandra said that she was going to get herself a firsthand look at his building, or it would be the end of their relationship. That's how she was. She was the kind of woman who once she made up her mind, there was nothing else to be said. Oh, she might play along with him, indulge him with some arguing or pretend she didn't notice when he tried to change the subject. In fact, she was so cool in her resolve, she would debate him just as generously as the wimpiest talk-show host there was, graciously conceding his points, and telling him that it made a lot of sense. Then she'd go on about her business, just as if she'd been talking to a tree stump.

He might get lucky, for once. Maybe Nita'd be gone. Wednesday she had those classes, didn't she? She'd be gone, he'd get Sandra in and out of there quick. He'd take her down to the St. Paul Grill, have some drinks and dessert, and that would be the end of it.

"Here it is," he said. He pulled his raggedy old Dodge into the space behind the building.

"You sure this is it?" she said. "This looks like a set from 'West Side Story.'"

"So that's gonna be the program tonight. Lots of snappy repartee. Sharp tongues on the attack."

"We aren't petulant, are we?"

"Is that the royal we?"

"You make such an adorable poor person." She snuggled up to him as he led her to the door. Her leather jacket was lush to the touch, as smooth and soft as the body inside it.

He fished for the key that unlocked the back door. He'd had a new deadbolt installed and furnished keys for the neighbors. He couldn't believe that there had been open access to the building. Even out where Sandra lived, if someone left a building unlocked it was very likely the mail would be messed with or someone would go around trying doors. How much had that lock cost, fifty dollars? Such a little thing. That was what didn't figure down here. So many of the little things that would make so much difference in the way people lived, in the way they looked at the place, and in how they felt about being there were not taken care of, like a lock here or a row of geraniums there or even the litter being picked up. It was as if they just couldn't be bothered. Or maybe they never got around to it. Or . . . he wished he had an answer to that "or." More than anything, there was a kind of inertia here, a way people had of just getting through the day and going along to get along and waiting until the dam burst before they headed for higher ground. He found it discouraging. As he led Sandra down the hallway past Nita's door, he found himself wishing there was a coat of paint on the walls, a warm cheerful color—and some nice bright fixtures to show the place off. He was shamed by it, and the shame caught him by surprise. It wasn't *his* home, after all. Not even his investment. But he did live there. For now. And he was showing it off to the woman he loved. He would have liked to be proud, but how could you be proud of living here? Why would you even bother to take care of a place like this?

"So far, so depressing," Sandra said.

"It gets better," he responded, wondering if, with her attitude, that would indicate more or less horrible. He opened the door to his apartment and flipped on the switch. "Viola," he said. At one time that had been a very funny baseball joke.

"Ooooh," she said. She strutted in like Mae West, one hand on a hip, sucking in air through her teeth. "All this for me? You shouldn't have."

Jesus, he thought. He hadn't noticed how cluttered the place was. He then realized what the apartment reminded him of, with its plywood paneling and coils of cable and desk smothered with copy. The abandoned coffee cups and tripods, various machinery. The room resembled the work area of every jury-rigged television operation in America. He hadn't noticed before because he'd been hunkered down in rooms just like this since he was a teenager. Places like this felt more comfortable to him than almost anywhere he could imagine.

"Well, make yourself at home," he said.

"As if," she scoffed.

He pointed to the sofa, the only even partially open-looking seating in the house.

"Oh my God!" she shrieked, jumping back.

"What is it?" He came around in front of her to save her from whatever.

"It's . . . it's . . . plaid." She shivered in mock horror.

"For chrissakes."

"Brad . . . that's you're name now, isn't it? Brad, back at the university, the girls in my sorority made a pledge. We would never go out with Kappas, never eat Velveeta, and we would never—as

long as we lived, under any circumstances, so help us God—
never sit on plaid furniture."

"Sit down, woman, and hush that mess for a few minutes."
Unfortunately he knew she was probably telling the truth. Those
uppity sisters she was in school with just would have a bunch
of rules like that. When they got together wouldn't a one of them
get up and go to the bathroom, because she knew the rest of
them would talk about her when she left. Enough designer labels
showing on them to peel off and sink a small ship. In a few years
those broads would be running this country. One or two of
them were already running state legislatures and various banks
around the country. Sandra here was the exception. She had
floated around from one marginal venture to the next, from city
to city. Afraid—ashamed, he thought—with her high-powered
background to admit what she really wanted: the nice house, the
important husband, the kids. It was like sometimes she couldn't
believe she had finally found someone who might give her that.
And he was having trouble with the notion that the person who
was supposed to make all that happen was him. But who knew?
Maybe each of them was the answer to the other one's dreams—
whatever they really were.

"Something to drink?" he offered, hoping there was something in the refrigerator to back up that offer. "You know, I don't
know what it is with you women and plaid sofas." He found a
pitcher of water and a bottle of Mendota Springs. "We got water
and water," he said.

"I'll have water," she decided, unhelpfully not indicating
which kind.

"And so you have some other experience with women and
plaid sofas you'd like to discuss? Well, honey, I guess we gonna
have to have us a little talk. Come sit down here next to Mama."
She patted a space next to her.

Oops. You had to be careful what you said.

Not sure how fresh the pitcher was, he handed her the sparkling water and sat, as ordered.

"Now, tell me about these other so-called women."

"Mindy," he told her. "Mindy was here. For a meeting. She hates plaid, too."

"Oh, that shriveled-up old witch. Tell me something: why is it with these white women—the blonde ones—they get to a certain age and then they decide they'll look younger if they go red. You noticed that?"

"That was Dexter's idea."

"Really, Brad?"

"Don't call me Brad. Please."

"That your name, isn't it? 'Live at Five, Newscenter 13, with Brad Wilson.' Or maybe I heard it wrong."

"So, how was your day at work? Shift a lot of papers today?"

"We *are* petulant tonight." She gave him an evil grin. "My day at work was fine. My paper pushing little-old-piece-of-nothing-job, such as it is. But your fancy diversions aside, what I want to go back and talk about now is all these women you know who don't like plaid couches."

Shit. It was as if they really did have some sort of deciphering device. He decided his best strategy was to play along with her damn game. Was nothing in the world better than a smart, catty woman. They never bored you, at least. Even if you had to be on your toes at all times. Like a prizefighter, you almost had to train for them. Watch "The Front Page" or any of those old Tracy and Hepburn movies. In a pinch, even "The Jeffersons" would do, though Sandra made Louise Jefferson look like a slow-witted old housewife. He saluted her with his glass. It was her game. Let her make the next move.

"Not talking, huh?"

He pasted on his evil grin

"I'll just have to let my imagination do all the work."

He lifted a hand, welcoming her to it.

"Let's see. Oh, you know who I bet it was? What was that little chippy's name you had on Friday night? That Laquita? Janita? The little dark gal."

Holy shit, he thought. A pro, however, he maintained his equanimity.

"Bonita."

"Yeah, that's the bitch. Yeah, I saw her all leaned up into you. Look like she owned you."

"Shhhh. They live right upstairs."

"Oh she does?" Sandra started up from the couch. "Let me go set her straight about a few things."

He pulled her back down. "Let her live," he said. "She did a great job on the show."

"Defending her, are you? Yeah, she did good. Got her some Dark & Lovely and fixed her hair up. Bought her one of them Jaclyn Smith K-Mart dresses. What are they, about nine ninety-five ..."

He cut her off. "Woman does the best she can, Sandra."

"I'm teasing."

Yes, she was, but somehow it didn't seem funny. Or appropriate. He'd worked so hard to put Nita—and the others, too—in a human context. Tried to show their wholeness, their decency. Maybe all over town folks sat and laughed at them, at their slapped-together wardrobes, weak grammar, and tired-looking hair. What if it had been for nothing.

A little hardball wouldn't hurt, just now. Pay her back a bit.

"What if that woman and me really did have a thing?" he asked. A risky strategy, but worth a try. Sandra didn't own him. Yet.

"Who? You and that Bonita?"

"I'm telling you, she's all right."

Fine, and sensitive, and smart, in her own way.

"Nigger, please."

"That's so hard to believe?"

"A silver-spoon Negro like you messing with that back-alley rag? In addition to whatever else you caught down here, you have picked up a sense of humor."

"I never knew you were such a class snob."

"I'm kidding. Damn. You really have picked up something down here. Remember, I'm the one suggested you tell these beautiful and heart-wrenching stories."

"You did. And thank you." He kissed her on the temple by her ear. She pushed him away, playfully.

"Damn," she said. "I come down here to have fun and you get all serious on me."

"I feel good about what we're doing. It is good. Don't you think?"

"Wonderful. Ground breaking, even. In the past two weeks I've seen more sizes and shapes of black folks than the whole time I was growing up. Since even on 'Roots.'"

"You think it'll make a difference?"

"Remember when we were kids and there was nothing but white folks on TV. Back in the sixties. There'd be one or two of us on a week at most, remember? Sammy Davis Jr., Bill Cosby. We used to look in the back of the *Jet* magazine to see who'd be on."

He sure did remember that. "At our house," he said, "*Jet* was like our other *TV Guide*. Sat right there by the set." That was the only reason the Wilsons got *Jet* really. His folks considered the magazine to be more than a little on the lower-class side, what with its stories about people who got buried in their Cadillacs and with that bathing-beauty picture in the middle.

She went on. "Remember when The Supremes would come on 'Ed Sullivan' and the phones up and down the street would start ringing with everybody calling everybody else up so no one would miss it. Each time one of us came on it was special. After a while it got commonplace. All those comedy shows and the music stars and the athletes. People like you."

Yes, people like him. At first, the only way he could even get on the air was by being groomed and ready and standing by at all hours of the day and night. They'd let him on, maybe, if there was no one else available. Maybe. Then came 1975. He wouldn't have had a career if the FCC hadn't made stations put us on the air. They made it the law, and he was trained and ready to go and in the right place at the right time. There were a lot of people out there in this business—women and minorities—should be pretty grateful there was such a thing as affirmative action. A lot of them who was turning their noses up at it now.

"You know, Brandon, even though we come a long way, we're still so far back in the shadows we can hardly be seen. You hear these white people talking about how they've got to hire blacks and therefore they can't do this and they can't do that. Then you look around their offices and see one or two black faces at the most. Will it make a difference? I don't know about in the rest of the city, but I tell you what. Up and down any street around here, when you put the folks on, it was 1967 all over again. You've made a lot of folks' days. You should be proud."

And he had done some good profiles, too, he knew. The woman over on Dayton who'd taken in eight of her grandkids because she'd lost her own children to drugs and gangs. The minister up off of Victoria who claimed to be curing crackheads through prayer. His treatment actually seemed to be working. The food shelf, the music academy, the theater company. He'd gotten a lot of information out in a short time. And he knew it wasn't enough.

"The rest of the city is what worries me," he said.

"A shame, really. You do your job with a modicum of integrity. That should be worth something."

"Toots, in my business integrity is worth about as much as a laxative in the diarrhea ward."

"The ratings are only fair, I know."

"The ratings are through the roof. Any station owner in town would give his firstborn to show the kind of improvement we have. We're up 50 percent. Fifty percent. The people in sales act like they've died and gone to heaven, and you know what. It's still not enough."

"What does he want, this Dexter?"

"My head on a platter. No, not really. Number one, baby. Number one. That's the only thing counts in this game."

"And so?"

"You need a coup. A scoop. A stunt. An exclusive."

"You got any such thing?"

"Maybe."

"Yeah?"

"Big drug deal. Right here. So I'm told."

She closed her eyes and a clouded expression eclipsed her face. He nudged her.

"Hey. I'll be careful."

"I know you will, it's not that. I just wish . . . Well, it's back to business as usual, isn't it? S.O.S. Same old shit, same old story."

"But that's real, too, you know. Just because drugs and violence is what they usually show about black folks, that doesn't mean it isn't real."

"That also doesn't mean that *you* have to do it."

"You got to give the people what they want."

"Some pickaninnies. A mammy. Hey, maybe you can have Uncle Ben and Aunt Jemima on too, while you're at it. Brandon. Don't."

"I have to."

"You *don't* have to. Your work's been so good. I know you'll win some awards. A Peabody. An Emmy, at least."

"That's not what I want."

"What do you want?"

"Same as Dexter. Same as the rest of them." He held up his index finger.

"It's not worth it."

"Yes, it is. And I've done nothing to be ashamed of. And I won't."

"You can't see the forest for the trees."

"Can't I? Did you see what I did in a few weeks? With just a little support and a little cash. Think what I'll do at the network. Think of the stories I'll do then."

"Deals with the devil. We already talked about that."

It was Brandon's turn to scoff. "Babydoll, I made that deal while I was still in high school. I want you to think about New York, Washington, London. The stores and the restaurants and the theaters. You've been wasting away here on the frozen tundra for far too long."

"Is that a proposal?"

"You want it to be?"

"I guess you haven't absorbed your lesson about trifling with me."

"Me? Trifle? With a smart girl like you?"

"Get me the hell out of this dump and take me someplace nice and expensive. A woman needs a good meal when she's being propositioned."

"You mean proposed to, don't you?"

"Whatever."

He helped her into her leather jacket. As he opened the door, Nita swung a fist in. She had been about to knock on the door.

"Oh. Excuse me. I didn't know you had company. I'm sorry."

"Bonita Sallis, this is Sandra Moore."

"Hi," Nita said. She backed away, grabbing behind her for the banister.

Be cool, girl, Brandon thought.

"Saw you on the news the other day," Sandra said. "You were wonderful. So poised."

"Thank you." Nita stumbled back up the steps. Brandon reached for her.

"Hang on a minute. Do you need something? We were just . . . hanging out."

"Naw. Nothing. I don't need nothing. Just hanging out myself."

They said good night to Nita and heard her close herself into her apartment. Brandon walked Sandra to his car. His stomach felt like it had been through the grinder. He needed something. A drink or a sandwich or a Pepto Bismol or something. He didn't know what he needed. He headed the car down the alley, let out the air he'd been holding in his lungs. For hours he felt he'd been holding it. It was over. Done. Like reading a retraction on the air. You sucked it up, swallowed your pride, and got it over. Forever.

Sandra didn't say a word, but she didn't let go of his hand all the way to the restaurant.

Common Sense

· · · · · · · · · · · · · · ·

Who did that heifer think she was, looking at her like that. "I saw you on TeeeVeee. Sooo poised." Nita mocked the words in her head. A stuck-up, yellow bitch. One of them thought her shit didn't stink. Let her walk up in here and wiggle that ass around alone some night. See don't she get herself knocked down a peg or two.

It figured she'd be the type he'd be messing with. The kind walked around flaunting they good upbringing and good education and they money, too. Jacket the bitch was wearing cost more than Nita brought home in a month.

Dammit, she'd missed her chance. She should have messed with the heifer's head. She should have gone up in his face and batted her eyes and made some remarks about how she'd see him later. Make her real crazy. Make her wish she'd never come up here in the first place.

Probably wouldn't of bothered her anyway. Her kind—these rich, snooty folks—they got different rules for that sort of thing. Nita's mama always said that the stuff you saw on them soap operas with rich folks hopping around each other's beds and cheating each other was true. Mama said don't even think them writers was clever enough to make that stuff up. They was writing what they knew, what really went on. Shoot, that Sandra probably had her two or three other men she fooled with, and she probably knew about his other little things, too. They probably got together sometimes and had a big orgy. Him messing with Nita wouldn't mean a thing.

There it was. Some more of them people out there enjoying everything that life had to offer. Apparently didn't have to worry about tomorrow, or even later today. That was Nita's problem—the very heart of it. Nobody never taught her how to go out and get her any of that fun, how to join that party, how to cancel her regrets. Everybody she knew threw caution to the wind. Not every day, all of them, but at least every once in a while. Dropping everything and going out to the casino. Picking up men in the laundromat. Buying everything they saw, even if they ain't got food on the table. Every time Nita tried that shit, hell . . . she never even got as far as trying it.

"Common sense," her mama called it. "My oldest girl, she's got common sense."

Not even the babies were an impulse. She'd planned even them. Thought about the careers and the choices in life, and knew even at sixteen that what she wanted more than anything was to be a mother. Looking back, what would she have done different? Choose a different father? Maybe. Wait a couple years? With what she knows now, maybe. Probably not. As with everything else, she'd made up her mind about something, got on track, and kept going. And by herself she did it. She had always done for herself, her whole life, since she was a toddler and wouldn't let her mama put her clothes on her no more. Right up to now. She was as proud of it in first grade when she taught herself addition as she was now. Who out there could say they could take care of themselves? Who out there could prove it?

When she looked around at these other folks' lives, and the choices they made, and the things they did, it knocked her from her stride. Grass always looked greener. That's what they tell you.

But could she honestly say she'd change a thing? Have more money? Yes. Have a partner—the right one? Yes.

A thought hit her and she smiled. Those kinds of things were not the result of her choices. Everyone out there had to deal with that shit. All these wenches, even that Sandra. Do I got enough money and can I find the right man? Can I have more time? And, could I be prettier? And, will the right man like me?

Wasn't no one free of doubts. The best you could do was make a plan and stick with it. Hope you could hold onto what you got.

She took it back. His Sandra probably *would* mind somebody messing with her man. She knew she would. It wasn't about love, or trust, or any of those things. It was about having something of your own. It was about needing to know in this life that you had something that belonged to you that you didn't have to share with anyone else. It was about the fear that one day you would look up and you wouldn't have anything at all.

She tried to find the guilt, but she had none. What happened between her and Brandon wasn't about none of that. What it came down to was a time came when she needed something, and at that moment he was there, and he made a gift to her. It had been good. Bless him. And she had gone back once. Out of curiosity. And again, tonight. Out of greed, she thought. Now it was done. She saw that. His eyes said it. Couldn't have said it better with words.

And I ain't even angry, she thought. Or sorry.

Sad, yes.

And lonely.

But that was not his problem. That was not his fault.

People like him and Sandra, they had looked at her her whole life like she was something less than she was. And she had believed it. And then he looked at her again. And again. And he saw her as she was, saw her in a way she could not even see herself. Him with his damn TV, he had held up a mirror to her, he had showed her that self. She had taken it and now it was hers. It was beautiful and it was worth something, and wouldn't nobody be taking it back, not ever.

So, let them go on, she thought. Let him take her back out there, wherever it was they wanted to be. They had come together only for this little while, Nita knew, and that was all it was meant to be. Like when you had the radio and the TV on at the same time and the songs were different but sounded good together just the same. That they ran into each other was an accident. But it had worked. And nobody was the worse for it.

So, good-bye and God bless you.

And thank you.

She hadn't remembered seeing anything under the door when she'd come in. She picked up what was a piece of white notebook paper, folded neatly four times the way her mother had done notes when she sent them to school. The note must have been stuck under there since she came back upstairs.

Dear Nita, it read.

Please read this. I know your mad but I wanted to say Im sorry again. Its my fault what happened. I did not want to hurt your little boy. Its okay if your mad. I know how you feel. On Saturday after I get my money Im leaving. Im going back to Mississippi. I talked to my mama and them and they are glad Im coming home. I am too. I hope my old car makes it. This is my notice I guess so you can rent the apartment again. Tell Mr Stretchy or whatever his name is to send me my deposit money to my parents house. Ill clean up good. Im glad I got to know you. I will miss you. If you change your mind and decide you want to come on down home just let me know. We got plenty room for you and the kids. You are a fine lady. I put my mama and thems address on the top of this page for my money and for you if you want it.

Your friend,

Joe Freeman (Sipp!)

Joe Freeman. She hadn't even known his name.

He was going through with it. Another man with a plan.

Best thing for him, too. Get his little bit of cash and get on down the road.

She saw him Thursday morning down at the machines, pulling some things from the drier.

"You up early," she said.

"Pulling it together. Mama don't allow you to come back home with a whole lot of dirty drawers."

"Mamas the same all over, I guess." She smiled at the truth of it.

She could see him stealing glances at her as she put in a load of wash. Mrs. Carter had said she'd come down and dry Nita's load while Nita was at work. One good thing had come out of the accident. Mrs. Carter was good for plenty more favors these days.

Sipp acted bashful. Awkward. Like they were just meeting, or like he was scared of her.

"You're on your way, then?" she asked him.

"Yes, ma'am. Leave out of here early Saturday. Be to Memphis by midnight. Everything goes according to plan, that is."

"You said you know your business."

"Other folks in it besides me. Folks mess with this stuff, you can't trust none of em too good. They be fine, though. I hope."

She measured in the detergent and slotted in the quarters. She sensed something chewing at her somewhere inside about where her heart should be.

"Maybe you should find another place," she told him.

"It's happening here. All set. Why you care?"

"I don't know. Them folks in and out of here with Mr. Wilson. You know."

"All that carrying on is good cover." He folded a T-shirt.

"It's perfect." He bundled a pair of underwear.

"Last place you'd look." He dug through for a mate to a sock.

"Won't nobody suspect a thing. Not less somebody tell em."
He put his face in front of Nita's.

She pushed in the quarters and reviewed all the dials. She avoided his eyes.

"You ain't been talking, have you, Nita?"

Better use cold water, she said to herself. She turned the dial to the setting and walked around him. She met his eye and he grabbed her arm.

"Be a big mistake."

"I'm late for work," she said. He let her go.

"These brothers don't play," he said. "Problems? Somebody gets burned? Won't be them. Won't be me. You know what I'm saying."

They stared at each other for what seemed to her like half an hour. She picked up her purse and started toward her car.

"Nita," he said to her back.

She stopped.

"You ain't wished me good luck."

She turned back.

"Now you hold one goddamn minute, nigger. Starting right now things are gonna be a little different than you thought."

Into
the
Sea

. . . .

On behalf of the Summit/University community
I would like to thank you for your efforts to
portray our citizens in a positive light. An
awards ceremony will be held in your honor at
the Martin Luther King Jr. Center. Tickets will
be twenty-five dollars a couple. Please let us
know in advance how many tickets you will be
purchasing for your table.

Mrs. Willimae K. Whitfield
President
Summit/University Community
Organization

"You wanted to see me?"

Dexter had his feet on the cabinet behind his desk. He dropped them and spun around.

"Sit down. We got work to do," he said

"No high five? No 'soul brother' talk? This some sort of holiday you white folks have I ain't heard about?"

"You surprise me sometimes," Dexter said. "By now you should have figured out why I do that crap. You know, don't you?"

"Cause you're an asshole?"

"That's what I like, a man with self-confidence."

239

Brandon snickered, feigning indifference.

"It's simple. I do that crap to bug people. Like some goddamn overgrown snotty-nosed junior-high kid. To get under their skin. Why? Cause my time is valuable and the world is full of fools. It keeps me entertained."

At least somebody enjoyed it, Brandon thought.

"You know, Wilson, I was 100 percent right about you. I didn't get this far without great instincts. When I saw your tape and when I watched you on the air, I knew you had it."

"Thanks."

"I'm not blowing smoke. That's your agent's job. I told you from the start. Your fate and mine are linked up like this." He crossed his fingers. "We're the same kind of people, you and me. We got the same drive. We want the same things." He came around the desk, sat on it. "And we're going to get them." He extended his arm to Brandon.

"I want to shake your hand. Congratulations. Great work, Brandon."

Brandon's jaw dropped open. He was stunned. "What happened to Brad?"

"I mean it. You have earned my respect. Not many people do." He looked him straight on, eyes almost a little moist. Brandon wanted to turn away, but didn't.

"I have to say something, man," Brandon said. "Maybe it's a mistake, but I have to say it." He took a deep inhale.

"Go for it," Dexter prodded.

"I heard what you said, and I understood all the words. I still don't quite get it. I feel like I'm waiting for that other shoe."

Dexter laughed. "Hey, I never said I wasn't a snake. You knew it the first time you saw me. Didn't you? Didn't you?"

A big slimy one, Brandon thought.

"You get places in this life two ways, Brandon. Nice and slow or quick and not so nice. And a lot of the nice guys don't get any place at all. I don't believe in hidden agendas. I make my mind up about something I want, and I go after it. It's that simple. And you're right. I'll work with you as long as it suits my purposes and when I'm done with you, I'll throw your ass out quicker than a used rubber."

There was the Dexter he knew.

"Not quite done with me yet, I guess," he said.

Dexter dumped something from his coffee mug down his throat and wiped his mouth with the back of his hand. "Far from it." He reached behind him and grabbed a stack of green-and-white computer printouts. Ratings. He tossed them onto Brandon's lap. "You know how to read those?"

"Sure."

"I mean really read them."

"It's not my hobby, but, yeah."

"Good. So you can look at them yourself and know what I'm saying isn't bullshit. We kicked ass. You know that. You knew it when I was giving you shit last week."

"But?"

"You know the 'but.'" He stared out the window. "I want out of this motherfucker. You can't imagine how bad."

"Dexter, it's taken me twenty years to . . ."

"That's you. That's *your* time line. And you're about out of time, aren't you, Brandon?" He said it to the window. Almost fondly, he said it.

Brandon kept his eyes on Dexter's back. Twenty long years. Thirty-eight years old. He couldn't even remember how many stations and assignments and career moves. There was a time coming soon when the algebra would go against him. Too old. Too many times around the track. Too many bridges burned. So close. So many times he had almost been there. So close he'd been burned by the lights even.

"You know anything about the *Spirit of St. Louis*?" Dexter asked.

"Just the movie."

"There's a certain distance out where Lindberg had to commit to the flight. There was enough fuel to come back, but beyond that point, it was on to Europe. Or into the sea."

"So this is the pep talk speech where . . ."

"No more games." Dexter made a stop sign with his hand as if he were one of The Supremes. "Here's where we are. We did as much as we could do with the cosmetic shit and the technical shit and the news shit. We played all the angles. We gave it our best shot. Everybody's happy. You and me, we still come up short."

"So what do we do?"

"You're still in this. Good." Dexter smiled. "I see we got two choices. We ease along like we are, climb up slow. New York forgets there was a Dexter Rayburn, and as the snowflakes fly and as the wind blows off the North Pole for another twenty winters, Minnesota watches Brandon Wilson turn into an old man."

"Or?"

"We go for it."

"How?"

Dexter gave him an incredulous look.

"Fine, man, no games," Brandon said. "But, I'm telling you, I don't fabricate and I don't do sleeze."

"Oh, bullshit. You're telling me you wouldn't put on one of those hooker porno stories if it put you over the top. You're a liar."

"Look here, I have never in my life done one of those stories and I'm not arguing it with you." Brandon examined his hands. He folded and arched them in his lap. As he spoke, what he said didn't feel like a decision as much as just inevitable. "I may have something we can work with," he said.

"Yeah?"

"I been sitting on it . . . I got my reasons."

"Out with it."

Why the hell not? he thought.

"A big cache of drugs."

"How much?"

"Don't know."

"What do you know?"

"Where and when. I have to tell you that this is just what somebody told me, okay? It could be complete crap."

"Do you trust her?"

How'd he know it was a her?

"Yeah."

Too much, he thought.

Dexter rubbed around his face with a hand. He was one of those should shave twice a day. Brandon could practically feel the stubble on his own fingers.

"If," he started. "If your source is right, this could be it."

"Maybe."

"No maybe. Definitely. And if not, it's worth a shot. We take every shot from now on, and we keep shooting till we get shot down.

"What do you got on for today . . . No! Fuck it. Cancel it. You're off tonight. We're done with that neighborhood shit anyway. Put Ted on this, too." He leaned back in his chair, eyes far away in thought.

"I don't know about . . ."

"Don't you give me that bullshit, goddammit." He sprung forward, the old fire back. "I need to know right this minute. Are we doing this? Are you committed? Are you? Cause there's no half-assing and there's no going back. Are you?"

Brandon swallowed deep. "Yes. I am. Yes."

"I want cops. Drama. Tension. I want it to be so hot I have an orgasm right here in this chair."

"That all?"

"I want it live at five."

"Well. Stay tuned."

"I'll see you in Paris, brother." Dexter said.

Opening the back door of the apartment house there he came, carrying out a big bag of trash. Your butt is nailed, was what Brandon thought. I'm nailing your nasty butt good.

"You grinning at something?" Sipp asked, grinning back.

"Nice day, is all. Here, let me help you with the door."

"I got it. Thanks."

"No problem at all." Brandon swung the door open wide, exaggerated.

"I said I got it."

"Sorry." Door resting on his foot, Brandon leaned on the frame and watched him sling the gunmetal gray bag into the dumpster. He was an oily-looking, blue-black thing. One of those you would expect to have a mouth full of gold teeth. He had his hair knotted up in a nylon stocking. Wiry and muscular—built like he'd been lifting sacks of potatoes his whole life.

"You waiting on something?" Sipp asked.

"Just enjoying the fresh air."

Sipp snatched the door, but only opened enough space to pass. Barely. He slithered through right next to him. Brandon smelled sweat, marijuana, cheap cologne.

"Folks don't like snooping," Sipp said. "Folks get hurt."

"That a fact?"

"Bet." He eyed Brandon all the way up the stairs.

Brandon kept his face calm, but his stomach bubbled with acid. Only so much cool a person could muster. You were supposed to get nervous, though. It was an animal thing—the nerves were there to keep you on edge, to get you ready to survive. People like Sipp, they made you nervous anyway. That was the kind of vibes his kind put out. So much for him, then.

244

He could put his intimidation skills to good use out at the state penitentiary.

She knocked on his door about nine thirty in the evening. He knew it was her.

"I was expecting you."

"You were?" She stood there, demure, hands clasped behind her back. His gesture welcomed her to come in.

"Have a seat," he offered. She dropped down on the plaid couch, folding one leg under her body.

"Can I get you anything? I don't know what I've got back there. I could make some . . ."

"You can relax. I'm not staying."

"Sorry, it's just that . . ."

"It's all right. Really. It's all right. Okay?"

"Okay." He straddled a dinette chair, facing over its vinyl-upholstered seat back. Facing her.

"She's very pretty. Sandra."

"Yes. Yes, she is. Thank you."

"How long you all been together?"

"Three years, I think."

"You think? Boy, you know you better remember them anniversaries."

"Yeah, I know."

Her yellow knit top was a tad too bright for her skin tone, but it fit her well. Maybe too well. Her breasts were fully outlined, almost exposed-looking beneath the ribbed material. She seemed nervous, so he tried not to stare at her.

"I was hoping I'd see you this evening," he said, then regretted it. This was impossible. Good-byes were never easy. And with her . . .

"We didn't see you on the show tonight. Mindy said you were on assignment. Whatever that means."

"She do okay without me?"

"We missed you. But, she's okay. For a white gal."

They both laughed. Then they were silent.

"Say, I have something to tell you and it's kind of hard for me."

"If it's about . . ."

"No. Not that. No, listen, please." He sat down on the floor in front of the couch, close enough to place his hand on her knee. "The reason I was off today is because we're . . . well, we're finished here. I thought we'd be around another couple of weeks, but, well you know how these things go. We've got other stories. Other places."

"You've got a lot of cleaning to do down here." She looked around and clicked her tongue. "I might be making me some quick damage-deposit cash."

"Don't you worry," he said. He didn't know what he thought he'd see in those eyes, but what he saw was some kind of jeweled warmth.

"One more story, huh?" she said.

He nodded. "Is it okay if I say I'm gonna miss you?"

"You can, yeah." She smiled.

"Okay. I'm gonna miss you. I'm not gonna miss this cave down here, but I'm sure gonna miss you. You are a very special . . ."

"Let's not go too far with this, now." she said, smiling, raising a hand in protest. He could see her avoiding his eyes as much as he hers. They both started to speak at once. He signaled her to continue, but she refused.

"About tomorrow night's show. I'd like you and the kids to be my guests down at the studio. Bring Mrs. Carter. Look around, see how it looks from the other end."

"I got other plans." Nita smiled.

"Mrs. Carter can bring the kids, then. I'll arrange a car. You can meet them there. We'll do dinner. You pick the place."

"Another time, maybe. Thank you. It sounds like fun."

"I think you'd better do it tomorrow. Please."

She smiled, pleasantly, tilting her head to the side as if flirting. "You seem mighty anxious." she said, almost a question.

"Well . . . ," he started. "It's just . . . I really can't . . ."

"You seem awfully nervous about something, Mr. Wilson. You know, on second thought, I think the kids just might enjoy that studio tour. My mother would like that too. Is it all right if she brings the kids?"

He struggled up and walked to his desk. Boy, she was a strange one sometimes. He could feel her eyes on his back.

"So, you'll arrange that?" she asked.

"Sure. I said I would."

"Well, good. Everyone should have a lovely evening."

He rubbed his scalp and turned to her. "Bonita, I can't let you . . ."

"Can't let me what? Go to work tomorrow? You know how they are over at the Monkey Wards. And a girl's got to make a living."

"Nita. I have to ask you something?"

"Shoot."

"Those drugs. That big shipment. Remember? You told me? They still coming tomorrow."

Nita's eyes followed a worn pattern on the matted carpeting. "Far as I know," she said.

"You know that's why I want you all out of here. Don't you?"

She nodded. "It's nice of you to be concerned."

"Are you absolutely sure this is going down? Tomorrow?"

"Well, I know what I was told. But you said it yourself. There's no trusting some people."

"It's just there's a lot riding on this."

"That's true for a lot of people."

He snickered. "If I didn't know better I'd think you were feeling sorry for the damn dealers."

She bit her lip and then opened her mouth to speak. She said nothing.

"Well, don't. They're scum. They're the lowest form of life."

"I guess that's true," she said, rising from the couch. She stretched her arms and yawned.

"Bedtime," she announced, batting her eyes. "My bed." She pouted and reached out to shake his hand.

"We'll be seeing each other?" Brandon offered.

"Yeah, I imagine we will."

"About tomorrow, Nita. You might want to let the other folks up there know to stay clear of this place. You know. About the time the news goes on."

"Big doins, huh?"

"It could get a little hairy."

"Well, I'll spread the word. Discreetly, of course."

"Good. Thanks. And, Nita," he followed her out to the steps. "You make sure you're in a good place, too."

"Don't worry, Mr. Wilson. Bonita Sallis has always taken care of herself."

Brandon nodded. That was the truth and he believed it.

Control

. . . .

Nita could never remember a time when she felt more nervous.
Or more exhilarated. Her nerves felt the way they had when the
gym teacher made her dive into the pool back at Central High
School—like inside her there were two motors twisting in different
directions, one for the part that wanted to jump and one for the
part that was chicken.

She packed the kids off to school and started down her checklist.
Her first call was to her job. She asked to speak to her manager.

"I can't make it today," she told him.

"That's not like you, Nita. Why, you're my most reliable girl."

That was part of the point, Nita thought. She didn't tell him
that, or anything else for that matter.

"Will we see you tomorrow?" he asked.

"Maybe." Maybe not. Maybe not ever again in life.

Sipp had been the easy one.

Mrs. Carter was the tough nut. Nita had knocked on her
door early.

"Who's that out there this hour of the morning?"

"Get dressed. We're going to breakfast."

"Got plenty food right here."

Don't have time for you today, she thought, but she said,
"Special treat on me, Mrs. Carter. You know Miss Nita don't give
out free breakfasts but ever so often."

Mrs. Carter swung open the door. She was fully dressed and already had her purse over her arm.

"Got some favors to ask you," Nita told her between bites of her Egg McMuffin.

"Favors coming fast and furious these days."

Nita smiled a smile that was almost a simper. She could humor the old thing. It would be worth it.

"I got a couple things, actually."

"I always knew there was no such thing as a free lunch."

"This is breakfast, Mrs. Carter. And I'll pay you back. You know your Nita takes care of you." Nita batted her eyes like a ho. Mrs. Carter rolled hers.

"The first thing is. I want you to tell Cece for me that we're spraying the halls. This afternoon. Tell her to take the kids and everybody over to her mama's. She can come back about seven."

"I ain't seen no bugs. You brought some roaches up in here?"

"Tell Mr. Reese and Mrs. Stephens, too. There'll be a car come for the kids right after school. Mama will be with them."

"This ain't about no cockroaches, is it?"

"Can't put nothing over on you, can I, Mrs. Carter?"

"You can tell me. What's gonna happen?"

"A few things. That brings me to your second job. I'm trusting you, Mrs. Carter. I want you to pay close attention."

The old lady leaned forward on her plastic bench as if she were a trained seal and Nita was dangling a fish above her head.

Nita beckoned her closer with a finger and whispered in her ear.

By noon she had checked off her entire list. There was nothing to do but wait.

She lay back on the couch and inhaled deeply. She was not

a religious woman, but as she exhaled she offered a prayer up to God.

Less a prayer, really, than an inquiry.

What did it mean, salvation?

What was greed and what was survival?

Was the line between right and wrong solid or dotted, and where did sin begin?

The phone rang. She did not expect it to be God. She knew there was no direct line, did not believe in burning bushes or fingers of fire.

It was Sipp.

"All right," he said. "All right."

Pas
de
Deux

. . . . 4 .

"Okay, there's Abromsky on two," Ted said. "Everyone's in place." They were sitting in a van disguised to look like a carpet-cleaning truck. Cameras aimed at the front and back doors of the apartment building, and another was in a house across the street. An old friend of Mrs. Carter lived there. The Minicam would follow Brandon in behind the police team.

"How'd you get the cops to play along with this?" Ted asked. "They usually hate this kind of shit." Ted's finger bounced back and forth between the monitors as if he were counting something.

"Are you serious? They love it. All those cops shows—those guys become stars. They get Hollywood agents and everything. I just called in a few favors."

"And you don't have any problem with this? This journalism-as-law-enforcement thing?"

"Come on, kid. You went to J school. You know about the fourth estate."

"I know that there's a difference between reporting the news and creating it."

Brandon cringed. "Jeez, don't get sanctimonious on me here. We're on in a few minutes."

Ted sputtered in derision. "Five ten?"

"Five ten, five fifteen. You know these guys. They might have to stop for donuts on the way." Brandon hardly sniggered at his own little joke, silliness being a long-standing nerve-covering habit. Here he was again at the part he hated the most, where everything had to go like clockwork and on somebody else's schedule. It would be fine. He had to believe that.

"They reconnoiter up at the high school," he said. "How's that for police talk?"

"What if they're early?"

"Then we're early. You guys," he addressed the crew. "Remember, its an unmarked gray car, and when it pulls up, we're hauling ass. They don't wait for nobody. And keep Mindy and Katy on the line, no matter what. When I say go, we're on."

"And you're sure there's even something going on in there to get?" Ted asked.

"What's got into you? I've never seen you worried?"

"Don't know." Ted said. "It's just, this feels like the big time. Don't know if I'm ready for the big time."

Brandon massaged his shoulders. "You done good, kid. And, in there . . . ," he pointed his chin to the building. "Well, there's always something cooking in there."

"They get a great show, no matter what?" Ted said.

Brandon hummed his version of "That's Entertainment." He felt his stomach turning over as if someone were stirring the contents with a spatula.

"You're not too cynical?" Ted hissed.

Two police cars pulled up in front of the building.

"What is this? Katy! Stand by!"

It was Dexter in his earpiece. "Wilson! You're on!"

"No! These are the wrong cops! These aren't my cops!"

"You are on live. Now!"

A squad of cops rushed the building.

"We're interrupting 'Final Jeopardy' with a developing story up in Summit/University. This is Mindy St. Michaels and we've got Brad Wilson on the scene. Brad."

Nita got out of the police car. Another officer started laying down yellow tape and telling people to stay back. He took Nita's arm and moved her to the other side of the car.

"Thanks, Mindy. We've got some action here, evidently."

Brandon had no idea what was going on.

"We're here on Marshall Avenue."

She had already said that.

"We've got several squads of police on hand."

Duh. Flashing lights, running policeman. Was this belaboring-the-obvious day?

"Just keep talking," Dexter said. "Just keep running your mouth. The camera's not even on you."

"Coincidentally, this is the same building in which we've been based for the last month. What you're seeing this afternoon is rare indeed. It's not very often you get to see our boys in blue in action."

Boys in blue! He couldn't believe he'd said that. What a cliché piece-of-crap sentence that was. That was the problem with this live shit. Who knew what might pop out of your mouth.

"I thought you were supposed to be some sort of fucking reporter," Dexter said in his earpiece. "Get your ass over there and talk to the cop and the broad."

Nita waved to him.

"Excuse me, officer. Brad Wilson, KCKK 'Live at Five.' Could you fill us in on the problem here?"

"We had a citizen complaint of some trouble in this building."

Great! Police-ese. At least the cops he had lined up knew how to communicate.

"Can you tell us something about the nature of the complaint? Officer?"

"That would be premature at this time. We're still checking the premises."

"Does the complaint involve drugs?"

"There's been word of illegal substances and some other problems."

He remembered Dexter had said there was no going back, that it was into the sea. He'd have to tell the story he'd intended to tell and he'd have to do it himself.

"Ladies and gentleman, as you no doubt heard, what you're witnessing here is police crackdown on drug activity in the area. Sources tell me that this, in fact, could be a major drug bust you're witnessing. There's no confirmation on that, but a major drug bust, in progress, perhaps, behind us, even as I speak."

"Keep talking," Dexter said. "Just like that. Talk to the broad."

"Just a second, I've got some information from the newsroom." Brandon gave the camera a questioning look.

"You heard me. Talk to the broad. She was with the cops. Talk to her."

Nita. He wanted to strangle her, was what he wanted to do. She was different today. Her face was plain and rough looking, hair tied up in a rag. Her clothes were mostly rags as well—a tattered sweatshirt and a greasy-looking pair of jeans.

"May I ask you a few questions, Miss?"

She was cool as a clogged radiator in winter, angry-looking, a sneer set hard on her face.

"You live in the building here. Tell us what you've observed."

She turned from him and faced right into the camera.

"I'm a working single mother. Trying to do the best I can for my kids."

"She's gold," Dexter said. "Just the kind I told you we needed more of. Wilson, go stand behind her so we got you in the picture with her."

"We have some retired people in our building and quite a few children. We just decided we'd had enough." She said those words into the camera, fiercely, like they were weapons, a hand on one hip, jaw jutting for emphasis.

"Talk to her Brad. You're looking like a dickhead out there."

"So you and your neighbors are in on this?"

"Yes, Mr. Wilson, and we'd like to thank you for the support you've given us these past few weeks. Here comes Mrs. Carter now."

A policeman escorted Mrs. Carter from the building. She was tottering on his arm, sobbing into a handkerchief. Brandon also noticed she was wearing one of her best dresses.

"Get the old broad now," Dexter ordered.

Mrs. Carter came and stood between him and Nita. She collapsed into his side, weeping and gasping for breath. Nita supported her and continued looking into the camera.

"Are you all right, Mrs. Carter? You remember our neighbor here, Mrs. Cora Carter. Tell us what you saw in there."

"It was terrible. Terrible." She sobbed into his chest. She was both convincing and totally unbelievable at the same time.

Dammit! They had rehearsed the whole thing, he realized

"Hug the old cow, Wilson. What's the matter with you? Anybody down there got glycerin? I want tears on his face."

"That's just how bad it's been," Nita said. Right into the camera. She said it right to them.

The apartment door banged open and pairs of officers hustled out two men and a woman. They were bedraggled and scruffy looking. A detective followed with bags marked "evidence." Brandon had never before seen these people—in this building or anywhere else.

"Narration, Brad," Dexter heckled. "This ain't no silent movie."

"The officers are bringing out some individuals in handcuffs. There are some bags of things that have apparently been gathered in the apartment. Drugs, perhaps. Miss?" He pulled Nita in front. "Do you recognize these people?"

"They're some people who moved into the building. Been making trouble for the neighborhood. Good riddance."

Right into the camera.

"Great!" Dexter cheered. "Okay, cut to the backgrounder. Now!"

Brandon heard the piece he had recorded earlier in the day about drug problems in the area. He was clear for a minute.

"What are you playing at?" he asked Nita.

"I quit playing," she answered. Her hard veneer cracked into a slight smile.

"Who are those people? "

"Crackheads. Don't you know a crackhead when you see one? Live down the block. We was sick of em anyway. Give em a little pipe, they'll do just about anything for you." Her smile threatened to get even bigger, so she sucked her lip in.

"Where's that Sipp?"

"Halfway to Memphis, I imagine. He told me to tell you good-bye."

"So you let him walk? Take down those pathetic losers and let the big fish walk." He eyed the addicts, trembling and nodding in the back of the squad car.

"Maybe they'll get some help."

He shook his head. "I trusted you."

"Ten seconds, Brad!"

"Oh, Brandon," she said. She pecked him on the cheek. Their assigned officer laughed.

"You be a big boy and do your job," she added.

"I don't get it."

The red light came on. She assumed her stance, hand on hip, scowl on face.

"You just keep looking in that camera," she said through her teeth. "We all got what we wanted."

Nita's Place

. . . .

The new curtains rustled like dry leaves in the upstairs hallway window. She had picked them out at Wards and the tenant who had moved into the place upstairs had helped her put them up. Mrs. Carter had said that the color was too loud, but Nita didn't think so and neither did Ray. They filtered the light in a way that complimented the bright lemony yellow she'd chosen for the halls.

Mr. Cornell—Ray—the new tenant had taken the place upstairs. He was a teacher's aide over at the elementary school the kids attended and was taking classes at night to get his teaching certificate. She liked having someone around who could keep her posted as to what was going on over at that school. You could never be too careful. Though he was young and liked to entertain, he was quiet enough. Sometimes, though, when he stomped around with his heavy-footed self, she longed for the somehow quieter thumping of Sipp's speakers.

She'd had no word from Sipp and expected none. Men like Sipp did not like being bested by women. He was hurt, maybe humiliated. Though Nita thought she'd been fairly easy on the nigger. Who knew where his poison ended up—in the lungs or arms or noses of some other mother's children. She ought to have had them all locked up. But, he'd gotten to her, with his talk of chances and possibilities and dreams. He deserved a shot, she guessed. She had sounded like the kind of person she would never have wanted to be. . . .

"You want your dream," she'd told him. "Here's the going cost of dreams today."

He'd balked, tried to get tough with her, but she'd played the part well, better than any of them soap-opera bitches.

"You want this deal at all, then you best get with *my* program. Cause I'm through playing with you."

She didn't demand much, really. The main thing was that he change his schedule to one that fit her plan—that he get his deal in and out of the house in the morning, that he be out of there himself by noon at the latest. She'd agreed to stand watch for him and keep her mouth shut. . . .

"Oh, and there's just one more thing."

"Yeah?" he'd asked, sullen, a lot of the glow washed away by her power.

"I want a piece. Just a little piece."

"How much?" he'd asked.

"What you think is fair. What you think my closed mouth's worth."

"Bitch, I don't know what makes you think . . ."

"What you think almost killing my son's worth?"

He'd winced when she'd dropped that on him. And though she felt guilty for the low blow, she knew she had him. And so what if it was a dirty trick? It was the truth. It should cost him something. She had dreams, too, didn't she?

People should be careful who they run their mouths to.

Skjoreski hadn't had much choice either. She knew the laws and so did he. The federal government confiscated less valuable property than his every day over smaller amounts of drugs than came through here. She'd warned him about those people and he'd blown her off. It became payback time, as it always did.

"Better tune in the news," she'd told him. She'd called him from the police station.

"What are you talking about, Nita?"

"You watch. 'Live at Five.' Then we'll talk."

And when they'd talked, he'd pretended like she was the ignorant one.

"I don't know what you want from me, girl," he'd said.

The "girl" part cost him.

"Just what's coming to me," she'd told him.

She had figured up her sweat equity and her inconvenience and added in a thousand of the money she'd gotten from Sipp.

"You draw up the papers, partner," she'd told him.

So, he was still majority owner—for now. She, for now, was rent free and had a say about how things went around here. Next week she would be picking up a new roll of carpet for the hallway. And a fixture for up by Mrs. Carter's door.

The police had been the hardest, really. You'd think they'd want a drug bust, but no, she'd had to go down there and talk and talk and finally—after a hysterical call from Mrs. Carter— she'd convinced them there was something worth their while going on. They'd changed their minds, she guessed. They had all been out there talking about how great this was looking on TV.

She was right, everyone had gotten what they'd wanted.

She lay back on her couch again. Same old tattered couch as before. That would change, too. Someday.

One dream at a time.

It appeared that the line between right and wrong was not so much dotted as it was wavy and ever-changing like the surface of a flag in a breeze. If you stood too close to to the line, it moved through you like some kind of magical fog. What mattered, maybe, was that you stayed mostly on the right side of it, away from the line as much as you could. And when you had to go near, you did so with your eyes wide open and with some kind of determination, and without blaming anyone but yourself.

Yes, there was some guilt. Some times more than others. She'd tried to do that thing they talk about where you put the good on one side and the bad on the other and then decide what was right. It didn't work. Her life had not come with scales and, regardless of which side she chose, the bad things were still bad and they didn't go away.

Some days the good things made the bad feel—well, not so bad.

She saw that Brandon on TV. That Brad. They had made him over different again, but he was still in there, underneath the makeup and the new hair. He somehow belonged in that box. Flickering and not quite real. She could not imagine him as the person she had seen and touched. When she had taken him to her bed she had run her hands along the solid planes of his back, across his butt, and back up his spine. He had been above her, inside her, and she remembered having the strangest sensation that though in many ways he was as close to her as a man could possibly be, he had somehow at that very moment not really been there at all.

Archives

. . . .

Don't forget the people who made you what you are today.

Mrs. Cora Carter
St. Paul, Minnesota

Even by seven, out over the park the sky had already lost the naive pastels of morning, had already assumed the concrete tones of hot mid-August. Air too thick to breathe most days, although it was cooled and filtered most everywhere Brandon went.

"Morning," Sandra said, coming out behind him on the terrace. She wrapped her arms around his waist, moist, her robe still misted from a steamy shower.

"Good morning."

"What are you looking at?" she asked.

"Oh, nothing. You know, the only time I really like Central Park is this time of day."

"I don't much like it ever," she said, swinging against him. "You hungry?"

"Nah, I'll grab something."

"That's good, cause I wasn't cooking."

He followed her into the bedroom and watched as she scrambled into her clothes. "Busy day, huh?"

"Mock-up always is."

Her worst days, in fact. After they'd arrived in New York she had talked her way into a job consulting on fashion layouts for a consortium of magazines that were trying to attract more African-American readers. The days they produced the magazine dummy pages were the days she spent fighting to get one more face here, another one there. A glorified people counter, she called herself.

"This wench today has got me until four. After that she can put gorillas in there for all I care." She snagged a fingernail on her blouse. "Shit." She was a bundle of energy, her pregnancy not taxing her one bit, hardly showing, even if she did say her skirts were getting tight.

"Slow down," he said. "One year and you're already a New Yorker."

"Never. I'll never get used to the way folks rush around this city. Can you see that?" she asked. She smoothed the blouse where the damage had been done.

"Not from here."

She peeled off the blouse and grabbed another. "Like I'd trust a blind nigger like you. How bout you? What's your schedule like?"

"Usual. Got an interview with the U.N. ambassador. Have to call some folks in the field."

"Yugoslavia?"

"Like I said, the usual."

"Remember, we got those tickets tonight."

"We do?"

"'Ragtime'? I had to all but sell this baby to get those seats. I'm seeing this show, and I'm not seeing it alone."

"I'll be here. Unless."

"Unless what?"

"Unless we drop the bomb on them or something. Or they drop it on us. Who's to say? You know, baby. The news business."

She kissed him on his forehead, rubbed in the red mark and grabbed her purse. "Whatever happens, your ass better be in that door and ready to go at seven fifteen. Or, I'll be the one dropping bombs."

"Have a super day," he simpered, squinting his eyes shut. She stuck her tongue out at him on her way out the door.

He lay back on the bed. This marriage thing wasn't so bad. It was quite all right, as a matter of fact. Better than the years of chasing around he'd done. She was a blessing. Sandra.

He rolled over, tempted to go back to sleep. No need to hit the studio until ten, at the earliest. His life was easier here. Easier than he had ever imagined. There were flunkies everywhere— enough gofers to move a mountain. People to do your hair and to do your makeup and to do your research and answer your mail. Hell, they had people who'd go to the bathroom for you if it was possible and if they thought it might earn them some points.

Dexter wanted him to take it easy, to lay low. Said it took time to build a national anchor and that you couldn't just go into homes all over America and expect people to love you just be- cause you were you. He said they had to wait for the right vehicle. They had spent hours—days, weeks—huddled around the table, Dexter, Ted and a bunch of other hungry punks just like them, trying to cook up the right project: a news magazine, an interview show, a regular panel. They had even considered another morning show—it had worked for Brokaw, they all said.

Meanwhile he sat. He did the newsbreaks between shows, filled in for vacations, did a regular high-profile interview. There was a publicist Dexter got who fed tidbits about Brandon and Sandra to the gossip pages. Being at the network wasn't so much work as it was activity, busyness and constant motion imitating substance. And the pay was good, too.

He clicked on the set to see what the morning crew was up to. Slow today—politicians and actors—nothing particularly eye-catching. Nothing worth staying around for. He was bored.

He could watch some tapes.

The tape.

Sandra said to lose that tape, but he couldn't. It was all there—
all four-and-a-half hours of it. From Mrs. Carter to the end. He
didn't know why he kept it. He had watched it so many times
that it was as meaningless to him as a cereal commercial.

He popped it in the machine and pressed play. There were only
two parts he watched.

He had indexed the tape to a warm spring day of a year when
he lived in a cold northern city in the Midwest. The sky was fading toward purple that afternoon and there was a yellow-green
hint on the trees. There he was and there was the woman in a
red dress. She was beautiful brown and almost as tall as he. He
remembered she was shaking and stomping—he was warming
her up to go on the air—and was kinetic, all movement and
energy. She was shy. He remembered his eye catching the camera
often, looking from it to her, as if he were trying to tell someone
"take a look at this." It was a habit, this looking from a thing to
the camera and back again, and it was stagey and self-conscious-
looking, but he had done it his whole career. They all did it as a
way of drawing the viewers in. On the tape the woman stood still,
angled up against him in that unnatural way that only happened
in pictures. He remembered her perfume, a common scent you
could smell on any subway and on any elevator in the city, and
how he could see the tracks that the comb had left in the dressing
she had used to smooth her hair back from her face. He fast-
forwarded to another girl. The same girl. Same lovely face, only
harder like steel, and raggedy as a mop in her discount clothes.
One face: a smile as rare as thunder in winter, the other, eyes diamond hard, black with light, cruel mirrors, reflecting back some
unquenchable pain. He juxtaposed them side by side. In his
mind, he did this. The two girls. The two faces. The two Nitas.

One was the act and one was the real Nita, he thought. Or
maybe there were others, as well; he couldn't be sure. These were
the ones he'd known. He merged their faces into one, or tried to,

but they wouldn't go together, somehow. He wanted to make her whole. He thought there must be a button on his machine to do this for him, and he looked at his remote control to discover again that there was no such feature, and that once again technology had failed him.

Books in the Harvest American Writing series